T0097147

MANLIO ARGUETA

Little Red Riding Hood
in the
Red Light District

a novel

translated by Edward Waters Hood

CURBSTONE PRESS

[English translation of the 1996 revised edition of *Caperucita en la zona roja* published by UCA Editores, San Salvador.]

Printed in Canada on acid-free paper by Transcon Printing / Best Book
 Manufacturing
Cover design: Les Kanturek

This book was published with the support of the
Connecticut Commission on the Arts and the National
Endowment for the Arts, and donations from many
individuals.We are very grateful for this support.

Library of Congress Cataloging-in-Publication Data

Argueta, Manlio, 1935 -
    [Cuperucita en la zona roja. English]
    Little Red Riding Hood in the red light district : a novel /
 Manlio Argueta; translated by Edward Waters Hood.
       p.   cm.
    ISBN 1-880684-32-2
 I. Hood, Edward W. (Edward Waters), 1954 -   II. Title.
 PQ7539.2.A68 C313 1998
 863—dc21
                                                98-51283

published by
CURBSTONE PRESS   321 Jackson Street   Willimantic, CT 06226
       phone: (860) 423-5110   e-mail: curbstone@curbstone.org
               http://www.connix.com/~curbston/

CONTENTS

TRANSLATOR'S NOTE:

Manlio Argueta was born in San Miguel, El Salvador, in 1936. He left his country in 1972 to live in exile in Costa Rica for nearly twenty years. His novels, which chronicle the contemporary history of El Salvador, have earned him an international literary reputation and have endeared him to the people of his homeland. Since 1970, he has authored six novels. The first two, *El valle de las hamacas*, 1970 (*The Valley of Hammocks*) and *Caperucita en la zona roja*, 1977 (*Little Red Riding Hood in the Red Light District*), present the social instability and political repression in El Salvador during the late fifties and the mid-seventies, respectively. *El valle de las hamacas* won a national literary prize in El Salvador and was published by the distinguished Argentine publisher Editorial Sudamericana. *Caperucita en la zona roja* was published in Cuba in 1977 after winning the Casa de las Américas' prize for best novel of the year. Argueta's third and fourth novels, *Un día en la vida*, 1980 (*One Day of Life*) and *Cuzcatlán donde bate la mar del sur*, 1986 (*Cuzcatlan: Where the Southern Sea Beats*), present the escalation of rebellion and repression in the late seventies that culminated in the protracted civil war of the eighties. Both of these novels have been translated into English and several other languages. Argueta's fifth novel, *Milagro de la Paz*, 1994 (*A Place Called Milagro de la Paz*), examines the legacy of the violence of the recent civil war in the lives of a family of three women. Argueta's latest novel, *Siglo de o(g)ro*, 1997 (*Golden/Ogre Age*), is a poetic novelization of the author's childhood.

Like many contemporary Central American writers, Manlio Argueta explores the themes of social injustice, political repression, and social rebellion. What characterizes Argueta's art is his use of a testimonial format, one in which authentic voices of ordinary Salvadoran citizens are introduced into fictional texts. Critic Linda Craft has noted that "for Argueta, testimony offers a discourse 'approaching a literary genre' that gathers together threads of a rich oral tradition and rescues voices that have been silenced and lost in order to give them resonance and relevance" (*Central American Novels of Testimony and Resistance*. University of Florida

Press, 1997: 106-131). In addition to the important work of documenting his country's recent history, Argueta's masterful use of this technique has influenced other Central American writers, breathing new life into the region's novel.

Little Red Riding Hood in the Red Light District is a complex novel. The plot revolves around the relationship between two young lovers, Alfonso and Ant (Hormiga), in a time of political upheaval. Characters and themes from the classic fairy tale are evoked within the wartime environment of El Salvador and its capital, San Salvador. The "red light district" refers not only to sexual exploitation but also to the political violence Salvadorans suffered in the late seventies. This is the area where the country's poor–most Salvadorans–live. Argueta's book is a testimony to their struggle and their ability to endure extreme economic hardship, social injustice, and state-sponsored violence against them.

In all his novels, Argueta is interested in presenting and denouncing the poverty, violence, and lack of civil rights in his country. Critic Ineke Phaf identifies the presentation of violence as his highest literary achievement: "He is not interested in increasing polarization but intends to give this violence a historical dimension, centered in a history El Salvador shares with other countries of the region. In this quality resides his outstanding relevance as a writer" ("Manlio Argueta." *The Dictionary of Literary Biography* (1994): vol. 145, 50-56). Manlio Argueta's novels continue to be relevant and timely: although El Salvador's civil war officially ended in 1992, the country is still one of the most violent on earth.

Structurally, *Little Red Riding Hood in the Red Light District* is a complex novel, with juxtaposed episodes, each with different time frames and points of view. This technique forces the reader to participate actively in the construction of the novel. Stylistically, the text reproduces the colloquial speech of its characters from San Salvador. Argueta has stated that Salvadorans consider this his best novel. They identify with its intimate testimonial nature, and use of the Salvadoran vernacular.

As previously mentioned, the first edition of this novel was published in 1977 by Casa de las Américas. A second edition was published in 1978 by Editorial Costa Rica. UCA (Universidad

Centroamericana) Editores published editions of the book in 1981, 1985, 1986, and 1991. In 1996, UCA published Manlio Argueta's definitive "revised and corrected" edition of the original text. This English translation is based on that edition.

—Edward Waters Hood

LITTLE RED RIDING HOOD
in the
RED LIGHT DISTRICT

I

IN THE FOREST

It is a sudden decision. It's inexplicable that I would abandon this hole in the wall after spending so much time here, surrounded by small objects, a book, a night stand, discarded ball point pens, old shoes. I enter Doña Gracia's room so she can tell me what I owe her. I think about leaving (apprehensively). I don't know how to repay her (fearfully). I wonder what Ant will say when she can't find me? Not being able to pay for the room is enough although that would seem a problem of conscience. Something makes me tell her without thinking it over very much. It would be better for me to go to live beneath the river almond trees, perched on the branch of a green lemon tree, the pinta bird of the children's rhyme. Making "coo, coo" sounds at people, on a branch with pink flowers, the branch with many flowers, like an upside-down necklace. So I have the courage to go to Doña Gracia's room to tell her I am leaving, but why, if no one is throwing you out? It's been two hours that I haven't sensed Ant's climbing-bird's steps ascending the stairs to the place where she hangs clothes, or passing a rag over the floor that shines with healthy filth. "When beautiful life is a tournament the best thing to do is to split forever," parodying a memorized phrase that says torment but isn't worth a damn. Who told it to me? Oh, Mamma, when she was alive, with her obsession of speaking in eleven-syllable verses. She is taking a siesta. Doña Gracia that is, Mamma never took a siesta. To leave now because you haven't come, pretty Peruvian Ant of reeds and *capulí* trees, your hair covered with a red scarf and your locks protruding from under your hood, the locks of hair that rise to heaven with the wind that blows. Sorry to bother you, as I knock on the door (terrified). My voice is like that of a choking dog. W-will you f-forgive me? I stutter whenever I speak from my heart. I push the curtain aside and tell her I want to settle my account, and she gets out of bed? Wait for me, I was lying down in bed, a headache, although it's gone now, thanks, through the curtain with blue tassels. Wait son, because she calls me her little boy. I make myself comfortable on the canvas seat of a chair, already wobbly from being sat on so much, the poor thing. She says to me: you don't look well. She pushes aside the blue tassels which flow down her back. Sit down, I tell her. Five months, makes five hundred, with your decent person's logic, of beloved mother and dead when I was seven years old, walking among the *amate* trees' brilliant green leaves. That's right, I tell her, it's five months. As I remember the time I moved the Honduran poet Clementina Suarez's piano, to celebrate her assignment as cultural attaché, and the piano got away and rolled downhill until it was smashed to smithereens on the Santa Tecla highway. And I: how am I going to pay for it? Not even the family jewels would cover it. Whimpering, with great big tears and every swear word in the book. There is no name for what you have done to me. And I, poor little poet. Doña Gracia would like to know what I am thinking; her what's-wrong-with-you-son eyes tell me so. I left you a note, nice-butt Ant, spearmint love. A goodbye forever note. Don't get upset Doña Gracia. I pull out my five-and-a-half ruby watch. If you want we can count the bread. Don't be crazy, I trust you, as she puts the bills away. You're not well. How do you know, I ask. You can tell, you look like you're sleeping the sleep of the unjust. I: what's that? Stop the nonsense because I'm going to take your temperature, as she touches my arm. "My God, you're burning up!" And then she places her hand on my forehead. Beloved mother on the shoulders of my uncles buried in the Chaparrastique Valley, by the bluest volcano in my country. "You're not leaving," leading me by the hand to my room, downstairs; each step is a tremor of weak knees. "Dear thing, you're trembling." And all your little children pour shovelfuls of earth on you, so your spirit won't come out to scare folks. "I'm not your mother." Her hand on my forehead, while I bring you water and an aspirin to bring your fever down. I wake up slowly; and at the same pace the window that faces the clothes-drying area opens, where I see you every day, Ant, love (madness) of my life, with poems dedicated to you. The window through which you enter my room. And further away, the buzzards circling above the garbage dump of the Soyapango neighborhoods.

— ii —

When I was in the Latino Café I knew you would arrive, but I acted like I was waiting for you, in order to play the part of the run-of-the-mill person and not a desperate individual. You know, there are situations known as cathartic, that is, when things are upside down and you have to turn them right side up, like in photographic negatives where people have their hands backwards. That's what you are, an inside-out image, a bat hanging in the air from a branch. Look at your truth and not the lies that appear to be true, you have the bad luck of not falling into any of the categories or temperaments, you are the exception of the exceptions. As they say, the normal among the abnormal. I am right aren't I, my dear little animal? We aren't ordinary people.

"Did you know I don't like this café one bit because everyone can see what we are doing and you have to watch yourself even when you make little noises as you sip your coffee, this place with its windows open, displaying you like a storefront window."

"It's a way of showing off our riches, turning ourselves into mannequins of conspicuous consumption, helium balloons of this beautiful medieval age with automobiles and window seats."

"You don't show up when you're invited. You have the courage to leave your Ant abandoned, watching my movements in the windows in front of me, stuck in this two-bit café for big-time thieves and merchants. Who knows where the heck you are. Al, searching for me somewhere. And you shall never find me. Speaking to me in your strange languages, you look for me somewhere else, in hidden places. As if you were an abstraction. And then you show up unannounced, a surprise wrapped in *papier maché*; and no sooner have you arrived than you are nowhere to be found, you are the invisible man who also goes after kids in the darkness of their bedrooms. The worst thing is that you go away and never come back; you take the final trip, abandoning everything, even this Ant that thinks twice before tossing a match stick, you leave me like a piece of old tortilla, inedible food, unknown soldier, dead animal. I wait for you in the Latino Café. Best wishes."

The likeness on the window in front gets up, exits through the front door, and advances towards its own image. I give myself a hug with my own shadow. Thinking that if we ever see each other again it will be never to part again and to find ourselves in the little room of photographs, with snot-nosed kids who belong to this world, kids who scream, who are a pain in the ass, who break dishes, who shall be different now and at the hour of our death, amen.

— *iii* —

At one time we went off to live as a couple.

"Don't you notice anything different about me, Ant, it just happens that I have been quiet for an hour. Who am I going to talk to if today I've already said everything? That's not all, we've gone through enough arguments for the next two weeks. You want to squeeze the words out of me one at a time. To be different is to speak to you less, to stop looking at you for a second or for a long time; because neither you nor I are always right on time."

"It's nothing..."

"You can't hide it from me..."

You are speaking to me from the kitchen. We are in different countries, making ourselves understood through gestures, because your word in the light of day sounds like anything but you. Your notion of telephone is lack of communication. I light one of those cigarettes that seem hideous to you. We are talking in a different language; yes, that's it.

"My lost fool, my wolf."

"I'm not a wolf, Ant."

In protest, you put up the folding screen that separates the kitchen and the bedroom. Now you separate the two beds. And you have left the kitchen naked. You know I don't like anyone watching while I'm cooking. Especially you, because I could become petrified, hypnotized by your velvety eyes. And, speaking back and forth from one side to the other can turn anyone into a sleepwalker. But every dark cloud has a silver lining: now you can't see me when I take my clothes off. Why do you always feel like biting me every time you see me naked? Why do you look at me that way when you see me naked? And you tell me the same thing: then, why do you take your clothes off in front of me as if it were the most natural thing in the world? And I tell you: taking one's clothes off is an original virtue, like going to bed or the bathroom. And you say to me, acting crazy: don't leave me, my feather skin. Who is leaving you, I say. Especially if we're having a baby.

We have great long-distance dialogues via radiography of the conscience. And all that remains of the cigarette are tiny, black, windblown ashes.

Did you know that I like to see your pictures stuck to the folding screen? Why are there so many photos of you up on the screen? Could it be that you're losing your marbles and so admiring yourself more than you should? If you have a mirror, you don't need photographs because with a mirror you can reproduce a thousand pictures a minute.

All of a sudden we come to the why's. Are we an interrogation or the same question as always? Is that the issue? Sometime we shall be together without asking each other questions and that will be when we no longer understand each other, when everything in the world has been lost and we are standing in the yellow sand in the middle of the desert and no one will know why we are alone. You will be standing in front of the kitchen and I will be chained to the chair within these four walls that are like our feelings. To ask ourselves the same question is to find the missing links that lead to the same cave; there, we have run into each other until we are stuck together, nose to nose, mouth to mouth, your lips and mine: a word in the darkness.

Ant lets out a little owl—or rather a little howl.

"What's wrong?"

"The saucepan is hot, I almost spilled grease on myself."

"One of these days you're going to get tied (I meant to say fried, why are we always making mistakes?)."

"There is something different about you Ant."

"Why do you say that?"

"The way you look at things.

"I'd like to call myself Sofia or María Elena, what do you think?"

"You're never happy."

"Perhaps I should call myself Virgin Mary mother of God..."

"What more do you want, your name is Little Red Riding Hood, you are the forest full of flowers and rabbits."

"And you are the wolf."

"I'm not a wolf." I end the conversation.

— *iv* —

Who would think of putting a folding screen between the beds of two lunatics who love each other? Now I would no longer be able to see with complete liberty her nude hills. Nor touch the smooth roughness of her pores. The fine hairs of her skin. The questions arise once again. Was it out of a lack of intelligence we fell into this desperate union? And all this is called love. The hope of being tied one to the other, an old overcoat, a hat hanging from a nail; you posing rigidly, covered with yellow lemons and the unfailing flowers in your lap in the photo; I shackled to one of your arms; or you piercing me like a hook in my life. Each is the coat hanger of the other. You leave me a note in which you say it's necessary—just like that, in a cultured, poetic tone—that we reconsider our differences of opinion and for that we must admit our mistakes; one of my errors would be not to remember anything about the time we have lived together—which happens to us for concentrating too much on ourselves. We think about nothing and faint. Your shadow gathers the papers from the garbage strewn about the floor, you wash the dirty dinner dishes, you light a cigarette and you sit on my lap. We get tired and we realize that to overcome the inevitable separations we should have been unequal and not these beings who look so much like each other, as if we were in front of a mirror.

"I imagine that they must be tall, serious, and educated, those pretty girls who show up to destroy everything."

"You're speaking about a spirit."

"Instead of all that suffering I bring you, she can give you what I can't offer you. I admit it. She must be a beautiful woman, chestnut hair and rainy eyes, the way you like them."

You throw blows left and right until you scratch me—I smile to myself. Sometimes I wonder if maybe you don't enjoy the roughness of your temperament.

I end up howling out one of the windows to get even with her impossible love. I bark at the sky and I feel like I'm her most cherished dog. Beloved dog, give me a paw. We are in the chiaroscuro of the room. In some way we are able to come to terms so that I will stop my howls. You're going to frighten the neighbors.

"I'd better go to my bedroom with blood-sucking insects, I'm going to try to forget everything," she says.

Some bell in a church tower always tolls at eight and it finds us in the same situation, Ant washing the dishes she didn't wash after lunch and I looking for a corner just for myself. If you knew everything that is happening. And what is happening? Repeating the Sermon of the magic mountain. I don't want to explain any more. Forget about the plates, the dirty clothes, stop washing them at home so we can go to the river to wash. If you don't make anything clear, I'm not going to know a thing, I'm not a fortune teller. And she raises her apron to her face. If you leave, everything will be different. Our crying is pathetic, for the love of the Magdalene. With so much resentment we carry, a Gordian knot forms in our throats.

"What will come of our dreams?"

The truth is plain to see, Ant, eater of fruits, I can't love anyone but you; after so many experiences, tell me, what path remains, with our cuddling, with a what-do-you-want-my-love look, with our saliva filling our throats. Your love is this half-light love, where each one howls like a dog through the window that opens to the clouds. Howling is a way of feeling important, and we howl when we are happy; to see the future, since otherwise we would be like irrational, ridiculous animals.

I receive each of your words with happiness. Have you realized how I adore you? Or are you blind or unaware that you are my finest jewel, my lapis lazuli stone. I would like to call you love in all languages, but it would be to no avail because I couldn't really love you in different languages.

She doesn't respond at all to my provocations.

"Why the quarantine-like silences?"

Our voices pass over the folding screen.

"I'm fed up with your ingratitude. I need you to leave me alone because it's the best way to be with you. That way I see you as more defined and I enjoy your beautiful words. But that doesn't mean I'm telling you to go."

Finally she starts falling asleep, exhausted from talking to the wall and the folding screen with the newspaper pictures on it. We sleep in silence. We don't speak but we understand one another and listen to each other. Asleep she is a peaceful animal, a small river bunny. Eater of water cress. Her mind soars to other places. Covered by a sheet, from head to toe so only the tiny windows of your eyes can be seen, Indira Gandhi, staring at the wall without noticing that I spy and caress, as if on horseback, your slightest movement. Spy of your dreams, that's what I am. Little smiles of oh-my-love-don't-love-me-so. Your little girl nose with a basket full of fruit for greedy, gluttonous grannies. Catching scent of the enemy that I am, trying to leave you forever without leaving tracks so that neither what happened to you nor where you went will ever be known, if indeed we did exist before this night that is so real. In this chocolate shack, a bedroom-kitchen-pisshole-dining room, and next to a miserable radio that gives news in a whisper. You saying in your sleep: If you leave, it's better that there be no farewell.

Until we get to the next day so fast we can see the trees flying by us on the sides of the road. Wake up my sweetheart, wake up, little cross eyes looking towards the sides of consciousness, asking what the hell have I got myself into?

Now you only talk to me under your breath because you have fallen in love with another, because you no longer love me and you have turned around five hundred degrees as if you were a toy animal.

The little wind-up animal has begun to jump: ten steps in the direction of the pisshole, another ten steps to the dining room. My eyes vent fatuous flames.

In back of me the noise from the toy animal's spring as it uncoils. Ant watching me strangely and that's enough! I keep walking. She lets out a howl—owl—to get my attention. I have left her behind me. And I see with the eyes of my conscience that she lifts her apron to her eyes. This always happens: when she wants to cry she doesn't and sometimes she cries when she doesn't want to.

"Sometime we should act like brother and sister, Ant, what do you think?" I say to console her. And my spring says tic-tac-tic. If you keep crying you're going to flood the house, Ant, pillar of salt, acting so obvious, with tears the size of *jocote* fruits from Usulután.

"We aren't children to be hiding behind strange games," she protests.

"Look at my face, my muscles, all of my expressions are dedicated to you. In these moments when we are content as Christmas and Happy New Year."

"You're making fun of me. Me, slave. You asshole. She damsel. And then those silences of yours that deafen me."

The spring continues to uncoil until I reach the back wall. I trip over the first obstacle and I stumble. I can only walk in a straight line, that's the problem. My nose bumps into the cold wall. There I stay until the spring is uncoiled. Ant swallows the mucous from her pouting. To hell with it my love, she says to me, why do we start playing if we're so sentimental. The spring's unwinding came to an end and I stopped moving.

"You used to lock me in the room in the house when I behaved badly."

"When you went out with other women. Besides, you decided to stay there to pay your debts of infidelity, but you're not going to deny that I served you your milk on time, your refried beans. If I'm lying, let me know it right now."

— *v* —

Every day we drink a beer at lunch time. She, ocher-colored short-shorts, crosses her legs while I talk to her about anything at all. She looks at me dumbfounded and with protest. I remember when we used to buy fried plantain on the corner by the hospital, and place stones beneath a hat so that the blue-bottomed, barefoot, buck-toothed Indians would kick it and stub their toes. The wide streets. To go out in the middle of the street to look for nails and little nuggets of gold and small pieces of flint. I remember the city of the *garrobo* lizards, San Miguel, cut a fart and eat it. The two-hundred-yard wall of the San Juan de Dios Hospital. The star apple tree and how we shook it at night so that the sparrows would take off flying and crash into the two hundred yards of hospital wall. We each caught three or four swallows apiece. Your beer is going to get warm. Mamma spanked me hard with a stick. And in the mornings we cured their broken feet or cracked wings. And when they got well, we'd let them go. She would take them from the cardboard box and they would fly away. Are you going to give me your Little Red Riding Hood outfit? What Little Red Riding Hood? What outfit? I try to remember my petitions and promises.

"Being locked up at home is for the birds."

The *pilsner* beer on the hot chocolate-colored pine night stand. Forget everything, you have me and that's the end of it. Seated on a chair made of iron with a seat of woven nylon. Do you like being naked? I like being comfortable, that's all. Her shirt has the same ocher color as her shorts, next to her heart she has blue embroidered letters that say YES, and on her shoulder NO. What's up, silly! Bird-face. You walk on the soles of your feet, palmiped bird; you go to the kitchen for any reason, you get bored of sitting motionless in the same place, you raise the bottle to your mouth before getting up and return with a few pieces of cheese on a platter. Eat up, it makes the beer taste better. And she sits down again on the seat of woven nylon. She acts like a stranger. She looks at the large photo stuck to the wall to hide filthy bricks; she leaves to walk through those streets. She sees me from one of the streetlights on the corner in the photograph. Hello little man, what are you doing so alone sitting on that yellow curb drinking beer and eating cheese at ten in the morning? With your obsequious smile that gives out free candy. I don't want to speak because it's Sunday. She knows it and that's why she is insinuating things and treats me like a king. Both of us closed in by four walls, sandwiched in; nothing else exists in the world except these four walls and these two iron chairs, the folding screen, the colorful stools, and the pictures on the wall, the paper flowers—flowers larger than our two heads put together—that have started to fade with time, the flowers placed in a pitcher of Orange Tang. I like Tang more than beer. She doesn't hear me; she's still strolling the endless streets of the photograph, I think it's one of Concordia Plaza. She's the one beneath the streetlight; she's waiting for a taxi. In the background, a sculpture unfamiliar to me. It would be better for her to get lost, for the two of us to get lost. We have nothing to do, it's Sunday and we can't go anywhere, we don't have any money for the fare to get out of this barrio so distant from any important part of the city. In the afternoon we're going out to walk around the *maculís* trees, which are in bloom. And we'll go farther to see the city, seeded with electrical poles, in the distance. If you want another beer, I'll buy it. She gets up in her sleep, I look at her bare legs, her calves, her skinny knees, her short hair sticking in her ears, and her eyes of a benign lunatic. Then go ahead, at least we have enough to buy another beer.

"Tell the store woman I'm very sorry."

"Aren't you ashamed?"

The store woman's husband died a week ago and I haven't been able to bring myself to offer an I'm-very-sorry. But I'm not sorry, because for him death was salvation; do you think it's nothing to be complaining for more than fifteen months, until he could only whistle his suffering? They gave him morphine. Why didn't they put a bullet in him instead? She knows it's just a joke, the matter of telling the woman I'm very sorry. Go ahead and be comfortable and don't get involved with anyone, but the day you die I'm not going to care if you die alone, you unsociable bastard!

And she leaves slamming the door behind her.

I remain unbearably alone.

When will you come back? But I'm just talking to the photograph. Some day we're going to put it on the wall. And there it is, hanging from a nail. Charles the Third Avenue, with no indication of place or date, four- to six-story buildings, a wide street with automobiles and a statue. Everything is well distributed as if the street began on the wall. Someone must have given it to you, perhaps you know the place and you're afraid to tell me about it. That's one of your ironies: you don't want to say anything, for reasons of intimacy, not infirmity. That's fine, if that's what makes you happy. And I grab her from behind, I squeeze her, forming a large ring around her abdomen with my arms. You're going to choke me, angry bear. I'm going to choke you by the abdomen! And we start laughing. I can't stand the laughing and I release her, she charges me, pushes me against the chair; she falls on my lap, the iron chair sticks to the cement floor. Can't you read the NO that's written on the back part of my blouse?

When will that beautiful day be, that great day of death?

And you start to tickle me on my lower belly. Please, no! I desperately shout at her. You can't take very much, can you? Death for you is a beautiful thing, but for me it's a way to continue suffering through others, if I'm not right let the store woman say so.

Beautiful day! BEAUTIFUL DAY! BEAUTIFUL day! Beautiful DAY! She repeats it as if she were crazy, placing emphases on one word or the other, and she throws herself on my lap baring her teeth and threatening me with her hands in the shape of claws, I'm going to eat you up! Leave me alone, I shout at her, stop those games that are only for villains and wolves, right now. They're not games, this is for real. Let go of me, cat, let go of me, tigress! I'm neither a cat nor a tigress, I'm the just judge of the night. Oh, you're that man who takes walks through the streets on moonlit nights. In that case I'm not afraid of you. I take her by her wrists and leave her disarmed. She starts to take little nips at me. A bite on the cheek that makes me let out a shout, and I respond with a shove that makes her fall to the floor. She gets up wanting to hit me and she does. You bit me, it hurt, I ask her to forgive me for pushing her. My tail hurts, she says trying to laugh, but with great big tears in her eyes. She's covering the floor with watery bread crumbs. You're going to attract the birds, stop venting your feelings, sit on my lap, climbing bird, come close, I'm going to massage you. Poor little tail, and, as if she hadn't done a thing, there she is, docile, wiping her tears with the back of her hand. You're to blame for this violence, you tried to kill me with laughter. Nobody dies of laughter; to the contrary, everyone dies of sadness. Why is it that way? Why doesn't anyone die happy? That's what you say, but those who aren't happy aren't in the shoes of the deceased. The living remain with their eyes extinguished; their muscles deflate and their skin reflects what goes on inside them, they are a nonexistent color, different from everything and unlike anything. It's the color of death, the color of life. I lower her short shorts and rub her buttocks.

Someone knocks on the door.

"I'm coming."

What are you laughing at, she says from the door with two bottles of beer, one in each hand. I was thinking about you, about your terrible games and your she-wolf bites and the times that you get angry for no reason, your lack of humor, destructive spirit, acting out comic roles. Your seriousness is one of those first-class ships; your eyes lit up, a fire in the forest. Your shorts, the room full of old newspapers and magazines. Absurd dolls kept from childhood, the photograph of Charles the Third Avenue and so on. Well then, finish your speech and let me in, still from the door with the beers in her hands.

My body prevents her from entering, she bumps into me.

17

"Come in, then, I hope the scene I was dreaming doesn't repeat itself."

The bottles are open. I sit down again, after having gone to look for the bottle opener. Still sitting in the chair with the nylon seat. She lies down in her favorite place, in front of me, a few steps away, but as far away as if I were seeing her through the wrong end of binoculars. I remember the *caimito* tree, full of sparrows, in Father Lapuerta's courtyard. Then we would skip along on one foot so he would give us some bread and honey. Well, the gang consisted of some five boys and three girls. Father Lapuerta would sit the girls—who were pretty little five or six year old misses—on his lap. I was seven. Lion Face was eight, he was the oldest, the Father would sit him on his lap and he was the one who got the most bread and honey. Father Lapuerta and Lion Face in a libi way. Lion Face with his sex face. We were some innocent dovi. Father was an angeli, who only lacked wings. We were all pin-pin, there went Berlin, pan-pan, there went Japan. Then we would take off running to go pull the dogs' tails. We would get hurt and then rub it to make it feel better. My father owns all the ships in the world. And mine is a military man who kills whoever gets in his way, with great big pistols. My mom owns this city. Father Lapuerta was an *ego sum lux e verita et vita*. You're going to have to tell me about your life to clear things up. Yes, sweetheart, drinking a sip of beer. Do you want me to rub your buttocks? She: you're crazy, what's wrong with you boy, we just got out of bed. Then we begin to breakfast on cubes of cheese and cold *pilsner* brewsky.

— *vi* —

I hope it rains, I like a dark night more than a starlit one. You always have crazy ideas, especially if you are in the back room, reeking of darkness, venting tidy urine water, rancid water, dirty sea, puddle of putrid mud, *cielito lindo* of a hundred thousand whores. "Don't use a lot of oil in the beans," I say in a supplicant tone. Ant is cooking, the spoon in her hand and the sizzling of the saucepan confirm this for me. Since she doesn't answer me I shout again: just a little oil with the beans. Shit! You've made me lose my voice, Ant, who never answers when I talk to you. "I am the cook, you wait until the order arrives," she says with a young-man-oh-how-much-I-love-you gesture. I take offense for no reason. Ant is a dirty sky. Please don't bother me, I'm going to burn myself, I can't be taking care of you and the food at the same time, understand. Bitch! She says her favorite expression in a low voice so she can't be heard. You are so cute when you say bitch!

Don't get mad, sweet bitch. I head towards her, moving my tail with inexplicable happiness. Stop bothering me, the rice is burning. Rice never gets burnt, it fries, as I circle around her, sniffing her, I put my nose to her insect butt. At first she takes offense and spins around avoiding me, please! she says in her home-learned English. You're going to make me spill the food!

She pretends to cry. Listen! You have turned into a luminous fountain of tears. I bark at her vehemently. *Amorrr* and I get stuck on my r's until she covers my snout with her ears. She throws the sauce pan on the pine table: boom-boom-boom, fucking pan. Sweetest bitch, give me a bite. She contorts her body backwards where I'm still sniffing her rear end. She sweats through her tongue, I lick her spearmint skin. The two of us keep licking each other, darkness arrives reeking of terror. I bathe her in saliva. She bathes me in saliva. Both of us covered in saliva. Blue sea of your tongue, vapor of thermal waters. Your tongue is a sharpening stone. Bitch of every day. The food is burning. Food is shit backwards. There you go with your two-bit graphologies. Do you love me, beautiful? I love you, handsome. Bow wow. Are you going to keep choking me? I've never choked you. The soul, that fine, timeless dust. I see her lettering with little flowers that says YES in large letters above her bellybutton, drawn with lipstick. For me, it's the only thing lipstick is good for. And I go around and around her body. Too bad I can't draw a NO on my hips. Hello witch, you turn into a *cadejo*, an evil mythological animal, at midnight, you throw your soul into a plastic bag and go off to wreak havoc in movie theaters. Neon witch, modernizing. I like being nude from the waist down.

"First and foremost we should be clean, and secondly, dirty. Life is something less than that thing you have on your wrist that's called a watch. And you think the important thing is to be with a woman, looking for trouble. Those seximental games."

"Don't think too much."

"I can't think of anything, because you are a stone: It goes in one ear but doesn't come out the other. You are leaving and poor Ant will stay at home, darning her husband's socks, poor Ant like a shitty Penelope, a saint who stays up waiting for her master, to open the door for him at two in the morning, the poor woman will beg for a caress and the gentleman will turn his back on her, he will belittle her, he will see her naked body, smudged by the sunset color of lipstick: YES! And this will go on every night until I get fed up and go out looking for another man; because my God, I'm not going to be alone like an immaculate virgin."

"You're crazy, Ant, just because it's hard to accept the news that I'm going."

"I'm the stupid one. And when I'm in bed with another man I'll think he is you and I'll say the same words I say to you, I'll caress him the same way, but I won't draw anything on my body, because that's special, just for you, when we lie down naked honorably, not daring to penetrate one another. I will jump all over him as I do with you and I will laugh when fatigue overcomes me and you will tell me that I am a fool and the stranger will laugh with his fierce wolf's teeth because he won't understand my reactions. He won't understand that I won't let him penetrate me in that manner, the way we don't do it. And stupid me, Ant, scratching his shoulder thinking it's you."

Ant's worst mistake is having run into me that day in Cuzcatlán park and having paid me any attention. Since then you dedicated yourself to harassing me, to telling me lies while I only gazed upon your naked body, with my naiveté.

"You are a bandit, a cynic with clay feet and forgive me for not respecting you, but I have to tell it like it is, if I don't I'll drown in this well of Saint Peter's tears.

"What I wouldn't give so that you too, in all sincerity, would say these things to me that I say to you, or rather, all that you are silent about when you are as if absent and you are as if elephant, saying goodbye to me in order to make me suffer.

"What's there to say when I don't have enough for a change of clothing and I'm forced to walk around the room naked, because that's what pleases you; and I don't even have any pretty phrases now, I must steal them because you have taken away my hope, know what I mean? You've taken away my dreams, you've stolen what's mine, all of my intimacies, my ridiculous habit of sitting at your feet to sing you a lullaby; or writing you imaginary letters, taking you out to eat rotten apples at the Jabalí Volcano. By the way, how would you like some rotten apples? And you correct me: ripened apples. I tell you it's better if they are rotten. You laugh, I laugh. You cry, I cry. You go hungry, I go hungry; you live in a pig sty, me too. You see, you are my other self, just of another sex. And you saying: The only

21

thing you have to complain about are my weeping of a luminous fountain and my mourning of the walls of Jerusalem."

"It's started to rain and because we were talking nonsense we didn't even notice, go close the windows."

"Now, why would I care if you left? If you are a notorious madman who starts howling when people are talking and you give the impression of a lost animal. I don't love you any more."

"Yahoo!"

"Before you weren't cynical, now you are, you should see how ugly you look, with great big teeth and fiery eyes and a grey pelt and your paws with great big claws ready to pounce. If you could see yourself in the mirror you'd be afraid. Your eyes are going to pop out with surprise and you're not going to be able to get them back, you'll be blind and go looking for them, feeling around, but I'll have the great idea of hiding them so that you won't find them and you'll have to find a guide, another dog, and that dog will be me who will take you from one place to another, wherever you want and I'll tell you the color of the flowers and the color of the seas and whether or not the leaves on the high branches of the *maquilishuat* tree are rustling; I'll tell you whether we are passing by a river almond tree, when you perceive that pink fragrance of its blossoms that scratch your sense of smell. I won't wait for you to thank me, it'll suffice to have you at my side, sick but mine. Now can you see how much I love you, I forgive you, I'm not selfish, it's the truth."

"And you'll lead me along the street where there's the most traffic and you'll abandon me to my fate, when the traffic signal turns red, the cars will run over me and you will lead me to the sea shore, you'll say that at five in the afternoon it takes on that incredible color, you'll give me a shove and no one will save me because you'll be careful to make sure that it's just the two of us. Then it'll make no sense for me to go blind, without a holy guide in my path, excuse me, but I don't play that way. I'd rather you not hide my eyes because if you did I'd kill myself. About my not seeing myself in the mirror, that's my business, I'm afraid I'll confuse myself and believe that the other one is me, the one whose right hand appears to be his left, the one who laughs when I laugh, that one is not me, but the image of another person who I could have been had I been lucky. Why should I look at myself in the mirror if I can see myself in the image that you have of me?"

"I like to hear you talk at great length, like now. It's an unending satisfaction, you start talking, you talk unraveling yourself, or as if you were removing my dress and that's why I let you pull down my shorts and end up naked from the bellybutton down. That's the limit."

"And when you take off the shirt that says NO on the back and you read the YES on your skin I'm going to start entering you through your bellybutton, through your mouth, your jeans, your nose, until I disappear from the Earth."

"Perhaps I'm mistaken, that when I make you speak, I only realize that I am wrong and that you don't have the gallantry to give it to me. Is it that you don't have any compassion for me, even if you don't love me? There are women who feel frustrated when we are objects of compassion, me too, I have fallen low, poor little me, I'm about to die of sadness and you don't notice it. If things go on like this, I'm going to have to say goodbye to you, just like that, said with indifference. The truth is we have sunk that low. Sometimes I wonder if we will make it to the next day and I am overcome by a mortal shudder, I'm afraid, I think I am ill, under a downpour of rain water in August beneath the eaves on the street."

"But I'll be with you Ant, because I don't want to be a

burden, much less make you lend me your eyes and have to share your images with me, because then we would be two blind people instead of one. I'd rather go where I don't smell your smell, or Magdalene complaints. For days now your presence has become an ancient tragedy, where tears substitute words and we look at each other in a manner as if it were the last day of life. That is unbearable for me and for you. Let's chat for a while instead and pretend we're saying goodbye so we can avoid a grandiloquent farewell; getting ourselves used to saying our goodbyes and you'll see it will all be easy when the real moment arrives. Let's laugh at ourselves instead, better yet tickle me, kiss me on my bellybutton until I tell you no more, dying of laughter; let's laugh instead, Ant, laugh and let real tears come out of you. Kiss me, Ant. I love you. Whose jade buttocks are those?"

"Yours, my love."

"And whose coo-coo-coo-coo is this?

"Stop now, you're going to make me die of laughter. It's mine."

"And that lavender tulip, I wonder who it belongs to."

"That's enough, you're going to kill me, I'm going to suffocate, stop making me laugh now. It's yours."

When I have disappeared through Ant's upper pores, I am she. I am woman like her.

— *vii* —

I want you to talk openly with me, to stop beating around the bush; to say, for example, it's going to rain this afternoon and know that you are lying terribly to me; even for lying you are not suspect. You'll dampen your face so later you can say you're crying, that's why every time I want to plant my feet on the ground your image appears; your just judge

24

of the night guides me to what I want to say. The star-filled sky! and it's not a product of the imagination, or just pleasant disquisitions. Your mentality is so screwed—you say to me—that you don't dare tell the truth. "It's going to rain this afternoon and there are stars in the sky." You don't spell things out. You see, Ant, one cannot speak seriously with you, that's the reason I prefer to remain silent when you are near and to shout when you are far away, so your kinds of dreaming don't appear. You're too obsessive, Ant, you want me to ask you for permission even to urinate and you watch me in order to inspect my underpants to see if they are stained with infidelity and may it be known, as you well know: when you see stains on my skivvies it's because I'm taking Witt's Pills, for my kidneys. You know very well that I am chronically ill, infirm; when I don't have a headache the tips of my toes ache; and if you come around with your abstract ways of being, you cause me greater damage. Talk to me about home remedies, coffee with biscuits, the meddler trees of Izalco, oranges of Juayúa, the looms of San Sebastián, the stones from Tablón del Coco. Speak pretty words to me, ones dressed in flowery cloth like you; lead me not into the temptations of remaining bedridden forever. Be my comfort, Ant, be good, don't break us apart, give me air through your mouth, because, if I'm this way, it's for you and not for any other reason; stop having those pink eyes that will tell me that you're crying, you're going to make me die of desperation. What good would I be to you dead? tell me. I don't want to see you crying because I'll think you have dampened your face and far from awakening condolences in me you'll evoke mercy. Help me hate you and we will have those hundred joys you desire and we will live happily, don't you want it that way, Ant? If you don't like that, tell me so I can start packing my bags and go out to breathe fresh air in the street, with my suitcase with five books I could carry in my pocket, my two pairs of socks, my other shirt, my second pair of pants, my toothbrush, the photograph of Mamma and Papa, poor things. Dead without memories. And you spent the best moments crying, today, for example, your birthday, we could have laughed at each other, but you get sentimental. What do you want me to do? Become weak? Accompany you in your sorrow? Stop crying and things will change, I can't start doing a jig to make you laugh, I couldn't do anything, because I've run out of jokes, just as I could run out of conscience and even love for you, Ant, climbing bird, daughter of your mamma, daughter of your aunt; it'd be better for you to commit yourself to caring for sick children and not for me, this animal full of life that acts sick. Go on, I invite you to look for a new occupation, I invite you so we can split up and each can go his or her own way, to make love in other places, but let's get off this tortuous path; perhaps we'll be closer the day that we feel far apart, one from the other, but then I'll think Ant is probably under the trees, smelling who knows what winter chills in her leather jacket, standing on a street corner, selling photographs. Then I will adore you and you will adore me, like characters in romance novels. Let's stop acting like ownerless dogs; let's be courageous so we can withstand so many of life's bad breaks, you are no General-in-Chief, no member of the Joint Chiefs of Staff, that's why you are in no way to blame. And let's not believe our tear-wrenching whining is going to change us; see what's happening, love less so that I love you much more, hate so that I can love you (and now you can see, if we keep talking I'm going to end up a composer of street music). I don't know if you can hear me, you're covering your ears, you fight the words that help, I think deep inside you want to hurt me. Your behavior is a refractory mirror: you take everything apart, you arrange everything to improve our relationship, only to say later things that we don't understand; to threaten us with breaking up or the evil things expressed with good intentions. Who then is the bandit, Ant, tell me, and if we want the ship to sink, here is the freshwater sailor ready to go down to the bottom. Let's stop tearing our hearts out, stop being the virgin of the miraculous medallion and let's live with everything out in the open. If you don't want to take care of me Ant, I'm leaving, my poems and little things, wish me good luck in this final farewell. From afar I will say goodbye to you and it will be the last time we'll see each other until we meet thirty years later, by then dying and different, but always lovers. If you keep crying I will no longer care if they're real tears or ocean rivers. I'll write you a letter.

And I left. I really fucked things up this time.

— *viii* —

It was Sunday when I left Ant. She kept her eyes closed, exactly like the children who die of hunger on the street corners of El Salvador. She didn't know that mine was a trip of no return, and that matter of not returning was for me a kind of intuition, only life would reveal the truth. "You're not going to return," I repeated to myself with a certain heroic pessimism. Ant will not believe it, I know, that's why I took advantage of her absence of several hours and I left her a written note stuck to the mirror. "Good luck, we'll run into each other some day." She'll think I'm hiding behind the door and that I'm going to scare her. We never would've agreed upon my departure and that's why we tried to be harsh with each other. The important thing was to get out of the house as quickly as possible, taking the suitcase, packed ahead of time, two weeks earlier, to help get used to the idea before the last day. The truth is that we never ever got used to the idea. So, when Ant goes to the pharmacy, I gather my things and leave. I know the place where my compañeros are waiting for me, they won't be able to tell that I sneaked away, they won't ask me a thing and I won't ask them anything either, because that's the heroic part, each one of us is in his own world—important, vital—but it's a world for only one; therefore, far be it for one to worry about everyone else. No one asks about Ant, I'm just Alfonso and she. Me on the train headed towards the border, she shut in, between four walls of hollow bricks, cooking her last meal that would be for the two of us. Are you coming at lunch time? she asks with calculated indifference. And just in case she prepares enough food for two. Three hours later I'll be far away. My other compañero is traveling on the same train; the agreement is not to speak a word to each other. We don't know each other; as long as some danger exists, and there will always be danger within our own country, we shall not speak to each other. Perhaps this is the best moment of my life, leaving everything behind in order to become part of something unknown, like traveling to the other side of the earth. I'm on the other side of the earth and I don't realize it.

— *ix* —

To be in reality is to come from one-knows-not-where and go towards where we ought to be. Papa died a short time after my birth, I wasn't even three years old. I'm sure of the date, Mamma was surrounded by flowers in the middle of a living room of mud bricks and in the corner there was a sewing machine; and there were people chatting softly as if they were afraid of waking the dead man. I played on the steps by the door, innocently. That's the memory I have of my father's death. Inexplicably they deceived me, they said that Papa had shot himself, because he was jobless and my childhood required economic responsibility, therefore I was to blame. It's true there was a gunshot, but he didn't shoot himself, he was shot when he intervened in a riot organized to sack the houses of rich people who had hoarded all the corn. At that point the people weren't just taking corn, but chairs, beds, mats, mirrors and, in short, everything they could carry, the proprietors had left their houses abandoning their possessions. But they took refuge at the barracks and demanded that the soldiers stop the looting. The gatherings of people on the street corners became larger and larger. A man stood up on a wooden crate and stirred up the crowd. Months earlier, the corn had disappeared from town, but it was known that it was in the granaries of the Arabs and the town's other rich people. Papa was the man standing on the wooden crate stirring up the crowd, calling for the looting of their houses. That day was my third birthday, the day the looting in San Miguel increased. Papa died from a gunshot wound to his head. They killed him as a thief. They shot him from behind. That's the reason they told me he had committed suicide. More than a hundred people died just that day alone. Thieves, they said, but all of them had been honest until they got the idea of attacking homes. What hunger does to people. The owners of the corn had convinced the soldiers that they should go hunt the people who were carrying away the corn and furniture on their backs. Papa would have survived, but when the first gunshots were fired the doors of the houses closed and strangers were not let in. Others were able to gain asylum, but my papa was felled by that shot never to awaken again. The little soldiers captured him with his hands up, but they didn't go easy on him, they shot him point blank, hungry dogs, thieves. There a hungry dog met his end. Bullet-ridden in an entryway in San Miguel. Nine years later my mamma died and I went to live with my godfather, the photographer, in the city of

Usulután. I had grown up, that's how I was able to eat by the sweat of my brow as the sentence reads in the Holy Scriptures. I was eleven years old and there you were, Ant, daughter of my widower godfather who lived with his sister Doña Gracia, that's to say we were brother and sister according to God's law. Ant was the family cook and I the one who ran errands and cleaned furniture and did other household chores. That's how it started. Ant began to take care of me as if I were a young kitten, although I was older than her and I could take care of myself, but Ant was always that way, attentive, and I needed that attention. Sometimes she would sit me on her lap to de-lice me or she would help me with my share of the chores. She took me on as if I were a motherless child. She must have been ten years old, but she already had the appearance of an attractive young woman. Having known Ant from such an early age also gave me the strength to disengage myself from her, unchain myself from where one binds oneself for love. Years later, the family left San Salvador and for a while I stayed again in Usulután, until they needed me to be with them, because my godfather had died, and so I went to be with them. Ant was already a woman of eighteen, her slanted eyes full of aromatic flowers.

— *x* —

Rodrigo went to urinate, to relax his nerves, the train had reached the border station. I was calmer, perhaps because I had lost so much. And I received your letters, Ant, the first two that I was never able to answer: you're going blind and can't read my letters. But I thought about the answers that I never wrote: how are you doing on those cold days? Do your fingers hurt from washing so many clothes? How are those hallucinations and little lights in your head? Do you still go to the market and return loaded down with parsley, onions, and radishes? For the family home. That's how Doña Gracia makes a living, by providing rooms for students. Which side of your window is the sun on when you get up? The sunlight that I get is a fried egg. Your poem letter is the only thing I receive, stuck in the pages of one of my books. I renew myself reading the pretty things you write me. "You're always in the mirror in which I see myself, you make ugly faces at me while I let out she-wolf howls because your image in the mirror frightens me. In the morning hours I remember you most. I don't write because sometimes I spend entire weeks in a state of abulia, I forget everything and shut myself in my room with music and I see what I can't see in the street, the photo of Jenny you left me. Then I practice breathing exercises. I try to absorb all the oxygen I can, because that's the way to live longer, to be able to wait for you." Yes, we should live longer to achieve things in this cathedral of dreams and misery called life. If you can't have anything else, the only thing left is to live. We know that to live is to be conscious of the existence of others. Although at times life is a fat lady who praises our defects and confuses us. "You had better be careful, do the right thing." You say so many nice things to me.

"Your big enemy is you and me. The greatest woman inside you should be me. The transcendent woman of my room is me and the man of the mirror is you. I feel like a queen surrounded by photographs when I'm alone in the company of the image in the mirror. Sometimes I hear the flute concert you gave me or I look through your old books, dusty as if they had arrived from a long, desert trail."

"Ant: Too bad I only have one chair that doesn't let me type because it's very uncomfortable to sit in a chair with short legs so that my nose is stuck in the keyboard. You could have even brought me one of those stools from over there, the kind that cost five *colones*. I would have already completed a book of poetry! Just imagine what a five-peso stool can do: a book of poems dedicated to you. I know, within five hundred years they'll talk of the book of poetry that I couldn't dedicate to you, because I had no place to sit. When I come back I'd like to have a set of Swedish furniture. No one will remember those books I shall write seated on Swedish furniture. That's life. 'What's worth more, a book of poems or Swedish furniture? It's the same problem that has existed for centuries and that no one can resolve.' One of these days I'll drink two bottles of beer and I'll jump out a window that will let me fall unendingly. I'll be dreaming then. And you will also be drinking a beer and you'll think that the one who has jumped out the window is you. Dreams intertwine, at least. Know what I mean? I've decided to forget about you for good. 'What are the streets in your barrio like, have the trees of Cuartel Park grown?' The future rulers of my country will wear loose slacks and they will love to listen to a flute and mandolin concert. There's no doubt that I'm privileged—imagine, who has that flute concert for now? Ant, life is an incurable illness. Starting tomorrow I'll make a formal promise: I'll never again make formal promises. What's it like to have a baby? You look like the world with your slanted eyes and round face while the sea surrounds you. If one day someone asks you about this silence, tell them that we already talk too much and that this silence is a tribute to our love. I'm an adventurer and I see how things are and how they aren't at the same time, like Heraclitus' river, the man who sells ice cream on the corner of Cuartel Park. Some day I shall return. I'm not forgetting how terrible borders are, but I will come back to see you. Let's forgive ourselves for writing in this fragmented manner, but it's the vacillation itself of not knowing if we belong to each other. I love you. Me too."

Why are we happy, Ant?

You ask stupid questions, you speak with an inscrutable brow. You dislike the unpleasant inquisition. Do you want me to say the opposite? For example, why are we so sad, Ant? Why must we turn these four walls into the largest planet? Perhaps you'd like to walk a little more and find yourself in beautiful jungles, visible to the naked eye from any window but easy to avoid, due perhaps to a false guilt complex or to avoid any complications?

"I don't know."

"You do, but you're afraid to say it, to recognize it."

"If I knew I'd tell you."

Being happy is a way of running away, and since you are my good conscience, you stop me with your conventional chains, distancing yourself from my intentions, heading towards places where we don't exist; worrying about a plane that flies above our beloved rooftops; a plane carrying beneath its wings an incendiary bottle and in its cockpit a young man who looks like you, but who at that moment isn't discussing trivial matters with a woman, but pushing multicolored buttons that will open the hatch that houses the devastating bomb.

"You don't say it because you think that happiness is a word that will fly away if it is released, right? Did I guess right, Ant?"

"I wonder why we started speaking dis-figuratively? A confused language. If we don't speak like people we're going to end up looking at each other in signs. Why do you want to know? One is happy or unfortunate and that's all there is to it: We aren't happy and that's enough. Why are you so curious? You like to peek through even the small slits of the soul.

But the war isn't our problem. It's easier to think about those rats that make a hole in each of the walls and that come to bite the uncovered tips of our toes. It's easier to think about these cockroaches, about the son-of-a-bitch mosquitoes, about the yellow-tailed mosquitoes.

"If you want I'll tell you."

"Go ahead then."

"We're happy because we've lived together."

"Yeah, beneath the same roof."

"And so many hours in the same bed."

"Do you think happiness is to be found in bed."

"I should think so."

And then there are more of our mountains, too many poisonous reptiles for so few inhabitants, that's why they get in and get under our beds and we don't know if the snakes that hang from the decorative facades of the houses are part of the nightmare. Or the lizards in the children's shoes. We realize the situation when the poison has already inoculated the brain with strange visions.

"Without realizing it we are incredible."

"Invisible too."

"I mean it."

"Me too."

"You make fun of our poverty. What do you say about this house, it barely has four walls and a door, which is the way out of the cave, and a few stair steps that lead to the world where yes indeed a table, chairs, a pot of geraniums, a door exist, a door like the mouth of a cannon."

"And for us, nothing, it is because of the ascending staircase that we started to live. Farther beyond, things have owners; we're not part of them. We just do the dirty work."

"I'm talking about all of that life. We should disappear from this house and start a new life, don't you think?"

"It's a fable without a moral."

"And you bring up the myth that the bed is the cause of

all happiness, it reminds me of those fairy tales I still dream about."

(Manuel the jerk walking through the streets of Tegucigalpa and behind him the barking of street dogs, and then drinking a coffee in the *Jardín de Italia* and then going to that affair where everyone comes out alive except you who looks like a ghost shrouded in a moon-colored sheet, your vacant, jail-cell eyes, with bullet holes in your head. So you're Manuel? You haven't changed much. You must be dead, probably because no one remembers you. The living forget with ingratitude, but the dead remember each other with magnanimity.)

"The day that we live in the same house we'll be happy, you don't believe it because you don't know what a family is."

"We've lived together, what more do you want, beneath the same roof, we've spent so many secret hours sleeping in the same bed."

"I've never been in a bed with anyone."

"Well, I dreamt it and it seemed real to me."

"You're crazy, my love."

"We're crazy."

"Let's just say we are beautiful."

"I was unfaithful to you. I've been sleeping in the same bed with a woman from the Río Blanco. But it's her bed and the bed of all that go at night to enjoy it. I've been one of two thousand, perhaps. The Red Light District, you know. For a few coins they lift their legs up, as if they wanted to scratch the ceiling with their toes."

"Aren't you ashamed to talk about it? What's her name?"

"She doesn't have a name. The times I've gone, I pick the one that's available, I forget her personality so I don't go insane. No one who goes to bed with a woman at the Río Blanco can be unfaithful, although I'm not very sure I know what I'm talking about."

"Then, so we can be happy, will you stop going to sleep with the anonymous Río Blanco woman? And will you stay to sleep in my bed and me in yours?"

"It has to be in the same bed."

"Doesn't that seem unhealthy to you, I'm talking about diseases."

"You're kidding."

"Think about the hot nights. I think your perspiration and mine won't get along. The sheets themselves will go flying off."

"You're sweeter than a caramel, Ant."

"I've never slept with anyone else, I tell you. Perhaps I never will, not out of lack of love but out of cowardice."

"You have to know men. You'll know them through their nocturnal hours."

"I think we're being fanciful."

"We shouldn't be such dreamers, don't you think?"

"We won't be when we sleep in the same bed."

"A woman isn't the same once she knows a man, Ant."

"You've got ideas from eccentric books."

"It's true, they're not my ideas, but what's the difference if everything said and done in the world has an origin? We're never going to be original."

"We're unfortunate, Ant."

"If we're happy we can't be unfortunate."

"I'm happy when I dream I'm asleep with you, with no one to bother us, no one to tell us anything or to know how beautiful we are when we are together."

"I'm afraid of men."

"You have to share your life with a man."

"Would you sleep with a man?"

"Me, of course not."

"My grandmother says there are men who sleep with men."

"She's out of her mind."

"And if I sleep with you will you stop loving me? Do you really need it, do you want me to see you naked?"

"Not just me, but both of us would sleep naked, you just don't get it because you're inexperienced, you're a little girl whose afraid of witches, I'll bet your grandmother got you to believe in voodoo dolls with pins in them. You'll get nowhere in life that way."

— *xii* —

At first it was just physical necessity. When I would pass the door to your room you were always looking at yourself in the mirror. You looked at your reflection forwards and backwards. To love that image in the mirror was to love a dead image of you, but I only loved that person who had her back to the window, the one who didn't see me when I went by on the way from my room to the dining room, the one who didn't pay any attention to me because she never looked at me. And the only thing that appeared were your eyes, the eyes of the image, in a room where there was nothing else to do except look at yourself in the mirror and look at the photographs nailed to the wall; from the beginning they pointed to an extravagant narcissism, but then I realized that you did it—according to what you told me—in order to feel like someone was with you and you could only be with yourself, Ant, wrapped in a hopeless mystery in those photographs that served as wall paper. There you were in different poses and attitudes, your love of flowery dresses and your stare going to poise itself, placing its dove feet in a place where you were, but that wasn't in the photograph, and it wasn't the lens of the camera either, it had to do with someone outside the scene, and if for some reason it was in the photograph, it was because it could be surmised from the eyes, in that look

37

there was something unknown to me that perhaps you knew. For example, in the one where you appear coming from among the young pine trees and you elongate like in a painting by Camilo Minero, surrounded by yellows and maroons in a rapid contradiction of colors. You elongate more than you really appear to; I notice it is your most authentic photo, competing with a fir tree and it's the same flowery dress every time you served a meal; then you said you liked orange flowers so much you had all your dresses made of the same fabric. You're wearing the same clothes. And everyone bothered you about having only one dress as if that were a sin and you started laughing, aware of your preference for orange-colored flowers and not caring what others thought about your going around in the same clothes, like in the song. At first I thought it was strange you always wore the same dress, but your dresses all smelled clean, worn for the first time, fresh and fragrant. Then you told me: "I like to go around the way I want." I thought then you were the oldest girl in the world. "I have ten of them the same color," with a smile in your eyes. It was like having just one. "I don't care. Do you think that's a defect?" And what difference did it make to dress in only one color, if the essential thing is to cover one's nudity, so be a naive painting; a way of adorning your skin and changing into a girl with orange-colored flowers on a light-blue background, ready to participate in Spring.

"What's important is being clean like the detergent commercials," you would say. Those phrases with two meanings that appeared to mean nothing, but that rang out louder than church bells, something that went beyond simple words: the main thing is being clean and luminous; and so, you, in front of the mirror, in front of your photographs, striking suggestive poses, looking at yourself every time you turned around, and your photos spying on you from a spot on the wall, watching the way I looked at you as if the two of us were desiring the same things: your image in front of the door, and myself stuck in the image too, pinned by your side. With such warmth we saw each other, the great desire appropriate for an age without reason. After all, it's the best way to perpetuate dreams. And how I loved you, cat eyes, turkey nose, I always stayed in second place in front of your door and you in the mirror, watching your beloved man pass by, planning to fix the world in your own way.

— *viii* —

"It's that I haven't told you my life story; if I did, perhaps you'd be on my side, now that it doesn't cost you anything to say that I'm possessive, that you don't need me, that I'm a caramel, you invent some words that only I can understand and now are nothing more than love on paper."

"Remember the last night we dreamed together? I arrived knocking in the darkness, I fell into your lap and you said another name. I paid no attention to it, I thought you were doing it to make me jealous, so I'd get angry at you and split."

"I didn't do it for any reason; besides, I think you're making it up, as an excuse to fight, look how you come to tell me about it six months later. Besides you gave me a great scare."

"Now's the chance; before you hadn't given me any reason."

"I can't live on the past, leave it alone."

"Sometimes I think you've played a dirty trick on me, with your vomiting and expecting a child, why didn't you take care of yourself? Now how are we going to take care of it?"

"You should have taken care of me. I don't know what

I'm going to do; maybe I'll give the baby my share of food and deprive myself of buying new dresses for four or five years, that's what I'll do, besides, I won't ask you for anything, I won't require you to change your life and you can come at the same time, you can go off with your friends, I think that a child won't be in the way for me, to the contrary, it will make you stay away from home longer, I'll take care of it, you should thank me."

"I think our dreams have played a dirty trick on us."

"In my situation, it's more like reality, you go out, you sleep somewhere else and you forget about the woman you left behind at home, Ant can endure everything, you must think. You don't realize that Ant needs to go to bed, to rest and sleep."

"Then you dream about your imaginary child."

"I'm telling you I have never dreamed about anybody, and if I did it would be a nightmare, I'd dream I was placing the noose around his neck or that I was stabbing my fingers into his jugular vein."

"It's not a pretty picture for people like you."

"Nightmares are always ugly."

"Keep talking while I put some water on for coffee."

"You don't play fair when we talk, you change the subject."

"I listen to you politely, I don't want to comment."

"If you listened to me with understanding, at least we would rhyme."

"I would build a house, I'd be an architect, I would build a small house where the two of us would live, and up above there would be nothing but stars, with no one to bother us, not even bad thoughts; but you see, we came to this house, where there's no room for another person, not even the little baby you're expecting."

"Yes sir, you are capable of anything, even of making me cry just for the fun of it."

"You get nostalgic, melodious, prudish"

"I get the way you want me."

"Let's just forget those dreams."

"Yes, that's better."

"Not really, just so we don't fight."

"If you want to eat dinner, come and sit down, wildcat."

"I want to eat up everything you put in front of me."

"I made a salad especially for you, I hope you haven't forgotten, well it's been so long since we've been together, enjoying a meal."

"Perhaps when I'm old I'll lose that tendency of disappearing."

"Why have you become serious?"

"I don't know."

"Are you okay?"

"I'm fine, I should get up."

"Aren't you going to eat?"

"I'm not hungry."

"The food is already served."

"I haven't eaten in the afternoon for years."

"I want to talk about us."

"We always talk about us."

"We need to talk more seriously, it's a matter of life or death, we have to understand each other."

"You speak first and I'll follow."

"I'm aware of everything, your infidelities."

"Really?"

"I saw you with her when you were going down the street, Tuesday, at five in the afternoon, tell me if I'm lying: They don't say Tuesday, blues day for nothing."

"That's true."

"I spoke ..."

"With whom?"

"With her."

"Who is she?"

"Juanita, from Suchitoto, don't pretend you don't know."

"It's not possible, because you don't know her."

"You'll see."

"I told her we were going to have a child and that you were a big bad wolf, that you liked to bite and that if you hadn't done so yet it was because you lacked confidence but that once she gave you her hand you'd bite her elbow and you were capable of eating her up. And further, that you were a hypochondriac, that you had to be given medicine in bed and that you had to be served meals of vegetables which have to be hand fed to you; that you suffer from kidney problems and you have to take Witt's pills every five hours, you should have seen how much fun I had telling these truths."

"You made it all up."

"I also told her something else."

"What?"

"I still love him, I shouted at her."

"And what did she say?"

"She started crying; but don't think she was crying out of love, but out of embarrassment, do you understand? There was nothing else I could do, especially when you are indifferent about that ball of smoke I'm carrying in my womb which, according to the tongues of gossipers and my own—which isn't exactly innocent—is your child."

"It's just that I've never known about balls of smoke, nor about children; what I do know is, your stomach looks as smooth as flagstone from Los Chorros or Tablón del Coco."

"That's on the outside, but you don't know what's happening to me on the inside, you see me beautiful on the outside and not the terrible inside."

"You've lied to me and you still complain; if you keep it up with your wailing walls of Jerusalem I'm going to end up crying."

"You're saying that because I'm here."

"You never believe anything I say, it's as if we were lost in space."

"You haven't said nice things to me, I hear you come to bed after midnight, you've erased me from the map."

"The thing is I've never understood your problems."

"I can't keep quiet all the time."

"Don't worry, everything might turn out well."

"Maybe you're right to see another woman."

"Tell me what time it is instead, I feel like drinking some coffee."

"I thought you got over the problem of drinking that crap."

"The problem I haven't gotten over is that I love you, I can go everywhere in the world, but you are my only love. Ant, fruit eater."

"You're a big fat liar."

"So are you."

"Your long absences, the fact you don't come home early because you go to see Juanita, the girl from Suchitoto. You haven't taken care of our love. And to boot, my Aunt Gracia is very worried about your late-night carousing."

"Know something, Ant?"

"What?"

"I'd better not tell you anything."

"You'd better tell me everything."

II

THE WOLVES

We were living in Santanita—the happier barrio—happier than when we used to play soccer with a rubber ball.

"Wasting time instead of studying," Old Miguel, or Old Man, said.

"You don't want us to spend our time sitting on our rear ends," Pichón—small fry—says as he kicks the ball against the wall of the house across the street. A mansion that went around the four corners of a block like a cat biting its tail. I: "On your mark, get set, go." Heading the ball.

"You can have the books, here are the ones I'm going to leave you," Old Miguel, taking himself seriously. Old, not because he's old but because of his temperament: "Change your ways or you're going to die soon." And he, with a go-screw-yourself laugh, was bequeathing them his library, if they don't want it, fine. His library is one in name only, it consists of a few pamphlets, magazines, newspaper clippings, all of which fit into a cardboard box. Junk! Academic stuff, we scoff.

"You guys think that in order to be revolutionaries you have to be illiterate," he disappears through the window.

"Let us play for a while," we, from the street, or the alley, because there's no exit in back.

"Don't pay any attention to him," Pichón says as he makes a soccer move.

Old Miguel came to ruin everything with his academic

discipline. "He'll be here a couple of weeks," Meme says. "That's right," we're resigned to it. Luckily for us, Old Man turned out to be a nice guy, except for his Napoleonic complex, which manifests itself in the inordinate amount of time he spends with his books, and his coming by all the time to give advice, behave yourself, be disciplined, don't covet your neighbor's wife, etc., etc.

"Well, guys, I hate to leave you. I have very important things to do," only then did we realize that three weeks had gone by and, in that short time, mutual sympathies and feelings of brotherhood had developed. He had been packing his suitcase since morning. Pichón, Old Man and myself, perhaps we couldn't hide the Indian sadness on our faces. "I'm going to a print shop, they'll understand things now," he was so sorry and had to tell us the truth even though he was breaking one of his disciplinary rules. He put on his Basque cap and dark glasses. Pichónidas, jokingly, with a stupid look on his face: "It's really sunny out," to make him see that it was nighttime. "It's a disguise, idiot." "You deserved that, Pichón," I tell him.

At four, Meme's car arrived. We shook hands. Earlier I was pissing every five minutes. Pichón, to get in the mood of the situation, was reading a Farabundo Press book. Old Man—I'm listening to Radio Havana—with his ear glued to the receiver, because it was always blocked with the sounds of five dogs howling on the dial. I had lain down to go to sleep. "Goodbye." The three of us had a banana-split feeling in our throats.

"He's leaving us his library," I glance at the pile of papers in one corner of the living room.

And Old Man rises to the occasion with his fifth-year philosophy education, in his farewell he says:

"I'm sure we'll be together again."

"At least we won't be playing soccer anymore."

Pichón, in bed, reads the Farabundo edition. "Why

didn't this Farabundo guy ever write anything?" he says out loud. "It is a mystery that repeats itself with Salvadorans," I respond.

Guapote—Pretty Boy—came for Old Man: "The car is over there around the corner." "Hey guys." "Hey Guapote." We don't call him Guapote because he's handsome, but because he looks like the fish with that same name. "Behave yourselves," is the last thing he tells us as Old Man leaves with Guapote behind him.

— *ii* —

"What a coincidence," says Guillermo, Meme's brother, "I've seen you pass by the Three B's several times." I tell him that I live around there. "Yes," he insists, "I was coming out of the Mexican Movie Theater when I saw you heading towards the bridge. "It's a coincidence," he went on, "because my hole-in-the-wall is in that area, on Venezuela Boulevard, to be exact. You know, when you want some bread just come by my house and I can give you what you need." It was the second time he had made the offer. The three of us (Pichón, Old Man, and I) in chorus: "Okay," without taking it very seriously, since these encounters with him only take place in the cafeteria and we don't trust him very much. "He's probably drunk," Pichón says a half hour later when we're headed towards Santanita. "Why are there such ungrateful people?" Old Man asks us (in a tone of protest). "If I were a baker and I ran into you guys I'd make you the same offer." Confirming how poor he looked, Pichón and I respond in chorus: "That's enough, Old Man, look who's talking, you're so stingy you shouldn't say anything."

"Maybe it's not wise to come to this cafeteria because he's already hanging around with us." Old Man: "You guys exaggerate, we have no reason to be afraid of him if we don't owe him a thing."

"That's what angers me about you, Old Man, you and your gratuitous sentimentality, we're not talking about being afraid of anything."

"He's saying you don't know who we're dealing with, Old Man," Pichón interjects.

"This isn't a game," he defends himself, with the look of a church choirboy

You really make one angry, I was going to tell him and don't when I see how relaxed he is drinking his *arrayán* fruit drink, at least it makes us feel secure about ourselves. Pichón changes the record.

"Do you like 'The Ballad of the Soldier'?"

"A poem," Old Man says.

"I didn't understand a thing," Pichón says to contradict Old Man.

Now it's Old Man who plays the same old record again: "The baker took off."

Pichón hysterical: "Your melancholy is a bore, Old Man." Three days later he ran into us again at Pavos Carlotas: "What happened to you guys, you haven't come for bread, if you want I'll have some delivered to your house." Old Man: "You'd have to go out of your way." The Baker: "Have a beer on me." I: "No thanks, by law the next two hours are dry ones for us." Old Man: "Perhaps I'll have one." The Baker, speaking to Pichón: "And you, dear poet?" Pichón, when the baker has gone to the bathroom: "He's a baker but he looks like an intellectual." The baker returns and insists upon a second round for Old Man. To avoid having to accept it, we decide to get up.

"You guys don't trust anybody," Old Man says as he takes his key from the door.

"You're angry, Old Man," Pichón says to pick on him. "That's why we call you Old Man, at twenty-two you've got more wrinkles than John Wayne." His temperament does him in, he turns into a mummy when he doesn't understand the humor. "Lay off, Pichón, you're going to anger Old Man, you scold him a lot." Old Man huffs from his room to let us know he can hear us, he may be old but he's not stupid. I motion to the poet to stop talking. Then Pichón does an alvaro mutis.

— *iii* —

"We shouldn't become impatient."

"I can't take this vagabond lifestyle any longer."

"Calm down, people."

They got the idea that we would have a print shop exclusively for the university. We found that out a month after Old Man had left. The FUAR—the University Front— paid for the house, our moms and dads took care of our other expenses; being alone in the house in Santanita was no party. You're going to be placed under quarantine, Meme tells us. That's the way it went for us, kicking a ball of rags against the wall; and sometimes we had books (we're on vacation); I had two final exams in March hanging over my head. I don't plan to study for them: "Remember, it's not just a question of revolutionary morality but of personal security." That time Guapote had to go find us at the corner store, where we were eating some turtle eggs. Meme was chastising us.

And we ran out of patience. We set up a press. Feliciano joined us. He brings and takes away the electronic stencils, besides being the printing technician. "Let's see if you can take the training," as he prepares the machine. Our press didn't even last three weeks.

"You're going to change your location and you're going to go to a family home."

"That's not possible," I tell Meme, although I know he means it.

"And I'm going to be the head of the family," Meme says. "We'll move to a place by Centenary Park, close to the Forest barrio."

"Since when are you the father of a family, my friend?"

"My private life, brother, you see, one has to be careful."

"And Al is another one who's got to be careful," Meme says to me in third person as if I were invisible.

"I have a wife and two children," Meme says.

"Well then, what are we going to do," Feliciano says, "You've kept it to yourself."

"The main thing is to lead a normal life," Meme continues to irritate us.

There are three rooms in the house. Two along the street and another one on the inside. There's a little patio paved with red cement bricks, a hallway for the table, and two columns where Old Man sets up his hammock. Guapote heads for the inside room, carrying the printing machines. "Give me a hand with the boxes of paper you lazy bastards." Pichón comes in from the street with two boxes on his shoulder. "Where were you?" "I went to help." "Move it, motherfuckers." "Not you, Al, you'd better stay safe and warm in the house, we'd better cool it." Meme gives us final instructions. A bell tower in the distance strikes: eleven o'clock at night.

That's when Old Miguel arrived: "I'm with you guys," he says cheerfully. And then: "I saw Guillermo, the baker, yesterday; he said he would like to work with the FUAR." (Surprise in everyone's eyes.) Old Man notes: "He can help by giving us bread, that's something." I: "Why didn't you tell him to go to hell? Tell him you don't know anything about anything." Old Man: "You're kidding." I: "I don't like it. We're not organizing a cell for the Front so we can deliver the bread Meme's brother brings to us." Old

Man: "We didn't know he had a wife and kids either, Meme is like that, a man of few words." I: "Well, romantic Old Man, Manuel is one thing and his brother another, those are the rules we must follow; besides, he never told us about his brother, there must be a reason." Old Man: "Being out of the country for so long has made you become very suspicious, Al," he said like someone setting off a rocket into the sky in a fireworks display.

— *iv* —

"Come and eat, boys," Margó says after a few days had passed and—among us—we had established the familiarity of five brothers living together with a female saint.

Meme comes out of the bathroom, a towel covering him from the waist down:

"I haven't seen you, when did you get here?"

"Hi, Al, I came in the front door and headed straight for the bathroom."

"And you show up like a kid with no clothes on."

"What happened to everybody else?"

"Feliciano went home, Pichón is taking a vacation until tomorrow, and Old Man went to the store to buy some beer."

"There's got to be a way to get Old Man to drink as little as possible, don't you think?"

"Would you like some?" Old Man offers glasses to us, each one half-filled with froth, half with yellow Meza Ayau urine.

Seated at the table: "Thanks, Old Man, you're from another world altogether."

"And this one is for Margó," Old Man adds, with a third glass in hand and only a trace of foam remains in the bottom of the amber-colored bottle, an ice-cold *pilsner* above all else, like the commercial says.

"I don't want it," Margó—who in this moment comes out in a pink robe, looking like the Queen of Sheba—says. "I just haven't had a chance to get dressed: first it was the kids, then the cleaning, and finally because I made lunch." "You don't have to explain, this is your house." Always a slave. "Come and get it, boys." With a plate in hand, coming out of the filthy, shitty kitchen. "Really, I don't want any beer, go ahead and drink it Old Man."

"I want some," Pepino the Brief says from his kiddie chair, a present from his great-grandmother who lives in Cojutepeque.

"I no want any," Negrita Cuculumbe interrupts, from the other kiddie chair covered with little birds and flowers.

"You're not old enough for love," Old Man says. We were laying the paper out all morning. Feliciano has decided we are to work at night because it's safer. He's an Olympian worker, he can get a Salvadoran *cambe* out of the machine, with the red-blouse rhythm. Pichón is his assistant. Old Man and I were stapling the pamphlets. That was last night. At midnight, the dry thud of the stapler. At one in the morning, Old Man moves his ghost shadow after drinking five cups of coffee Margó had left in the Aladdin thermos and the kerosene lamp. "That's the bad thing about you," Feliciano jokes: "You drug yourself in order to work, you have to play fair you grouchy, respectable Old Man, like us," he's talking about Pichón and himself; both of them in T-shirts and underpants. Feliciano: "I don't even smoke, that should give you an idea how resistant I am to sleep." Old Man: "I've slept since nine at night, I don't know if you have material to put together now. I go to sleep early and then I have coffee from my thermos. Compared to me, Feliciano is a child, it's not that I want to brag, that's just the way it is; And it's not a virtue for you not to smoke or drink. I fell asleep with one of Trotsky's books over my face, but I was listening to the nonsense you guys were saying." Lying in the hammock hung between the pillars in the hallway. "The most important thing is not to give the body any rest, to get it used to the cracker rhythm crunch-crunch, and you'll see, you wake up fresh," says Feliciano. Old Man opens his mouth: "You can't work without bull-shitting." Feliciano defends himself: "I only speak when the machine stops, you can't deny that." Because once the mimeograph machine is put in motion he turns on the transistor radio, they turn the volume way up to drown out the sound of the machine that lets out its red-blouse rhythm as it spits out sheets of printed pages. One night they threw rocks, or perhaps it was a gun shot from next door: "Let us sleep, you drunken, partying sons-of-bitches," they shouted. And we: "Fuck off," from our side, but softly so only the voice of conscience could hear us. "We'd better knock off." "Okay." Once we heard the shot. "Or let's turn off the radio, because it makes more noise than the mimeograph machine."

And that's they way it was for us, amidst the subtle perfume of orange blossoms, like Rubén Darío's sad princess and other adventures. Another day, we had to cover the walls with egg crates. If we mess up, it won't be the police who come but our neighbors. "How can you work all night with the radio on full blast, Feliciano?" "You see, I'm the deaf Beethoven." At four in the morning Feliciano and Pichón go to bed. At eight, Feliciano is on his feet, that's the key to production, no rest. For breakfast, he has a cup of coffee and fried plantain, the way Margó prepares them; and then a walk, "I'll be right back, I'm going to take a walk through the Forest," and he leaves. In the afternoon he sets aside time to write an article against the military government, while Pichón sleeps to his heart's content—face down, ass up.

"Sometimes I think you're wasting your time," Old Man says to me. And I: "There you go again, I'd better not pay any attention to you." He continues: "Meme says you are

ready to do more serious things, not student jour-
nalism." "I'm ready for anything," I respond; and I stop
paying attention to him, because at that moment I am
writing the editorial for the next pamphlet. "Something is
better than nothing," I say in a didactic tone.

— *v* —

And her mother told her: "Watch out for the wolf because
if he shows up in the forest he'll eat you up." But Little Red
Riding Hood, who was disobedient, replied: "If the wolf
comes after me I'll eat him up." And her mother: "Don't be
foolhardy, take these fruits and this meal to your
grandmother." She takes off and on the path she runs into
the wolf disguised as a policeman, with his forty-five in
hand and if she didn't give him her basket he'd eat her up
with bullets. She responded: "Don't come at me with *Juan
Charrasqueado* threats, if you want, do whatever you think
is right." The wolf responds that the proper thing to do is to
shoot, but that he doesn't want to waste gunpowder on
buzzards and even less so on a snot-nosed runt. Then Little
Red Riding Hood says to him you should eat shit with your
left hand so you don't lose any, you son-of-a-gun copper.
And the policeman: "Look what a insolent little wench,
that's the reason why this society is corrupt and heading
towards bankruptcy, with so much disrespect and poor
manners towards authority," and that if she wanted, he
would accompany her, after all, that's what we are here for,
and that what he said about the pistol was just a joke, he
did it to scare you and they pay him to look after snot-nosed
brats like you that walk through the Forest on their way to
see their grandmothers. And Little Red Riding Hood: "Get
out of my way, wolf in policeman's skin, can't you see I'm

in a hurry to see my dear grandmother who is ill?" And the uncouth animal let her go, only because of who she was, because they know not what they do, like in the Bible. Juan Charrasqueado: "Well, if you don't want me to accompany you. It's every man for himself." But the police wolf hid and then he ran off to get that grandmother whore. Now he's knocking at the door of the little old grandmother. "It's me, Little Red Riding Hood," with a disguised voice. The grandmother opened the door and the wolf pulled out his forty-five, emptying its magazine: bang-bang-bang-bang-bang!

— *vi* —

We've been working hard printing for four months and everything is going well. Guapote comes on Fridays and he takes away the packages wrapped in newspapers to hide the stuff to be distributed on Monday in the university departments. Margó is in charge of preparing the packages: on Thursday she works all night with us. "They say a lot are sold," Meme affirms, "and that's good, the fact we print ten thousand copies and don't have to throw away any is good enough." "It's not that they all get sold," Old Man points out. I say: "The copies that are left over are probably left behind in the classrooms, in any old place." "Some of them are bought in bulk and then are handed out gratis." I: "The newspaper gets read, but it's necessary to sell each copy separately, but of course that means being exposed." "All the boys have their own trustworthy clientele, there's no problem with that," Old Man says. On Thursday we don't do any printing, we help Margó wrap the packages, the poor thing spends almost all night working, but we don't leave her alone.

Margó gets up and goes to see Negrita. "She's wet herself, she's wet herself," she says from inside the bedroom. "Where did so much water come from?"

"From her bladder," Meme-Manuel shouts with the understanding smile of a good daddy.

"Bring her here," Old Man shouts, "I'll take care of her for you."

Negrita appears with her hair full of flowers and butterflies.

"You're always peeing on yourself, be quiet, my love. Go to sleep now," Margó complains: "She's like a clock, at twelve midnight she releases her sacred father Lempa river; if I didn't put a bundle of diapers on her we'd have to sleep in a swimming pool. Pepino sleeps like a log, fortunately."

Manuel says to Alfonso:

"She inherited it from me, I wet my bed until I was twelve years old."

"Aren't you ashamed to admit it," Margó interjected.

"By then I already had a girlfriend."

"I can just imagine the way you must of reeked," Margó says.

"Mamma didn't tell me anything, just that she had to take the woven blankets to air out. My grandfather would say what a little jerk you are to have that problem at your age and if your girlfriend Marinita were to find out she would be ashamed to have a bed-wetting boyfriend." And Mamma: "Don't feel bad, my little boy, you can wet yourself as much as you want, I'm the one who washes your clothes."

Margó has sat Negrita down on her lap: "I'm going to change my little gillyflower bud. I'm going to put dry diapers on her, clean her up and then I'm going to start packing pamphlets," remembering the song of the Virgin Mary who washed as Saint Joseph hung.

We're sitting on the floor, except for Margó. "If you want I'll take Negrita for you," Old Man with his paternal instinct. "No, keep working, I'll join you guys later," and she gets up, because Negrita is kicking, "let's go beddy-bye. Wait, you spoiled little girl. I'll be back in a few minutes, I'm going to put her to bed."

"Sometimes I think we don't do these things with the joy they deserve," Old Man pulls out his student manual of philosophy. Meme: "Explain yourself better. In other words, you want us to get Feliciano's radio so we can listen to music." "We're tired of hearing so much late-night radio and so much *cambe* from the machine playing the red-blouse rhythm. We want something that makes us feel worthy to be involved in this," Old Man finishes. Meme introduces a discordant voice: "you should see how with this work I receive all the love in the world," mocking. "The important thing is to work when you enjoy it and when you don't." "I've just packed three hundred copies for the School of Dentistry, which is the most conservative of all. How can I feel happy about it when it's like wasting buckshot on buzzards? We wouldn't do that even if we were masochists." Old Man: "you guys don't understand anything." "We understand, Old Man, but why should we make our life any harder than it is by getting wrapped up in philosophies? The thing is you are a poet like Pichón." Meme falls into his trap: "Talk of happiness at a time like this! As if we were speaking of freedom, forgetting that we are in chains." The conversation continues in this fashion until Margó reappears: "Pepino is awake, I'm sorry I can't stay with you guys." Dressed in a vaporous common-market-industry exploiter-style robe. Meme: "I can see that you've already disguised yourself, so we're losing you as an helper. What happened to Negrita?" She finally fell asleep, but she wet herself again and Pepino is still talking in his sleep. What time is it? Twelve-thirty. Damn! It's getting too late to finish everything. Heat some water so we can drink coffee. We all agreed. Two hours later we had the shipments ready for all the departments. Good night. Manuel slowly entering the nuptial room. Old Man sleeps in his hammock, with an arm hanging down, still holding a book in his hand.

— *vii* —

I caught up with him about four blocks from his house, as he was going into the Forest neighborhood *pupusería* for some *pupusas*—Salvadoran tacos. It was him, it was enough to see him from behind to be able to tell, twenty-four, with an athletic build (he had played soccer in high school, that was one of the things we knew about him). *You know, it's inevitable, you have to follow them. We're going to give you a car and a companion.*

"I guess that's them over there."

"It's not a question of guessing, you have to be sure."

"One is 5'8", has a Guatemalan accent, brown hair, and studies at the university."

"Your job will be to identify them, nothing more, later we'll tell you what you have to do, you don't have to worry about it, little friend."

"Of course I'm going to worry, having you guys nearby."

"You're a funny son-of-a-bitch."

It's enough for you to remember the color of their eyes, of their skin, the way they walk, any special gesture, height, you have to memorize their bodies, understand? So that you could paint a picture of them in your mind, describe them, so that a drawing of them can be made based on your descriptions.

"For me, everyone walks the same way."

"You're a brute, I don't walk like you."

"I'm not a photographic camera."

"We're going to turn you into a photographer with an ass-kicking."

Keep in mind that they are political enemies of the

government capable of anything, so you're relying on our protection, so you don't run the risk of waking up one day with a bullet in your head, understand?

And he tried to say he understood: "Clear as a bell."

I was passing by the beer hall and I took a liking to them and what's the name of the song they were singing and if that wasn't dangerous. And they didn't give a damn, they kept singing and then I learned that they were friends of my brother: I don't know why I took a liking to those fellows. (Don't call them fellows, call them individuals, or at least sons-of-bitches, maybe you sympathize with their ideas?) *How could I be a sympathizer of anything, if I barely know them, I don't know what they do, how they spend their time. I only know they are students and two of them are poets. God save me!*

"Not even your mother is going to save you."

"Look, we're not accusing you, the way we work is different from what you think. But one thing is certain, with us you'll always be safe, it's up to you. Make up your mind."

I headed home thinking about retaliation: They told me to lay low and to come at their first call, but you know, no funny business. And I went. No, not on my own, they came to take me with my hands and feet tied, like a *garrobo* lizard. No, they didn't beat me, they've always been good to me that way: Their tying me up is not important, they tie people up as a precaution, they're not the authorities for nothing. (You know, we have to deal with criminals.) My brother isn't a criminal. (They threw me into the pickup; they struck me on the head, but it didn't hurt much, although I was knocked unconscious; they struck me with a rifle butt. Sorry, we confused you with a subversive.) And I forgave them, although I knew there had been no confusion, they had come looking for me.

"Here come the bums," Margó teased her compañeros.

"Forgive us, Margotita, for being so late."

"Forgive us, (imitating him) Old Man you bum, our dear Old Man."

"No one prints a page today until the dishes are washed and you help clean the house," with a Holy Child of Atocha smile.

Pichón enters, but he walks right past his compañeros. He went directly to the printing-room bedroom. He doesn't like for Margó to stick her nose in his wanderings or his free time.

"Are you going to eat right now, boys?"

Everyone at the table. Pichón puts in for the first time, just to say something: "What happened to Manuel?"

"A compañero came for him."

"We'll help you with the dishes, don't worry, guardian angel," Feliciano says.

"We promise," Old Man adds.

"Don't warm up any food for me, I've been sleeping and I've lost my appetite," Alfonso says.

"Look who showed up," Feliciano adds.

"Poor Al, he can't go out on the street."

"Because he doesn't have a father or a mother."

"If you don't hurry up, the food is going to get cold," Margó shouts.

"Feliciano comes to eat at the house in the Forest. There are political problems in the streets and it's better for us to be together. There's more and more to print."

Margó complains:

"I don't know why you guys have to go out wandering given the present situation. And if you're doing it in order to drink a beer, that's even worse, you're going to turn into alcoholics without a mission," as she approaches with the frying pan of warm food.

"Don't serve me any," Old Man says as he heads for his hammock. "I'm going to sleep awhile and then I'll fix something for myself."

"What's wrong with Old Man?" Al asks.

Feliciano with a duplicitous gesture:

"Leave him alone, he drank five beers."

"But how is that possible, if we're so poor?"

"By invitation," Old Man clarifies the situation before anyone else can respond.

"I've burnt the noodles," Margó says with frustration, more than anything in order to divert attention away from Old Man.

"Don't worry about it, at any rate you're not obligated to be the cook all the time," Al interjects.

"The same thing happens at the end of every month, we run out of everything, there's no money, and the food gets burned," she cannot hide her frustration, "And the worst part is that we have almost nothing for the last days of the month," she hears the crying of Negrita Cuculumbe just as she is getting settled at the table.

"Quiet, my child, come and eat with your uncles."

And then, speaking to Al:

"You guys aren't going to forgive me for this terrible food I'm offering you."

"Don't worry about it, no one pays attention to these things, what can we do if we don't have anything, long as there's milk for the children."

Margó finishes setting the table and goes to the bedroom.

In their five months of printing they had developed a beautiful familiarity with one other; dinnertime is a ritual, except for Negrita's interruptions. Margó places napkins under their glasses: "So it'll feel like we're eating in a first-class hotel." Someday you'll be able to serve wine instead of water from the aqueduct or drainage ditches, which is pure shit water.

"Why do women worry so much about food?" Al wonders and answers himself cynically: "We do too, it's just they worry about preparing it and we about eating it." "Has Guapote arrived yet?" Margó asks from the bedroom: "Today is the last day of the month, he ought to be coming." On the thirtieth day of the month we no longer have food and that's why we must wait impatiently for Guapote's arrival.

"Are you going to work tonight?" Feliciano asks Pichón.

"Maybe not, I want to go to bed early, even if it's just once a year, the lack of sleep is wearing out my patience."

"Manuel said he was bringing some sardines tonight," Margó tells them, as she places a serving of rice on each plate.

"I hope you didn't have any beer," Margó says to Feliciano.

"I was with Old Man and Pichón, I went along with them but I didn't have any beer."

Margó interrupts again:

"I like to be hungry when I eat," she says with a feminine gesture that does not go unnoticed by the men. She gets up and goes to the bedroom. Everyone eats. She returns a few seconds later: "I have a surprise for you. I haven't forgotten about you," and she shows them a giant purple avocado that's too big for her two hands. I don't forget about you," she struts, with the air of a triumphal march, as if the entourage were already arriving and the pure sound of bugles could be heard. And to think a few minutes ago she was shedding tears like colored balloons. At times she exaggerates. It is as if lately she has had a presentiment she's going to lose Manuel or one of the compañeros of the house.

"Where did you come up with money for beer if there's not enough to buy food?" Al demands to know.

"Don't worry, we're not inconsiderate, what happened was a friend invited us. I mean, someone who befriended Old Man, and we tagged along with him," the baker had invited them. "Sometimes I wonder if that baker isn't a fool, think how much it must cost him to earn his money and he blows it on us, people he barely knows."

"At first he offered bread, as a contribution to the cause, and now he's buying beer."

I remain silent, dipping a piece of tortilla in the purple avocado that Margó served us.

— *ix* —

The convalescent bear appears through the screen door, "I'm going to eat you," he says. "Hello bear." "Hello, Al, what are ya doin?" "I'm just here reading this book." "Why?" with a Chinese accent. "Because." "Because why?" "Because because." "And why because because?" "Damn, little bear, you never stop." "Why?" "Where's your mother?" (It's better not to pay any attention to him.) "She's washing daddy's crows." "And your daddy, where'd he go?" "He's in bed, reading." (It's so quiet, as Margó works, he says to himself.) "Were you left all by yourself?" "Yes, cause Feliciano and Pichón went out." "Come over here, bear," he interrupts the child, "I want to check your temperature." The bear approaches. He takes him by the paws with great care and, grabbing his wrists, takes his pulse. "Be careful not to strike me, you're okay. How many times have you gone poop poop today?" "Why?" "Because that tells whether you're well or not." "A thousand times, then." "Oh, you're dangerous then. You're the only crapping panda bear in the world. You have to take care of yourself." "My mother takes care of me." "Good, bear, don't be out in the air because it will harm you, go to your den and bundle up." "Why?" "Because if you don't they're going to give you a suppository and that is unpleasant." "Mamma said I could come out of my room, that I'm already better." "You shouldn't take any chances, can't you see you're the only one of your kind, panda bear?" "I'm going then," the child leaves. "Go and don't come back until your mommy has finished washing. And don't come back until this wind has stopped blowing. Remember that the continued existence of the pandas depends on you, because when you're big you'll have baby bears, we can't risk losing you because you are a universal spectacle." He backs away moving his arms as if he were steering a circus motorcycle. "Okay, I'm going, ciao," he goes out the screen door. He waves goodbye to him with his hand and goes inside his den. Pretty bear, lazy bear. Stuffed teddy bear. Poopy bear, beloved bear. You almost died, Pepino the Brief. What would have happened to your mother and all of us. Margó doesn't like to remember it. Your temperature reached 105 degrees. You were like a sweaty coffee pot. Margó with her eyes full of tears, "don't say that, can't you see that if he dies I'm going to die too." He was too hot to touch. They took Negrita to stay with her great-grand-mother. Meme-Charrier—he was frightened—he had left at six in the evening and returned at six in the morning. "We haven't slept at all, we put compresses of cold water and cubes of ice on him, he was delirious for four hours and then he began to get better. It was terrifying to see death up close." "Imagine, I wasn't going to see my son again because I've been working for everybody else," Meme-Charrier laments. Pichón left at twelve midnight to go looking for some medicine at the twenty-four-hour Pharmacy, to buy some suppositories for you." We weren't careful enough with the pure shit water that comes to us through the pipes," Meme-Charrier complains with his hands on Pepino's head. "My poor little *mondongo* stew, you'll be better soon," Margó seated on the edge of the bed, tears pouring from her eyes, and she decides it's better for her to go to the kitchen. And when he was completely well they held a party in honor of Pepino. "We have to bring Negrita back from Cojutepeque," where they had sent her to stay with her great-grandmother. "Let's take advantage of this opportunity and celebrate his birthday too." "But it's not for four months." "That doesn't matter, we should be happy," Margó wipes away her rain tears with the back of her hands.

"Mommy, if I die, where will I go?"

"Child, don't think about those things."

"Am I never going to die?"

"No, child, I'll die first, panda bears never die and if they are in danger of dying they're placed in the hands of rich friends so they can have the best doctors in the world take care of them, to save them."

"I don wanna go with the rich people, Mommy."

"It's just one possibility, I won't let it happen."

"Where do children go when they die?"

"They don't go anywhere, they stay here."

Meme-Manuel-Charrier:

"That's enough, I'm going to take his temperature. It was a simple intestinal infection, he's no longer in danger."

He puts the thermometer in Pepino's bottom.

"Papa, do you wuv me?"

"Yes, bear, I love you, don't ask me those unnecessary questions."

"Do Alfonso and Mommy wuv me?"

"Yes, and so do Pichón and Feliciano."

"Good, I wuv all of you too, so I'm not going to die," his eyes look like two sputniks orbiting a grapefruit.

— x —

Dear Mamma. A prayer for all. Mamma, full of Grace. Vender in the markets. Mamma buying bottles from door to door. Mamma whore. Mamma who runs through the streets pursued by the police. Mamma, how are you? Mamma like all things when they are from the heart. Mamma searcher of treasures in garbage cans. Mamma traveling by train with large baskets of ripe fruit. Stupendous Mamma. Mamma with her face painted like a rainbow. Mamma, coffee picker. Mamma who picks flowers along the roadside to arrange them in tin flower vases. Hot Mamma. Sick Mamma. Mamma Virgin Mary mother of God. A sacred name like the deer. Mamma lighter of candles for the Holy Child of Atocha and for beautiful San Antonio. Mamma through these dark streets. Vender of dark *atole* and pineapple rolls. Mamma marching through the streets with hats made of newspaper to protect herself from the sun and with a bag of refried beans and tortillas just in case the march goes on for hours. Mamma of the Union of Slum Settlers. Barefoot Mamma. Mamma ready to take off running if there is gunfire. Tough Mamma. Cotton picker beneath the agrarian sun of the coast. Where are you? One of these days God has to love me a little bit, I'll build a house where the two of us will live. Hi, Mamma. Bad mother. Go to sleep, my little child. One of your days, a day starving to death. Mamma, pleader so that they will release my son, he has not done anything, shut up you old whore. Mamma, I be back late. Mamma in the morgue. My mamma. Mamma searching among the dead. Mamma Virgin Mary and nothing more. Mamma saying it's my body that's trembling, not my spirit. Mamma return the body of my son. Mamma man, grandmother, grandfather, mamma mamma. Your mother. Good Morning entire universe.

"Well, what's happening is the band is drunk," he thinks of the phrase that justifies everything. He was playing with the flowers in the swamps along the road. A little rabbit here, a *taltuza* over there. A little worm over here; ants carrying green leaves along the paths. Birds of sweet enchantment. Opening the rose, closing the carnation. Her multicolored basket. Blue the sky painted blue, a shitty little song. The glowworm's light bulb ass came be seen. It means it's getting late. The sun entangled in Little Red Riding Hood's hair; the last bit of red sun at dusk. Singing the song about the days of the week: Monday, Tuesday, and Wednesday, I see grandmother's house, she could lower the stars one by one. "The poor thing is so ill." The red dress leaving threads in the dry brush. "Good morning, Grandma, I have brought oranges for you to suck on." "Oh, my child, why did you go to the trouble, the woods are so dangerous," she thinks that her grandma must be thinking. Ding-dong, the electric doorbell rings when she pushes the button. "Who is it?" a hoarse voice like when it rains fish in Yoro, Honduras, although she thinks perhaps her grandmother has a sore throat. "Me, Grandmother, let me in, I'm freezing," and the ferocious wolf puts on slippers in order to give himself a grandmotherly air, wrapped up in a Guatemalan made, Lana Turner woolen blanket. "A tasty morsel I shall eat," the bandit-faced wolf thinks, fondling the pistol at his waist just as a precaution.

"Coming, my dear." The bastard.

— *xii* —

In the early morning, we were sleeping when we heard the miniature dogs bark. Bow-wow in the distance, cutting the bitter oranges of the night. We had no idea the National Guard was going to come. I saw when they illuminated the window with the headlights of a jeep, but I thought it was a maneuver to turn around in the street. The guards got out. They went grrrrowl. I look out the window and they say open because if you didn't they were going to kick the door in. And I: "What's wrong with you, what do you want?" And with the first blows the door falls down. And bow-wow, the miniature dogs barking. The kids start to cry. Then the men enter the rooms flying like supermen. Rip, rip, sticking their knives in the mattresses. They broke the children's medicine bottles and they went inside the room where Feliciano and Pichón were sleeping. They came out in their underwear. Pichón also had his thumbs tied together, let me put on my shoes and blow after blow. And the children grasping at my clothes made me feel like crying, my poor little ones come over here, I don't want them to hit you. And where was Manuel, that this is the house where enemies of the government held meetings, that we were guerrillas. And where's your husband? You were involved in dishonest acts with these sons-of-bitches. I live with my grandmother, but it got too late so I stayed here to sleep, in the house of my school buddies. And they: buddies, my ass, they don't even respect authority with ass kickings, imagine, saying compañeros in front of us. I don't know how to go to Cojutepeque after seven in the evening, believe me. Click clack, the men gnashed their teeth together. Bow-wow, the miniature dogs in the distance. Who the heck pays for the house. I've already told you that I don't live here. Tie up these two sons-of-bitches well, with their hands behind their backs. Hush children. Mommy, mommy, the children. They are sure Manuel used to live in this house, please don't lie to us because you'll pay for it dearly, because you don't lie to authority. And I: I had been living at my grandmother's house for about two months, they couldn't take me away and that I was separated from Manuel, I don't know where he is, we each went our own way. Don't tell me that you're fucking one of these assholes, or both of them. We've had bad luck because the big bird has flown the coop. And don't try to fool us about your grandmother in Cojute, because you've always lived here in the Forest. Manuel is your husband, what happens is that these assholes change their names, Manuel is Meme and he is also Charrier. If you won't tell us anything here, in the black palace you're going to spill your guts and we don't care if you leave your children behind as orphans, they'll end up in our hands. They took us to their car. I: Should I take the children; and they: Leave them if you want, but they would be left alone, you're not going to say someone is going to come and take care of them. We all get in the car, but first they put rubber masks on us and I didn't let go of the kids, crying, what was going to happen to them with these crazy people? When we got to the black palace they put all of us in the same cell, except for the children. Don't worry about the kids, we're not going to do anything to them, but it's your fault for getting involved with mischief. Pichón and Feliciano were thrown to the ground after being struck with rifle butts, with their thumbs tied behind their backs, face down, unconscious or pretending to be unconscious so they wouldn't hit them. They beat them harshly with a stick, although they hadn't done anything. And tell them where Manuel is and who belongs to the group. At last two lieutenants arrived, we knew they were lieutenants by their uniforms and because they were young, yes, Lieutenant Sir, they ordered the men to go away and to leave them alone and they started to offer me advice: How was it possible that with two small children I would get involved in this mischief, perhaps out of fanaticism or they had brainwashed me, how much did they pay me each month, if I was living with one of the two they had captured. And the Lieutenant: Don't worry about your kids, we'll make sure nothing happens to them. As you can see, we are well-mannered people, we're not criminals, or bad people. Later they brought me food. But I couldn't eat. Sometimes they take me out of the cell, always with a hood over my head, perhaps so we don't see anybody and so no one sees us, but what does it matter if they recognize us or not. The hood is green, with tiny holes at eye level so that at least we see the ground to walk. The Lieutenant says do you want to die, because you're not eating. And I'm thinking, why does this dog with knife-like teeth care? It's easy for you to get out of here, your kids too, but you must cooperate. And I thinking, eat shit you bastards. Where do you have my children? I asked. You think we are criminals, your children are okay, don't worry, we are fathers too. You have to tell us where Manuel is, and you can be out today. Anyway, I didn't know anything and having been at that house with my children was a coincidence, because it's Manuel's house, I admit. I did know Manuel was going to arrive the next day, in the morning, but I say nothing, luck saved him. And I decided not to tell those assholes anything else, excuse my French, but those fuckers force one to curse. And they found only a mimeograph machine, some fliers. And that was proof that it was a clandestine press for producing subversive materials. They insisted they wanted to release me, but that I must cooperate with them, the authorities. Later, I found out my grandmother had come from Cojutepeque to the black palace to ask about me, but they told her they didn't have any whores here, so you'd better leave if you don't want us to give you free housing. And they asked me about Pichón and Feliciano. And I imagine that they show up at night to study. Another day they took me to see my children and they were very happy, Mommy, Mommy. They wanted to see me break, but I barely had tears in my eyes that came from down below, from the putrid waters inside my heart. You too are guilty, so it'd be better for you tell us something important or you'll remain here with your children. I don't know how long I was held prisoner. They finally released me. I never saw Pichón or Feliciano again, they disappeared.

— *xiii* —

Feliciano finished an article for the newspaper and then went to the kitchen to eat some *pupusas*, the ones that Margó had left for him wrapped in a table cloth. Feliciano, your *pupusas* are going to get cold. I'm going to finish, I'm in the best moment of giving birth. Feliciano says that he must write from time to time because he doesn't want to turn into just a printer. I like to operate the mimeograph machine, but not that much, he says. Meme: save some *pupusas* for Feliciano, because he fell asleep. Leave me some *pupusas*, Feliciano shouts from his room, showing signs of life. Hurry up, then. Dammit, rest comes first and then my stomach. Minutes later he approaches the table. It turned out good, I think I'll read it to you, if it doesn't bore you. You go right ahead. He hands it to Meme who looks it over quickly:

Prehistoric animal remains are found in this country, all of them are well preserved as if they had been kept at a hundred degrees below zero. Researchers have established that these rare beasts lived during the latter part of the second half of the twentieth century. They are all characterized by their large double chins, an unequivocal sign that these animals were gluttonous, voracious eaters. It was during the time when the *barbarians* lived in the *trees*, during the time of the *apostles*, who climbed the *trees* in order to eat the *birds*. Here are some examples of these animals with their scientific names which, by the way, are unrecognizable, but that doesn't matter, their descriptions will suffice:

Rubenecus rodrigus, an animal of gigantic proportions, white, like an Indian with *bienteveo* disease that turns their skin white, his brain is barely the size of a small turd; nonetheless, for catching prey in flight he was like a hungry buzzard, he is also known as the ambusher because when it came to doing away with his own kind he did not waste any time scratching his balls;

Taponescus terrestris, unlike the rubenecus, was of smaller dimensions, with a primitive intellectual's complex, a missing link which, although you could not call him a beast, had some humanoid characteristics; adept at taking from others, forefather of the art of bullfighting because he was a natural *matador*, I'll kill anybody who gets in my way, he would shout;

Armadillus molotus, awkward and tough, as stubborn as a Honduran mule, they say that even when he was small blows to his head with sticks did not bother him and that is why his head shrunk, they called his mommy and daddy *jíbaro* indians because they had shrunk his head by pounding on it; and the worst part was that was that instead of going ha-ha-ha to laugh, he went grrr, like the lion at Metro Park;

Gonzalutecus mondrigus, a relative of rubenecus, a black beast that genuflected as it walked; he was living proof that the monkey had descended from man, but because he had been pushed and had fallen, his spinal column had been broken, creating that *sui generis* species of hunchbacks and crawlers, which, however, are not reptiles;

Herculón salvatoriense, as his name indicates, had a herniated ass, he had a light-colored hide, like the wise monkeys, praise God he left no descendants because if he had the Salvadoran jungle would have been full of herculones, and, as the inhabitants of the aforementioned jungle are so macho, we had better drop the subject.

Sanchus religiosis, a climbing animal, from informer he became president and it is always better to follow the crowd; became extinct because he was among those that could not survive, he was too backwards to take care of himself;

Geramus racimus, prehensile paws, stupid to the point of saying uncle; although he thought he was top dog, he was never more than a flea, conceited, for sure, no one was going to take his position away from him.

That's enough! I don't think this will get by the censor. You've used up almost all your tricks, Feliciano, you are offending the political class, the elite of our fucking nationality, but you know that everyone has his heart, and they don't put up with these things even if they're in a good mood; besides, it's not up to high academic standards. Go to you-know-where, Meme, this is the best article I have written and I'm not going to throw it away. If the tribunal of the inquisition, I mean the editorial board, tosses it in the garbage can, they can eat shit; if you don't publish it, it's because you guys belong to the language academy and all that other crap, Feliciano defends himself.

Hours later we have voted on his article and it wasn't accepted: Pichón and I, plus Pepino el Breve, voted against it; those in favor: just the dog's owner, Feliciano, that is; abstentions: Margó, Old Man and Negrita Cuculumbe. Meme said he wasn't participating in the tribunal because he didn't want them to say that he was censor. The children were sitting at the table and they wanted to vote, no one objected. I wanna vote, I raise my hand, they say. And in the end, the article is a piece of crap, believe it, Feliciano. Stop picking on him. Fucking revisionists, Feliciano says defending himself. And that he wasn't going to work that day, then, that he was going on vacation until tomorrow, you guys can produce the newspaper, with two-bit poems that don't question shit. He went out slamming the door behind him, like in the novels with little flowers, love stories and little birdies, as lonely as a street dog. But, before leaving, he let out a Count Dracula guffaw. Then, if Feliciano doesn't come back soon, I have nothing to do tonight, I say, they're showing a Tarzan movie today, at the theater in the Forest and I'm not going to miss it. With these guys we're screwed, Margó says. Leave them alone, it's another way to have fun, Old Man says. And what are the two of us going to do by ourselves? Nothing. Because Meme-Charrier won't come to sleep here tonight. Then we'd better go to bed, it's little kisses for the children and then I'm going to my hammock to read a while.

— *xiv* —

I saw Old Man today, he's so kind, he's so delicate he's like an angel. I saw the others too. Old Man is different, he treats you as if he were talking to you as an equal. I sat down beside him. Pull up a chair and sit down on the floor, Al says. Just to play with me. They show no courtesy, except for the Old man. Feliciano, for example, starts to pick and pick: putting salt in one's pockets, serving a glass of beer that's all foam, touching the waitress' ass. In a word, he keeps it up until you lose control. Well look here, friend, Felix the cat says to me, drink a glass of beer because we're leaving and if you don't hurry you're going to have to stay here by yourself. And I just smile at them, going completely crazy. Oh, you guys like to make light of everything, I complain, pretending I hate to do so. I, I can't deny it, harbor proletarian prejudices, my conscience is proletarian too; I play dumb. "If you guys want to take care of serious matters, tell me and I'll go." No, says Al, who really seems to be the best mannered of all of us although sometimes his angry side comes out and he starts in with his innuendoes, or with concealed attacks. "We're not going to say anything you can't hear," he says. He's one of those people who look you straight in the eyes as if he were saying: I hope you are fucking with us you little asshole. Sometimes he throws out a difficult question, and you can't tell whether he's serious or not. He's something of a busybody, I mean he likes to judge others.

But Old Man is another story altogether, he's the only one who objects to my paying for a round while the others play dumb, waiting for me to pay. Of course, I'm the one to insist I pay. It's in my interest, after all. Although sometimes Old Man is quarrelsome: You are really a coward, he says to Alfonso when he tries to keep drinking and it's better for him to go. Old Man says that you're afraid to live, give yourself completely to life—he speaks philosophically because he studies philosophy—you're always nursing your drinks.

When we're on our fourth ice-cold, foamy brewsky, Al starts writing on a napkin. I don't trust anyone who doesn't drink. I try to avoid conflict and I offer to recite a poem for them, one by Miguel Hernández, and they stop arguing because that's why they are brothers and soul brothers. It takes balls, Feliciano admits. I make a face of resentment. Pichón realizes that I am upset and tells me not to pay any attention to it, that it's just a joke. Let's hear the poem by Hernández. But I can't start as long as Al is entranced by the girl in the sweater with a drawing of a Bentley on it where her breasts are, or keeps writing, I want his attention. That is what I say, those little punk students are sons-of-bitches, and big bad bitches at that, they're not used to breaking their back working, like proletarians, busting their asses. And I start with "Winds from the town carry me off, winds from the town bring me back." When I finish, Felixiano threatens me, he tells me to recite another one, if you don't recite one I will. He lets out a tiburcio telénguez or count-dracula-novel guffaw. I pretend I'm crazy. Al intervenes: I'm surprised that a proletarian like you would know those poems by heart. Why? I ask tenderly. Because in this shitty country I thought only students knew those poets. I don't know if he's saying this to praise me or if he's fucking with me, but I still have to act crazy. You see, we proletarians are clever too.

I have my teeny-tiny library, always using diminutives. And how did you know that you had to buy those books, Old Man asks. I read Toruño's literary supplement in the *Diario Latino* newspaper, where you guys publish. Do you know Felipe Toruño too? Of course—proud as when they sing the national anthem—don't forget that Toruño was also a proletarian, a shoe smith by trade, and from there he rose to where he is today, an intellectual, perhaps that's why he supports you guys.

"Well, let's go," Al insists. The session is closed. Wait, have another round on me. You guys don't know what it is to suffer, picture yourself in front of the oven, which is the hardest part about being a baker. Oh, I forgot that you make bread! Felixiano interrupts me. B-a-k-e-r, I second with deliberation. Is there a difference? Alfonso asks. Of course there is, I tell them, we bakers are union members and those who aren't organized are bread makers, shitty bread makers. They play dumb, I know I'm impressing them, although judging by the look on Felixiano's face it would appear he's thinking: this son-of-a-bitch is crazy. Just imagine, I change the topic, with this hot summer and me in front of the oven; after five years of working as an oven man, your eyes are almost cooked and they turn into baked pumpkinseed eyes, diced eyes, green corn tamale eyes. "You poor thing!" Old Man sighs. Being a baker is a man's job, I brag. Alfonso has become silent, I think he admires me. You must have started working very young, he says. From the time I was ten years old, I respond with a medal-of-commendation tone in my voice. You must have eyes like a cat, Alfonso says. Eyes like a strangled ox, Felix says softly, but he doesn't know that I have the keen ears of a fox. Well, I've worked a lot of years, but not always at the oven: sometimes I knead the bread. I deliver bread and buy the ingredients. We all take turns. "How old are you?" Al asks. Twenty-four, I answer. Wow! Felix says, I thought you were a hundred, because you look older than Old Man.

Alfonso asks the girl with the Bentley painted on her blouse for more napkins. They kiss in the air. A dog looks in the door. We drink beer, but at heart we are bored. Well, I'm going, see you later, alligator, Al says, leaving me with the words of the poems stuck in my throat. If you're going, we're all going, Felix says. When we reach the corner, one by one they shake my hand. He says to me: We're going another way, but they fucked me over, because, they asked me which way I was going, then said they were going in the other direction and that I couldn't go with them. *Ciao.* They go away, but I circle around the block and start following them until I see them arrive at the Forest.

— *xv* —

Feliciano just turned in his editorial for the paper. Here you have my work, compañeros, or masters of censorship; and he throws it on the table. Stop acting like a child, that's what democratic centralism is for, and don't blow a gasket every time we review your writing. Eat shit, assholes. "This isn't an editorial," Old Man protests. "It's a postcard, a letter." "Yeah, but a shitty little postcard," Feliciano says. Feliciano goes to the printing room to avoid having to participate in the voting on his article on the antediluvian period of this century section. Come on, don't be a jerk. You guys decide, I'd better work, he shouts from he other room. You read, Pichón, you've got the voice of a reciter of poetry in the moment of surrender.

"How are you, Armando?" I ask you this question in the company of several friends who always ask about you, rabble-rouser; in the name of our offspring, we ask you, we remember you when you were a tiny tot and we gave you the nickname 'Shixty, Sheventy,' not because you liked to count and you stuttered, but because we called you 'Shixty, Sheventy' with tenderness, that was the nicest nickname we gave you. We also called you fat ass with fleas, Barabbas, in short: we call you ox instead of bull, in other words, a bull with no balls. First Minute News:

"Reports, Society: congratulations. The nation's first lady, who yesterday added another *guarismo* (which means figure and should not be confused with the word *guaro*, or liquor) to the population statistics, is in room 303 of the Salvadoran Polyclinic. You can take *guarismo* any way you want, with lime or straight, you are bad! Second Minute News:

"Socials, condolences: the day before yesterday, Saturday the twenty-fourth, Nicolasito Dueñas died of a bullet wound to his heart, the brother of Remberto, of the same last name; just yesterday the news appeared in *La Prensa Gráfica*, a serious newspaper with two daily editions: in one, the news was characterized as "of unknown motives or causes," the other edition made no mention of it, instead, it carried a soccer schedule, what do you think of them apples? Third Minute News:

"Gossip: they say that they changed mustached troublemaker's name. Now they call him Sotero Guirola, because he's tried to push through the law of agrarian reform; and those most affected, no matter how angry it makes them, can't call him Shitty Gorilla in public. Fourth Minute News:

"Politics: The Cockle-doodle-doo rooster crows the way he does because he has no balls. He could not even stand the idea that an agrarian reform law would even be discussed and preferred to resign. He was replaced by another fine-feathered fellow of evil omen: the Floripondio Crow. Ministry matters are for the birds. Fifth Minute News:

"On this note, we say goodbye to you, wishing you a great day, may God bless you and make you prettier for me, as Roque used to say about Saint Salarrué. See you later, alligator, and, until next time. Signed:. Melara Brait. A pseudonym, of course."

"Felixiano the Cat fucked up again," I tell Pichón. "I don't know why he's writing that vulgar crap. They're not going to take us seriously. We'd better censor him because if we fall into the clutches of Don Armando Rabble Rouser he won't forgive us and bang-bang-bang-bang, he fires his machine gun, two promising figures of Salvadoran literature disappear, their bodies have not been found, their names in life were Pichón and Alfonso. But if we don't publish him they're going to say we don't have any balls. It doesn't matter, why don't we think with our heads instead of with our ovaries? Then, he's censored. We are intelligent people, right? Or intelligidiots."

— *xvi* —

Margó opened three cans of sardines. At that moment Pichón arrived, a magazine under his arm, carrying a raincoat because in the Panama barrio, where he had come from, it was raining. You're welcome to eat. Thanks. Thanks yes or thanks no? I've already had some *pupusas*, I was with Manuel. Sit down, then, did you see him? Yes, we had made an appointment so I'd go to another print shop and he prefers not to come to this house, at least for the time being, I have to tell this to Margó.

I went to repair a mimeograph machine that's not working right.

You always arrive as if you were being pursued, breathing heavily, with that mole on your nose, on the spot where your glasses sit: taking them off and squeezing your nose. Great long-distance eater, pursued by the cops dressed in blue with their rubber nightsticks to strike heads without leaving any marks. Putting on an apron so you won't stain your shirt, because if you don't, your mother-in-law, who busts her butt scrubbing dirty clothes, will kick your ass. Hard-working Poet. You're an Indian who has come down from the Izalco Volcano; grandson and great grandson of José Ama and Chico Sánchez, those shot by firing squad in 1932, those hanged in the plaza.

I'll accept your offer of a cup of coffee. Old Man is in the mood to cause trouble, something rare in him. We are celebrating Negrita's birthday (she's seated at Pepino the Brief's side, eating a soup that has macaroni and stars in it). How old are you today, Negrita? "Tree," she raises her carved, wooden-doll fingers. "Six," Pepino corrects her. "Two," Margó says, "You're still little, eat your soup my love." "You got anything to drink?" Pichón asks. "Here," Charrier says, pulling out a bottle from who-knows-where, perhaps from his shirt sleeve, in Mandrake the magician style in the time of the jocote fruit that explodes when you sink your teeth into one. And the bottle of diabolic spirits starts to takes its toll. "Pour me a glass of poison," Margó says. "I can't drink it without lime," the poet says, "it's my antidote." Drink it straight, don't be a faggot. Old Man (aside): I only drink beer, so I'm going to get a bottle of beer from under my bed. You see what an asshole he is, he brought his own special drink. You want some? With foam so it goes farther. It's meza ayau urine, no thanks, I don't like sewer water. "Me wanna saldine," Negrita shouts. Don't give her any, they've got chilies in them. Then what are the kids going to eat? Old Man gets beer and the kids have nothing to eat. "Me wanna beel," Pepino says. Don't be such pests, eat your soup. How are your eyes doing Pichonidaskaya? Pass me the beans. Horrible. Don't worry, two drops of lime a day will cure that. What happened to Feliciano? Pepino needs to pee. Damn it, you're a pest! They censor Feliciano a lot, they won't let him develop. Give me some, even if it's just a little foam of Meza Ayau urine, you old cheapskate, individualist. Go to hell. Read me a poem, Pichón. Some poahtree for me. But not one about little birds and flowers, but a protest poem. Go to hell again. I'm going to recite "The Jukebox," then. But stop being a pain, pay attention. It's not finished yet, it's still rough. You read it. Well: I propose to paint this form, these roots of the popular character in almost all the films from Mexican cinema, of corín tellado in her light-blue Cadillac. Music comes out this music box like poems, made up by cantina poets, the songs loved by the patrons of kicsi place, the lighthouse, commonplaces of popular culture that nourish terrestrial hopes: the jukebox, like a vacuous nebulous metaphysics. To watch it swallow the coin and one discovers Azalea Flower by Negrete, which is L7. You have to see her battered, behind bars, hoarse. Write poems to her, draw her with your senses open and her rainbow lights, it's the furniture of the future, full of tenderness, nostalgic, interplanetary vessel, lunar module where the whores often fly to the stars. Damn Poet, I almost didn't understand you, you're too philosophical; you have to be a populist like the jukebox itself, so that you get it right. I told you it was a rough draft. Don't explain anything, Pichón. I'm going to read you another one. Applause of Pepino and Negrita. No! "Don't read another one or I'll start reading," Old Man says in a threatening tone.

Okay, friends, I leave you. A goodbye kiss to Margó. They stay home. Goodbye Papa. Goodbye love. See you, Manuel. Right then Feliciano shows up. We thought that you weren't going to come back tonight. You missed the birthday party. If I'm not back by six in the morning you'd better go to Cojutepeque, Meme says to Margó. Why so early? Because If I can't come back by then it's because I've decided to stay all day at the other printing center. Ciao, then. See ya later, alligator. With Feliciano here, we can work a while so we don't get bored. Never, we must respect Negrita's birthday.

I'm going with you, Meme. But where are you going, Al? I'm going to go sleep wherever. You are a mystery, you don't have to go. I want to change houses just for tonight. I don't understand, but it's your decision, too bad I can't take you with me. Don't worry. You wouldn't even if you were crazy, Alfonso. Anyway, we're not working tonight and I'm going to go out and have a good time. You're the only one who can't go out, but that's not our fault, Meme says, as he finally says goodbye. You guys are almost shit-faced, maybe we won't be working so I can go too, Feliciano says. Don't go, have a drink too. See you another time, Meme says. *Ciao.*

"Uh hum, tell us what you got!"

"I see that you guys don't respect feelings."

"Bah, cut the crap, spill your nuts for us, sorry, I meant to say guts, and thinking about it won't do you any good."

"I got something, but I think it's written in code, I don't know if it'll be of any use to you."

"Give us what you have, nothing more."

He pulls out a piece of paper, a napkin and another napkin.

It looks like a play:

"Quit taking your time and pull out all the papers you've got."

His hands get stuck in his pockets:

"The way you guys act makes one nervous."

"There's no reason for you to be nervous if you are honest with us, and don't try to give us lessons."

"Here's the most important paper."

"Whose handwriting is this?"

"Alfonso wrote it when we were in the beer hall, that's why it's written on paper napkins."

"Give it to me," says the policeman dressed in blue carrying a nightstick for striking heads. Surprised:

"And what's this shit?"

"Better let the baker read it," says the other policeman disguised as a wolf with his forty-five pistol and four clips in his holster.

"Yeah, you read," in duo, the two policemen. He reads in a flute-like voice, like when he recites poems by Miguel Hernández. What a mess one gets into to protect his children. I'm not getting out of this one.

"Hurry, we're not asking you to recite by memory."

Reading:

"A scene in Copas Bar (cantina and beer hall)."

Toño the bartender (looking out through the windows): This is a dead end.

The Bentley *Girl:* Fortunately for me...

Germán Arestizábal: Life is a dead end. (The *Bentley* girl smiles at Germán.)

Bartender: That's why we live peacefully in this country.

The Bentley *Girl* (sadly): If there were any cars around here they would've already run over that dog that comes to spy through the window. (She is referring to 'Eros,' the dog that always comes to peek through the windows looking for a bone.)

Customer wearing a tie (entering): A drink...

Bartender: Was that *guaro*?

Customer wearing a tie to Germán: Could you pass me the salt, please?

Germán Arestizábal: It would be a pleasure, young man... the pepper as well.

Customer wearing a tie: Who knows what lime with chile will taste like.

Germán Arestizábal: (romantically): Perhaps like one's first kiss.

The Bentley *girl* (smiling through the mirror at the back of the bar): You have to try it to find out.

Bartender: Like that little dark-skinned guy the other day, he drank a glass of beer with an egg and hot pepper in it, he started to turn green and left here all shook up. I saw him later in Barrios Park dressed in an odd manner, barefoot, even though the man has got money.

Customer wearing a tie: He probably doesn't wear shoes so they won't mug him.

Germán Arestizábal: Probably.

Eros (our national breed of mutt): Give me a bone, I don't care what people say.

The Bentley *girl* (trembling, to the beat of her heart, her car painted on her bountiful breasts): A speaking dog doesn't die, ain't that right, Javier Solís? (She speaks to the customer wearing a tie.)

The radio playing full blast: "The only thing left for me to do is to blow you away with my shotgun."

(The curtain falls with a crash. Applause and rotten eggs on the stage).

"Shit!" says the cop with the friendly nightstick. "This is a Russian code. Or these sons-of-bitches are crazy."

"The thing that had me the most intrigued," Meme's brother says, "was the part about the shotgun, that's why I brought this stuff with me, I was able to pick them up when they weren't looking, when Alfonso threw them on the ground."

"Perhaps so someone could pick them up later."

"Do you think there's some hidden message?"

"I don't know, you guys are the brains of this outfit."

"Cut the crap! We're going to beat the shit out of you if you don't help us interpret the message," the cop dressed in blue says.

"Didn't I tell you that you guys are pathetic."

"Shut up if you don't want us to knock your teeth out."

"Leave him alone," the policeman with four clips says, "He's cooperating with us. The best thing to do is to take this paper to our superiors and let them figure out what it means. You never know what to expect."

"What's happening is you guys are impatient, neurasthenics, I do my duty."

"You're right, perhaps if our superiors scientifically analyze it they'll discover this message's code."

"But I wouldn't be so sure of that, you think like a civilian."

"I never said I was going to become a soldier."

"You'd better get out of here fast if you don't want us to beat the crap out of you, go ahead and get on your way."

And I go away. They were delighted with Alfonso's poem.

— *xviii* —

Goodbye Feliciano, goodbye Pichón, what ya doin so quiet, like million-dollar bills, sitting on a hard rock. Forever quiet, forever sleeping like two little brothers. You survived the nose cancer, Pichón, son of your fucking mother, bigwig of Cuzcalteca poetry, gustavo adolfo vallejo, printer of subversive materials, hard-working, revolutionary poetmaster, pecker of the Salvadoran oligarchy's rotten fruit, gnawer of the trembling pilasters upon which El Salvador's *Guanaca* democracy rests. Goodbye, brother. They took you away on a stretcher, starched and composed, dressed in white. Several months after your disappearance you still smell of subversion. Where then is your corpse? We don't have it here. Or here. We didn't even know him, that's enough already. Here either. We would have wanted to get our hands on him if he was indeed a subverter of public order. And his cadaver, oh, it kept dying. Why don't you look for him on the mountain? All those dead, all the disappeared ones climb the mountain and then they blame us, the pigs, as they call us. Go to hell, shitty students. *Let us salute our fatherland with pride*—singing the national anthem. *To call ourselves your sons-of-bitches*. And the police beat him hard with a rubber stick. Goodbye, goodbye, forever goodbye. *And we joyfully forswear our lives*. Full of animal worms. Stupid boys, can't you hear them saying get out of here. They were asking for it. Why are today's youth so idealistic? We old people don't understand. Why do they die just for the hell of it, if things are the way they are and aren't going to change? *We shall tirelessly consecrate ourselves to you*. For the good of the Oligarchy, Oligators. Who thinks they're stupid? *Oh! Ligarchy, my stepmother. Oh! Ligarchy, full of hate like the bird of falconry.* If they are disappeared, why don't you go look for them in their hiding places? You spared yourself a lot of trouble trying to make them change. *Oh! River alligators, expoliators of my fatherland.* Goodbye Feliciano. Goodbye Pichón. They spared themselves work by getting a *charamusca* cumbia rhythm out of the small, inky motor of the mimeograph machine, the round drum going around and around, and the hurry, hurry up, all night long. "Down with the dictatorship." "Shitty Government." "Don't make fucking waves, make Revolution." *Oh! rogues, how long will you take advantage of our cowardice.* We could call ourselves your children, but they call us sons-of-bitches, go to hell, father-landless son, Godless and lawless, and leave us alone, with our small fortunes that have cost us so much to amass, our little factories that we constructed with the sweat and blood of others, don't bother us. One step forward, march, just one step forward. Goodbye boys and girls, compañeros of my existence, beloved land. The little soldiers marching to the beat of the drum, ta-ta-ta-ta, ta-ta-ta-ta, ta-ta-ta-ta, ta-ta. And you guys so silent, sitting on such a hard stone. They were seen in the Zacatecoluca jail. They're alive. Then, where do they have them? Look for them in their hiding places and don't blame us, the ones who are here to safeguard the sacred interests of the fatherland. *Oh! Cold claw, you raise heaven and earth in order to impose your holy tyranny in this world and the next.* One step forward, march. Pretend that they never existed, forget. Goodbye poet Pichón, goodbye Feliciano printer, drinkers of dark *atole* at the end of Independence Avenue. Friends of the whores and of the early-rising drunks. Forever silent, forever asleep. And looking at us always the way the dead do. Those who never existed, the invisible ones. One step forward, march, the small, landless, peasant soldiers. With one eye on their rifle sight and the other on the heart of someone else's son. *My compañeros, my brothers.*

— *xix* —

"Look Meme-Charrier."

"What?"

"Why didn't you tell us you had a brother?"

"I didn't think it was important."

"Of course it's important."

"I don't care about it."

"I do..."

"That's your problem."

"He says you don't get along with him because he's a worker; I know that that can't be, but I'm telling you for your own information."

"Look, Old Man, forget about him, we're brothers, but we're totally different. Or don't you realize that?"

"I don't like the way you ignore him, I think you're prejudiced against him."

"Listen, Old Man, it's better for us not to mix family matters with our political activity."

"I don't see the contradiction."

"It'd be best for you to forget about him."

"We can't forget about him, he's your blood brother just as we are your brothers of the flesh."

But Old Man doesn't tell him that the whole group was with his brother in the beer hall. If you only knew, he even recited poems by Miguel Hernández for us. He didn't want to belabor Meme's refusal to talk about his brother.

III

LITTLE RED RIDING HOOD

A little more of our scarce resources are needed to make the house payment, electric and water bills, street paving tax, cleaning, right to view a few yards of the volcano covered with mist at night (a surcharge of ten percent for a view of the Jabalí Volcano), the stars cooking in its cloudy vapor. They charge us a lot to see this sitting animal—the Jabalí Volcano—along the length of the entire city. And inside, the house has walls of exposed red bricks.

"Just imagine if we had a child," Little Red Riding Hood says to me. "It would die of cold, the poor thing; without a warm blanket for these November temperatures," she says to herself, singing, from the sink where she is washing dishes. "Yes, it's possible it would get sick and we'd have to pay for a doctor and medicines and where there's smoke, there's fire," I reply, speaking to myself.

And that's nothing, just imagine what the food would cost, have you thought about how much we'd pay for a month's supply of *Pelargón* baby formula? Milk, just like that from mother's breasts, and then you have to go to *Carnation*. Not to mention the crying in the night. "Just thinking about it gives me a headache," I think to myself, desiring intensely to be with her.

Little Red Riding Hood has stopped washing the dishes and she heads—with her choppy steps, galloping, a horse of wind roaming our countryside—towards the dining room, with clean dishes in her caressing hand.

"And you complain about not having a child," she says,

getting one up on me. I've fallen into the trap, my feet are pressed together and I'm about to lose a leg. I suffer, trying to get free. "Really, Little Red Riding Hood, why can't we have a child?" Now it is she who has fallen into the trap, into the depths of a well with no water and no bottom. "Why can't we have a child?" she repeats in a long, drawn-out fashion as if she had fallen into the well. And the silence is prolonged. My eyes revolve around the letters that I'm reading. I wait for her response that will come from the dining room, from the other side from where I am now, reading a book, in the living room divided by a folding-screen wall barely six feet high. The wind blows in through the shutters. Little Red Riding Hood remains silent, a century more or less of silence and absence. And now I can't hear her at all because her words come flying out in gusts through cracks in the window that looks out on the Jabalí Volcano.

— *ii* —

You should see the pretty face I have on this rainy day that is like our days. New day. Birds hidden in the branches to listen to a song that comes out of your mouth. You should see what pretty rain, the little worms falling in spurts, gargling, with black dust from smoke. The park is two hundred yards away, the park's gardens. Thunder running along the tiled roofs and your face behind the window pane. I wash my face, I see myself behind the window. You should see what pretty hair I have. For you I am pretty, I know, although I'd like to be pretty for the whole world. That way I'd look better to you, no doubt. I'm pregnant, you'd find it fascinating to see the skin of my belly tremble, as if Carmina wanted to come out of her treasure chest. The poor thing! I can see her, in her dark corner, without anyone to cover her, folded up, without eating, with just her umbilical cord, kicking desperately with her little feet, a duckling in its shell, uttering softly through the telephone line of blood, da-da, ma-ma. She has only me to be her vessel, container, she breathing through her oxygen cannula, taking trips through space. There she remains, quietly, until the time comes. Poor thing! And what about you, you get lost; for no reason you disappear. You just say a well-intentioned goodbye: "Good luck, someday we'll see each other again." A paint stain on the mirror, an imprint of my lips, a "good luck" sharper than a kitchen knife. And I see myself between the red letters, spying on myself or perhaps your eyes are behind the mirror, stuck to the sign. I now realize I was never more alone than when you took our clothes outside to hang them in the sun to get rid of their musty smell; and I've never had more company than now, now that I have Carmina in my pretty stomach, swollen, a multicolored circus balloon. You take the cake for being conceited, scarecrow, scare-death. I, in the room looking at myself in the mirror, waiting for you to appear touching my shoulders, caressing my belly, asking: whose cute belly is this and whose little wildcat leaps are these? I am a fool who's just come down from the volcano, selling flowers, those illiterate girls who don't know what it's like to be behind a mirror, reading a goodbye sign from dusk to dawn. "Good luck and I don't know what," the phrase, painted with lipstick, says. Brr, it's cold. If only you were here, Al, so you could sing a song out loud. I settle for the masks on the ceiling, the noises of animals in the night, the pillow with a bat inside it, the one in the horror story by Horacio Quiroga you told me about. And remembering Juanita, the girl from Suchitoto, nicely dressed, along the cobblestone streets, smelling like flowers, like in the Argentine song "At Five on Florida Street."

— *iii* —

What could you have seen in that woman, with eyes, teeth, hands, feet; different from most people in her gestures and in the fact she's always asking things that aren't important to her—with notorious defects, of course, laughing at someone, biting her fingernails. She covers her head with a green cap, wild, mountain parakeet. As far as love goes, certainly she behaves like a real whore. That's what some of my friends who got to know her well told me, intimately, I mean. I wonder what you've seen in Juana, the one from Suchitoto, who's so special. She walks like a tired ox and then suddenly takes off straight ahead, and her artificial ass, they say that she stuffs two soccer balls in her panties, that's what you like, the part in the rear, because you're good for that, you don't believe in spirituality, only in material things, pragmatist, as long as there's something to touch, you say laughing to yourself, grinning with your great big pearly whites like the teeth of a young horse. And then she took you to Guatemala—the big slut!—and she kept you locked up in a room of the Hotel America. There was nothing you could do, that's the worst part. You spent a lot of money and you didn't do a thing; from Chalchuapa to Guatemala, the two of you hugged on the Tica Bus, like two little doves just out of their nest, wearing each other's skin down from so much touching. "You won't believe it, he had his hand under my skirt from the time we left Chalchuapa! He's insatiable."

You're happy as long as you're touching, you should have been a mailman, touching doorbells so that they open for you and delivering everything. There's no cure for your vocation as a flute player, touching your ocarina. Juanita herself told me. I don't know why, maybe she did it to make me suffer, or maybe she didn't know who I was, or perhaps she's just a great storyteller. Her eyes, like two birds in a cage, moved back and forth as she told me about it. The rest of it doesn't bother me, she said, the important thing is that he went because I wanted him to, and I never thought I was hurting anyone, I didn't know there was another woman involved, she insisted with a hoarse chabela vargas voice. Well, I don't care about that, I thought. She became silent, a monolithic Mayan of the pre-classic period, without the slightest expression on her face, without the slightest movement, she barely blinked her eyes, and more than once I raised my hand to my nose to scratch the nervous tingling that ran through my skin. "You should write stories, you're a great storyteller," I finally said, almost asleep on my feet like a parrot on its pole. And she, with all the gall in the world, with no desire to desist. "That's enough!" I was thinking, but at the same time curious to know about your affairs when you're unfaithful and then show up with your honey-sweet hugs and caresses that leave me sticky, a fly on flypaper, or a horse-biting spider caught in a honeycomb, breaking free but leaving its legs stuck in the wax.

And who could stop her? She was a bulldog: "Then we went to the hotel after strolling around Centenary Park, mingling with vendors selling combs and small mirrors." Because she has a tongue on her, that Juanita, like the one on the poor little crocodile that said it was a toad in the contest to see who had the biggest mouth. When you weren't looking she went to get it on with the priest who showed up looking for her with the pretext of wanting to see colonial churches. "Yes, my children, in Antigua, Guatemala, there are tunnels connecting the nuns' rooms with those of the priests. Of course, those were other times, when the law of God was not respected; cells where they buried the newborn babies, children of impure priests and nuns I don't need to tell you about; in short, all those things that now pertain to the nefarious history of the Church." And you, with your mouth wide open, dunce-like, startled, idiotic, drooling at the mouth, you believed it. "Yes,

Father, if you want you can take Juanita to see all the colonial churches, because I have some things to do and I don't want her to get bored." She herself told me how she spent the whole night in the sacristy; filled with sins, she tried to rid herself of them in one fell swoop and that's how night found her, removing and inserting sins, what's a body for if not for that, and, that's why the hen clucks. She came and knocked on the hotel door when it was already early morning. Of course, for her to enjoy her vacation, one foot-long hot dog wouldn't be enough.

You telling me:

"In the room next to ours there was a German couple who spent the whole night wrestling and screaming; I thought about my responsibility for Juanita, it was midnight and she hadn't returned, fortunately she was in sacred hands."

I telling you:

"You got what you deserved for acting like an idiot."

You defending yourself:

"These are mistakes one makes without realizing it; besides, I never imagined that someday you'd find out, much less hear it straight from the horse's mouth."

I:

"You thought you were so cool when you were no more than a child drinking water from a baby bottle. It was my fault, perhaps, for having gone to my grandmother's house."

He:

"You left me alone, sad, like a *bolero* song; I had no other choice than to go to Vindels' place, where I met Juanita, and that's why all those things they sing about in Mexican songs happened to me."

Little Red Riding Hood:

"I remember that before I left for my grandmother's house I almost killed you. The knife passed whistling above your head. Then you took your favorite books and a wooden mask by Chico Gavidia; for more than four months you lived off the Vindels. In a few days you were going to Guatemala; you've been a great fool; saying my grandmother's face looked like a bitter orange when you knew that it was just the opposite: face of orange sweet lemon, split in two, give me a kiss, I ask you."

You:

"Your furious statue-face, the face of a president of the Republic."

I:

You went to Guatemala when I was dying of love. And she sent you flowers, what a whore: "Here the girl Juanita sends you flowers; so they don't go to waste, you should put them in a bottle with some water; and she also sends you these *chilacayote* candies." Tell her thanks, you're very kind, but you shouldn't go to so much trouble. She says it's no trouble, just the opposite, she's at your service. But my God, what could she have been after with so much attention?

It's a good thing I didn't stick you with the knife or neither one of us would be here talking about it. Nonetheless, revenge was had: She herself told me everything, without knowing who I was. The vile things the two of you did! I waited on the wooden bridge, at the same spot where I met you. He likes to see me in a robe before we go to bed together, a flowery robe with light-blue petals, to be more precise. I was furious that day of the knife. Now I understood those telegrams supposedly signed by your mamma: "I must see you. Period. Bring me poetry books. Period. It's a matter of life or death." And I believed that your mother was crazy. And then she signed: "Your mommy."

She was married to a medical doctor. Then you heard her husband's car pull up: What, it's impossible, he's in San Vicente! The poor man working his ass off at the hospital so that his wife could cheat on him in his own home and in his bed. With a scoundrel like you. "If you want, hide under the bed." And I had one hand covering in front and the other in back, Adam-and-Eve style. "Put your underwear on and turn off the record player because I've told my husband that I never listen to music when he's not here." Her gestures revealed her fear of her husband. And it was impossible for you to hide completely beneath the bed. And when do you think you'll leave, silly, you'd better hurry up if you don't want him to kill both of us. Put your pants on, then, and jump over the wall, be careful you don't break your legs. This isn't the time for jokes. What a mess I've gotten myself into this time! Beep-beep, the car driving into the garage. Plop, plop, the sound of footsteps at the door. Wait Facunda, don't open the door yet. And the maid doesn't know what to do with herself because she too has a right to get upset. Anyway, I don't have the keys, Juanita, my child, Facunda says, feeling like she wants to go sit in the presidential armchair, because fear has drained the strength from her ass. Great, that gives us more time, Juanita replies, arranging her hair and putting on her panties. And you, put on your pants, don't just stand there like a Michelangelo, that man is going to kill us, this isn't the time to be poetic, leave barefoot, there's no time to put your shoes on, don't be stupid, perhaps you were contemplating taking a little bath before you go running off! You jump over the wall. Knock, knock, he's at the front door. Just a minute and I'll open, I can't find the key. What's this mess, it looks like a hurricane has been through here. Facunda's legs were trembling and she was crapping in her pants, obsessed with running over to the presidential chair. I just haven't had time to clean up anything and the lady of the house has been a little sick. "That Facunda, she gets lazier and lazier," Juanita pretends to complain. The shameless maid: "Since you sent me to go get tortillas and I spent two hours waiting, it was afternoon before I knew it. You're incredible Facunda. And plop, you fell from the top of the wall, like a *garrobo* lizard on its back. Did you hear that noise, Juanita? Yes, it must be an opossum looking for chicken eggs or eating the cashews. And I really fucked up my leg. Limping down the street. Pick up this room, I want to sleep. If you want, you can take a bath before lying down, Juanita says with honey-sweet words. The doctor: There you go with your insinuations, can't you see I'm exhausted from work? saying this with the greatest annoyance.

When you got home you had your pants on backwards. I told you: You're hunting ghosts. You: But how could you go out looking like that. You see, you get crazier and crazier every day.

— *v* —

I look so good pregnant, you don't know what you're missing. I spy through the apartment window, while outside it's nighttime and raining so much, over there in the park, and farther in the distance are the buildings of the university. Tomorrow you'll come to tell me to open the door for you, to forgive you, that you are an angel of God. I'll be in a place where finally we'll remain separated, totally free to think, facing each other, but apart. I won't hear you say that you are coming from someplace, because my secret place will be a tomb with only one key, and that will be my impregnable home, watching the grass grow upwards and downwards, inside those tunnels with only one entrance so that the wireless pressure waves you use to communicate over thousands of miles and dozens of years will not reach me, with one foot in the grave, toothless, more on the other side than this one, disappeared forever and you think that it's a joke because I've never done it to you and because you know this Little Red Riding Hood, eater of fruit, and with a smile on the tips of your fingers, I mean, the other Little Red Riding Hood who disappears and makes herself invisible so as not to see you, not to have to give explanations and not to have to tolerate the tedium of your memory getting inside my head, the fly's egg in the fruit so that the larvae will be able to eat it up from the inside out. Remember these words.

I've learned to sit in front of the window, glued to the window pane, being on the other side of the mirror watching the drenched children go by as they return home from school, watching the dogs stuck together after coitus; the women from the little market, the crazy woman across the street with her eyes covered with honeysuckle and other kinds of luminous climbing plants, with a green scarf, waving at my window with her parakeet-colored scarf, without knowing that I'm observing her, intrepidly, glued to the window pane, the most beautiful entertainment in the world, the street and the green zones, a little boy pissing and shitting on himself behind a group of Madonna lilies planted in the communal garden; those who return from work with their fierce countenances, repentant for serving two masters. So I am at the window, and other rooms observe me: behind each shutter, a pair of eyes; in each cornice, pairs of eyes disguised as little paper birds and kites, the water tank on the fourth floor, on the terrace, spilling its liquid beneath the sun. And me with my gut, my stomach in motion, waiting for you to show up from somewhere and to look up, to the third floor, looking behind the windows and I opening the shutters to see you better and not be behind a mirror; and the pure air enters; a smell of fried fish from the food stands below, the voices that before belonged to a silent movie; and to see how it has stopped raining before I realized it and to hear your shout: "Hello, can I come up?" I, asking that you go around back and take the stairs. "What other way is there to get up there?" And I explain to him that he could be a bird; but no, then: "Go around back and come up." He rests here for awhile. Now that the sky is clear we can go to the terrace, to the water tank, like we had done before, to give each other a special kiss or have corporeal relations on our feet, I, inclined like the leaning tower of Pisa and you like San Vicente's tower, without supporting yourself on anything, trees abused by the wind, your hundred and fifty pounds on top of my body, a special sensation, a taste unlike that of the fruit stolen from someone else's garden.

But you don't show up anywhere.

It's better, after all, soon it won't be hot, that's what happens once the black clouds clear up giving way to the blue of strobe-a-delic lights. Once again I will have forgotten you. "Hello, my love!" I repeat: "Go around and come up." The sound of his footsteps, boots full of water coming up. "Come right in, young man!" You, in a towel, drying your Savior of the World curly hair in a gesture of surrender, asking me to take off your boots which are full of mud and water; and we die of laughter, go take a bath, come so I can take off your shirt and pants and you wrap yourself in a towel, son of Indira Gandhi. The water falls from the shower in spurts, the cold water, and I hand you the soap over the top of the shower curtain. As you shower, I'm going to heat some water for *Listo* coffee. "I barely had time to catch the bus. It's raining cats and dogs. Hard as hell." "Take this aspirin, my love, with this hot coffee and bread roll, I don't have anything else to offer you." You seated on the iron chair with the woven nylon seat, I wanting to burst out crying. Out of joy. "I am crazy and I don't believe in luck: See how you show up all of a sudden and with no notice as I was thinking about you; sacred telepathy." The coffee's ready, dry your hair, put on this un-ironed shirt: it's just you show up unexpectedly. It's the smoke from the kitchen, I explain to him when he mentions the big tears streaming down my face. It's the green firewood. What green wood are you talking about, aren't you cooking with electricity? That's right, I answer. It's just that that's the way the poem goes: It's the green wood that makes me cry. I clean the buggers from my nose, the big sad sentimental buggers, and all that salty seawater that flows when I'm dramatic and amorous, I'm such a fool!

"Who would have thought I would see you from the window?" she says.

"You see," I reply, "I was watching you even before you showed up. Magic telepathy."

— *vi* —

The rooms are more or less spacious, separated by walls that don't reach the ceiling, a kind of divider of red bricks and cement, unpainted; ventilated by four windows; in the back there's a kind of room for drying clothes, an extension of the living / dining room. Three miniature dogs live in the clothes-drying room; Little Red Riding Hood takes care of them as if they were her own children, she gives them *Cinco Molinos* milk in a baby bottle; she has made them cushions from old sheets. The dogs don't let anyone sleep because as soon as they hear the noise of cockroaches they start growling at them in the darkness. I tell her: Give those dogs away, Little Red Riding Hood. She: If it weren't for my dogs the house would be full of cockroaches. And who can convince her? I: A cat would be better, don't you think? She:

Cats are pigs, they shit under the bed and you can never get rid of the stench. I really wonder if one of these apartments could stand the stench of cat shit. Looking at it that way, the miniature dogs are better; she takes them out so they can take care of their necessities in the green zone, and if she forgets to do this, the dogs themselves take it upon themselves to remind her, nipping at her legs and scratching her. "It's time to take them out to shit," I tell her. Little Red glares at me with a don't-be-vulgar look, respect the little dogs.

The dogs have become part of the family: They go to bed the same time as us, they like to sleep with the lights out, they prefer a marimba concert with drums and flutes to ranchera music, they express their taste with some anxiety, running in circles in front of us, trying to speak: "Turn the light off." "Can't you put on some nicer music?" Little Red has to please them, because, if she doesn't they won't leave her alone. "Excuse me, it's time to turn out the lights now," she says to me. I may be glancing through the newspaper. "The dogs are calling me, they're tired." "They can eat shit," I say to myself. Little Red Riding Hood thinks that I'm including her in the banquet, she yells that if they are in the way they can go out to the street, to the green zone, herself included, of course. I tell her that the invitation to the scatological party is only for the dogs. "It's all the same," she affirms with a dam full of tears about to inundate the room. I turn the light off and fall asleep. At six in the morning they start to bark. Little Red gets up to give them their bath. "It's too hot for them." And for us, I think. I tell her that the dogs are too spoiled and that creates problems for us.

To show Little Red Riding Hood I care about her, I've taken the miniature dogs out for a walk, so they can do their thing. And I feel like a man, a new man, showing understanding towards the animals that won't let me sleep, that wear out my patience. I'm, well, good to my enemies. Maybe I am just the man that's needed.

— *vii* —

(Little boy, I don't know where you are, but I write to you just the same; I had told you that if you didn't answer my first letter I wouldn't write you another word; later it occurred to me that you might not have received my letter. You haven't gotten sick, have you? I'm not going to ask you if you miss seeing me or if we miss each other, because it would be a tongue twister. I know that you're happy in your solitude, for having gotten rid of me in such a pathetic way. As for me, I can't say the same thing. It's hard for me to live alone, you know it, and one of these days I'll show up in your house no matter where you are or someone other than you will come to me.

I want to write you every day as I did some time ago, that was when I thought that I adored you adoring me. But it's better not to play the fool. I want to talk with you, tell you how well I'm doing. I get back on my feet admirably— like the movie artists. I live a restful life because Aunt Gracia visits me and you can't image how well she looks after me. The heat isn't suffocating lately, sometimes it gets cool and rains like in the Bible, it rains until you start to feel like building a Noah's ark. The neighborhood has changed, now I have some talkative neighbors, storytellers of tragedies: I'm going to tell you something in confidence: I still love you very much, even with the harm we've done to each other. I want you to answer the following questions: Is our separation final? Should I forget you? Be honest with me, no matter what your reply I'm going to sing a song like those that I used to coo to you before going to sleep and that you said were the saddest songs on the planet.

Well, little boy, take good care of yourself and always take your medicine when you're sick. It's no problem for me to write you, so I will not forgive you if you send me a classified ad-style letter. Oh! Remember, when you're with another woman I'll be doing everything possible to please another man. Many kisses from the one who hasn't forgotten you. Little Red.)

— *viii* —

I love you very much, it's true, but not enough to keep my mouth shut. Your behavior forces me to accept that peachy my-love, my-love with disgust. If you believe you can forgive me for it, forgive me, in any case I'll say whatever I must. In the past few days you haven't kept me informed as to your whereabouts, where you go at night to come home in the wee hours of the morning. I've learned to scold you about it and I'm giving you an ultimatum, I don't want to be alone nor do I want you to come provoke me with your stinking Ambassador cigarettes. If you don't love me, don't come to harass me with smoke and I'll stop loving you. You confuse me, you walk around haughtily, as if you were a freed slave. You say that you went to so much effort to seduce me and refuse to admit that it was I who seduced you. When you were coming down the stairs to spy through the hole in the plywood wall, maybe you didn't notice that I was looking at you from the mirror. If I had really felt alone, do you think I would have acted the way I did? When I was alone in my room, you were accompanying me through the hole in the wall. I would dress up to look at myself in the mirror so I could exhibit myself; you observed me observing you; your eyes wandering in the darkness, your eyes of a caged cat, your eyes were the slash-and-burn fires of March on the volcanoes. The look of a snake hunter. Mirror mirror on the wall, who's the fairest in this kingdom of darkness that is my dark room? And I would dance around. In a certain way, I was making fun of you. I was doing it for the unknown neighbor in the room directly above mine. You were dying on the other side of the mirror, you remained hidden somewhere on the staircase, breathing with reticence as if you were fed up with life.

— *ix* —

Let's forget it then, I say. I ask you where did you leave your new handkerchiefs, why are your underpants stained. Tell me once and for all if you've decided to continue this war of words, tell me so I can put it behind me and stop thinking that we are going to be together again, lying in bed, with your shadow still there because you never get up as I pass my hand over your head, blowing in your ears until you shout *no more!* and we laugh and laugh.

Tell me if I should forget about your shadow. If I should erase it from my bed, if I should remove it so that someone else, who has the courage, will come sleep with me. You know that that's been my life, being with someone: From the time I can remember I have been with someone. You started to have strange dreams, dreams that coincided with mine, and there in those corners of the soul we found each other.

I'm telling you all this from Tablón del Coco, watching the carts pass over the sonorous slabs of stone. Once again you'll have your room dark, without anyone to wash your clothes, without anyone to give you teaspoons of syrup when you're sick, without anyone to clean your shoes, without anyone to wake you up when nightmares threaten you. I mean to say, without this slave who loves you, without this Little Red, servant, that one day thought she wore your initials on her forehead branded there like on an animal and that I'm having a hard time removing now. I pretend solitude when I look at the sea from the upper hallway of the big house. You're nearby with your unpleasant odor of poisonous cigarettes. I touch you through the bars in the window that looks out on the pine forests of Tablón del Coco. You rock yourself on the tip of my fingers when I point at you or in the palm of my hand when I want to erase you, a wake on water, tepid mist, an image somewhere. Behind the dividing screen you hear me take an aspirin with a glass of water.

— *x* —

(Dear Al: I've come to the end. I still can't stop feeling the nostalgia that cherished things produce. What do you think? I've come home and I am greeted by one of your letters. It has filled me with happiness, because once again we make contact and I will try not to break it. My house in Tablón del Coco doesn't surprise me, they've fixed it up quite beautifully, they've placed a giant Christmas candle in the living room, it was one of Aunt Gracia's ideas.

Aside: Don't you think things have changed between us? I do. Your being part of my imaginary world is not the same as being part of my real world. I say this because yesterday, not the day before today, but that yesterday when I felt I was your friend, everything was different. I understood that I have always been crazy about playing with fire, I have a cook complex and that's why I've burned myself several times. I don't want to play anymore, I'm tired of behaving like a little girl, I've grown up, I'm going to be twenty; you know me well, from the time I was a little girl.

Sincerely, Al, do you think you're doing the right thing writing to me? You should forget about me. Because, don't think that I'm going to play along, no, I'm going to quickly get out of this vertigo and *thanks for everything*! I tell you this with a trembling voice, my hands tremble as well, as they write this letter. With greetings from Little Red Riding Hood.)

— *xi* —

Seated on the iron chair with the woven nylon seat, drinking a glass of *pilsner* brand piss, the pause that refreshes, more than anything, a *pilsner*. Pretending to be reading the newspaper, but you're not reading anything. You see that I'm thinking about you, with that benignity that unites us. I'm leaving forever, too bad if you stay at home. I realized I ought to leave and I went to Tablón. The climate of the pine forests is paradise; besides, Aunt Gracia got work at a nearby farm. I'm not sure whether or not the baby will be born, I don't even know if it will ever turn into a person that says Mommy I'm hungry. This child will never be born. With tenderness, I feel its little kicks in my belly as if it were in agreement with me. No one has congratulated me on my future child, you know? Because nobody knows about it, just you and I. *A child is one's shadow, when we're not anywhere and everything seems to be covered with a ghost vegetation above our heads.* I say her name will be Carmina; if you'll go along with that I'll go along with you and we'll call him Alfonso. *I forgive you for everything, Little Red, I understand my eternal illness, always desiring a strange freedom, especially upon being something of a victim of these waters that seep through the mud walls, now I won't escape even with a miracle, with this solitary darkness and confinement.* Now you see, I am condescending towards you,

you have to thank me. Al, we should keep in contact from both sides of life. I tell you and I repeat it, this day of birds and pines and distant sea wind.

— *xii* —

"Chickadee of God in my path," I proclaim. You think I'm kidding. I say pretty words to you, that's all. But you become hippopotamus—I mean hypothetical—and here comes the war. Tears once again and the screen comes crashing down. You start saying things from the other world, unpleasant and imaginary things. And she: Don't say stupid things, it'd be better if you kept quiet. Don't put me on, you cave man.

You are not just any old chickadee—look carefully: God knows what he's doing and if we take this as a sign from above, there's no reason to feel offended. She: I know that it's not a joke, but you're obliged to say grandiose things and not stupidities. Why, if I'm not grandiose? That's just the way things are. You'll go away forever, that's the problem. But if you think I love you, you should promise me that you'll love me, even if you forget about me, it's like committing yourself for life and for death. And I reply to her that I'll no longer say philosophical things to her. And right then I start calling her hibiscus. At first you think I'm talking about a flower of the carnation family until I explain it to you, then you called me *papaturro* fruit tree. Camino Real *papaturro* fruit, that sticky fruit that even the birds turn their noses up at, in other words it sounds poisonous. Whereas hibiscus sounds harmonious. I love *papaturros* snitched from someone else's garden, she says without thinking very much what she's saying. Okay, I'll never call you chickadee again, and you won't call me *papaturro* either. It's ocrow, meaning it's okay with her too, as she looks at me with her beautiful eyes, like a dream, like the lakes of

111

Cuzcatlán, alias El Salvador. Do you know what I mean? You're my country and that's why I traverse you from your head to your toes, passing through ravines and depressions, through vines and fields of wild flowers. "They ought to give endurance awards for being Salvadoran," he says, remembering the poet Roque Dalton. You don't understand me, I tried to call you village bellflower, hibiscus, because you are colorful and musical, and you come up with other things.

— *xiii* —

(It's been months since you've sent me any letters telling me about your situation, if you are free of evil premonitions, out of all depressing farces. I write you with a certain amount of happiness attributable to rest. When I sleep I become different, I dream sad dreams about you, I go looking for you in a two-story wooden house, but I don't dare enter to see you, and I wake up terribly sad because I can't find you in the recurring dream I have every night or perhaps it was only once and I dreamed that I would have the same dream every night. In the dream, I visit, alone, the marvelous countries of other worlds and I know that you are sitting under the leafy mango tree, surrounded by dragonflies, shaken by the nearby aroma of the pine forests. But I don't see you. I discover that you are listening attentively to the electric company's six-in-the-afternoon concert, you look at me and I dream that you accompany me along with other women laborers who are going to pick coffee. I don't forget anything. And then I go to meet you in a second dream, I see you surrounded by friends who are going to execute you for betraying their ideals, you are locked in an cell of mud, in a cage for armadillos, I go down several narrow steps, to meet you, and I see you as if you were an opossum in its cave. Sometimes a ray of sun blesses you. You tell me you miss that red brick house and sitting in the iron chair with the woven nylon seat, and you tell me that you are an eternal prisoner, and perhaps they're going to execute you, they're going to apply the same law that you have believed in, but you doubt that it should be applied, the scorpion eats its children and vice versa. I wake up and go to work, there where I can watch you over my shoulder, as you walk among *pepito* trees that provide shade for the coffee trees, drinking fresh water from a *tecomate* fruit or eating pickled rabbit with diced onions and vinegar. Sometimes I think that "vicuñas produce wool for others." What does it matter? It's just a bunch of nonsense anyway. I see you in the emptiness of our special clouds. I invent these dreams to be close to your nose and to offer you my sunflower eyes, my chubby cheeks, my burnt Uncle Coyote butt. I make things up so I don't feel sad like the Sally who used to sell sea shells by the sea shore. Don't believe anything I say.

If I hadn't written you, Al, it wasn't because I didn't have time. Truthfully, I have a lot of things to tell you. If only you could have seen me in white shorts and surrounded by flowers, in a pretty photograph with Carmina. Well, I'd better not mention her. It's when I'm waiting for the trucks full of sacks of coffee to take me somewhere, because Tablón del Coco bores me, if it weren't for Carmina I'd be an invisible person. One of these days I'm going to take a two week vacation to go on a diet of peasant *guaro* liquor and coconut milk, I'm not going to do it in order to escape, but because it's delicious and because some medicine men recommended it to me so that Carmina wouldn't be born, however, she was born nonetheless, but I continued to like the medicine men's medicine. Don't worry, I feel better, weeds resist fire, my head doesn't hurt any more and my celestial eyes don't get red any more either. You caress me in dreams and that is enough to bring me relief, because you reach the bottom of my blood vessels. Don't worry, my love. There's a remedy for everything, except murder. But that's another thing. I'd better say goodbye. Kisses from Little Red.)

— *xiv* —

Tonight I've been vomiting. You tell me to stop, as if it were a voluntary act. I tell you, it's not my fault, but then you tell me in a dream whose fault is it. I answer that it's Father God's fault. You angrily, going around the world: stop joking. Because you see me sprawled out on the bed, my poor dinner tossed in a little plastic bucket that serves as a chamber pot. I: It must be the liver we ate at noon. You: It's probably something (with that beautiful logic you sometimes display). I: If we had a telephone we wouldn't have problems, but the closest public phone is over a mile away and it's a terrible night.

I watch the hands of the clock, it's ten till two, how can I go out at this hour? You're not going to let me die unattended. I: Maybe if we knock on the pharmacist's door he'll open for us and prescribe some medicine. She: You're only going to find aspirins and condoms. I wonder if they'll open this late? They'll open for me because they know me, but I can't even move, if you go they'll think you're a thief. And I: I've never been to a pharmacy, much less this one, you're right, they won't open for any stranger at two in the morning. Living so isolated is a calamity.

Why haven't they installed a telephone around here? Doctor, could you see my compañera? She's been vomiting for two hours, I want you to recommend something that will make her well immediately. I'm sorry, but I don't give advice over the phone, give me your address and I'll be right there. Asshole! No, nothing, Oh! The charge is triple because it's late at night plus the charge for delivery. Just come, and later we'll arrange the money problem. First I must be sure you'll pay me for the consultation. Look, my compañera is dying. Who the hell isn't dying in this life? Besides, that means more income for us, excuse my bad manners, but I can't keep talking. He hung up! He didn't even ask where I live, the son-of-a-bitch.

"Is the pain any better, Little Red?"

"I'm telling you it's not pain, it's vomiting."

"That's true, no one has said anything about pain. You'd be better off with your Aunt Gracia, she would have come up with something to cure you. Let me make breakfast. Okay?"

"It's getting a bit better," Little Red bats her eyelashes, moves her head to one side; the candlelight falls on her entire face. "Fine, tomorrow will be new day," I nudge her with my buttocks. "Move over a little." It's three o'clock, I hear the San Ramón Church bells.

"Sleep, my little girl," in a tender but drowsy voice.

The dogs start barking. They bark at the *nixtamalero*. They bark every night. In November and December, the *nixtamalero* shines like a great big sugary *jocote* fruit in the sky. I get up to urinate. Fucking dogs, let us sleep. I notice that there is Little Red urine in the *Salvaplastic* bucket. You're saved, miniature dogs, because a shower of hot water would have come down on you. I push the curtain aside and I see moonlight on the dog's heads. And the great big star lower in the sky, shouting out gunpowder sparks. The threads of the *nixtamalero* and the moon enter through the cracks in the glass panes of the shutters, threads of water that moisten my eyes, my hands, the heads of the dogs. It is a fine rain. I lift up the bucket and start to urinate with difficulty. Ant wakes up, what an uproar you make when you urinate! I don't answer. I was dreaming that some policemen were hitting you on the head with their night sticks, she tells me. I see your dream. Ant: it's not my fault. I: your dreams come out and affect me. The stream of my urine competes with the stars illuminated by the light of other stars. Outside, in other apartments, in dozens of buildings, there is silence. The purple-colored night, green-colored, in Technicolor. And the *nixtamalero* in the east, bombarded by some space projectile, shines from many thousands of years ago with the same light that bathes my face and illuminates my urine. I close the curtain that separates the bedroom from the dogs, perhaps that way I won't hear their barking so much. Ant protests again, that she's sleepy. I take out the flint and light the candle. I feel it rain in Ant's eyes. I: are you crying? Four bells. The dogs stop barking. I: don't get sentimental, you know all too well that the dogs only exist in our imagination, tomorrow you'll see the otolaryngologist, or something like that. Ant: don't hog the sheet, it's freezing. It's four o'clock in the morning. When I hear her snoring sweetly, I get out of bed and slowly head towards the miniature dogs' bedroom, I take them from the cardboard box and one by one I toss them from our fourth-floor window. They don't even let out a whimper. I close the window. Move over a little, I tell her again, because every time I get up she takes up the whole bed in diagonal position. I nudge her, I lie down and I'm already asleep.

— *xv* —

(An employee of Telecommunication, alias Antel, is identified as the perpetrator of the damage done to a Saint Bernard dog, property of Mr. and Mrs. XX, who reside at the end of Los Abetos Avenue, in the San Francisco neighborhood of San Salvador. The dog's owners affirm that on the tenth, at around four in the afternoon, an employee of alias Antel arrived on a motorcycle to deliver a telephone bill and that the dog, upon hearing the noise of the motorcycle, barked; the employee then took out a thirty-eight caliber pistol—as was ascertained during the dog's surgery—and shot the animal in its nose. The bullet remained lodged in the animal, to one side of its throat. Mr. and Mrs. XX state that, in all the houses of the San Francisco neighborhood, there are dogs that serve to protect the lives of their owners. They point out that the canines' presence keeps thieves away. About the Saint Bernard, which today is near death, its owners state that it was imported from the United States and that it is seventeen months old. By their very nature, dogs are born to protect humanity; they say that this kind of animal plays with all humans, except with thieves. Mr. and Mrs. XX will file a complaint against Antel, no matter whether the animal lives or dies.) Moral: He who hangs around with dogs learns to die.

— *xvi* —

(Please forgive me for not having written to you earlier. I assure you that months before, days before, I had written you everyday, a letter a day, of course I was never able to put them in the mail. I hope you're doing well. I got your news. It was a great surprise to hear from you. I have many things to tell you: I listen to a lot of music. I don't go the hill any more on Sundays, but instead I've devoted myself to charitable works, some women friends invited me into their group, and I'm happy. You should see how much poverty there is around here. We don't have any choice but to do good to our fellow man. I take Carmina with me. She's in my womb. You know, I hate to spend Sunday at home, I go crazy, I have to go out. I'm getting pretty again, I behave myself, although at times I like to get away from Aunt

Gracia. My recuperation has gone very well. In December I started to get fat again, I looked like a balloon, I went so far as to hide myself from my acquaintances. I'm ashamed to let them see me fat. Except for charity meetings, I didn't go anywhere. But all of a sudden I've started to get skinny, and here you have me, as pretty as ever. Besides, I'm becoming more cultured: I read a lot. Especially historical novels or great romances, remember that I'm a great romantic. As I was telling you, I stopped helping Aunt Gracia count sacks of coffee and it was precisely that inactivity that made me get fat. It'd be better for me to tell you about my new personality later. I've changed a lot, maybe you won't like me this way. But remember that I've fallen two times, got messed up, not to use a bad word. And here you see me full of life. You should see how much fun I've had: Last November I started going out with a serious fiancé, he's an older, light-skinned fellow, a real ladies' man the son-of-a-bitch, divorced, with two adult children living in San Francisco. At first I was very interested, so he ended up asking me to marry him, with fireworks and everything. In January he traveled to San Francisco to tell his daughters that he was getting married during Holy Week and that we would go on our honeymoon to who-knows-where. I spent two whole weeks thinking and remembering you; I thought so hard and remembered you so much that upon my ex-future husband's return I'd already decided to send him to hell. My Aunt, who, just like grandmothers, can pull the stars down one by one, nonetheless remained enthusiastic. She threw parties, with *pupusas*, tamales, *guaro* and hot chocolate. But I left him stuck with the tickets he'd bought for our honeymoon trip to who-the-hell-knows-where. Aunt Gracia went to war, along with all the old women of the charity group. I shouted at them: Fine, if I get married, within a month I'll leave him, I'll divorce, If I have a child with him, I'll abandon it and I will go away with Carmina;

still in my womb, imagine. I almost started swearing; besides I didn't even know what I was saying, because, how was I going to have a child with the older, light-skinned fellow if I was pregnant with Carmina. In short, I've become strong. I've had to be reborn, I've turned into a mature person, practical at times, implacable at others; although my guilty face still betrays me. Apparently I lead an empty life, however, I'm enriching myself; you'd have to hear me to realize how nice I talk: with flourishes and metaphors. Dear, don't forget to write. Tell me anything, decide to come back once and for all, don't make yourself invisible, and ask about me so you don't lose the habit. Remember that in the end all commitments between us have been erased; but that's why I dared to tell you about my breakup with the older, light-skinned gentlemanly fellow, otherwise I wouldn't have even mentioned it. Well, dear invisible love, just judge of the night, annoying little boy. Hugs from Ant. Oh! I almost forgot: I'll never forgive you for what you did to my miniature dogs. Ant.)

IV

THE RED LIGHT DISTRICT

The dead are becoming more restless every day.
(Roque Dalton)

— *i* —

The bad thing is to fight with your compañero leader: to disagree with your soul. He dissents with his cojones. *"My orders aren't open to question," he shouts at me. And I begin to realize that he needs help.* Manuel was furious all afternoon, we tried to play a joke on him and he responded with the eyes of a killer of enemy soldiers. "Get prepared, we're going to run," he says. And we: "We are only going to run?" Run and crawl through the countryside. When he's in a bad mood he makes us run with the rifle in combat position, squatting down, I feel like my heart is going to break into two, three, five pieces. My legs tremble and we can't end the exercise because Manuel threatens to put a couple of bullets in our heads. I don't think he would. Sometimes we run in zig-zag, going around the mango trees until we reach the river; from there we return, and that's how we spend the afternoon in this country club. I busted a gut. "Let's crawl!" I hear him shout when I've started to vomit. This time, as we ran, I watched as barbed wire was put in place for us: Rodrigo had brought some rolls of it in the jeep and was helping to plant stakes. They run wires between the stakes, tightening them up at ground level. "To the wire," he says, playing with his forty-five, watching us run from where he's seated on a wild coffee tree trunk. He's in a bad mood, I mutter to the compañero at my side. We suspect Manuel has it in for us today. He places his boots on the barbed wire and moves them as if were playing a guitar. "They're loose," he says, "They should vibrate when

I touch them." "These guys won't even get their heads under it," Rodrigo observes. "I'm in charge here, tighten the wires," the leader compañero takes charge. Manuel's eyes are bulging out, while our lungs are jumping out of our chests. I feel like I'm going to fall; I see Jorge vomiting, crashing to the ground, tied into a knot. Jorge had been the best in the group, before he had to run hunched over and in zig-zag. Manuel shouts at him and fires his gun into the air. Jorge curses and sighs at the same time, moving his hands to his abdomen in fetal position; he can't get up or go on. I lack the energy to continue circling the five remaining trees, I hope that's the end of this. Manuel has a lot of respect for Jorge and won't leave him there on the ground. What we were hoping for occurs, he gives orders to suspend activity. He leaves his seat on the wild coffee tree trunk and heads for the barbed wire, he touches the wires with his boots again. "What's going on here? These wires are looser than your legs." Rodrigo protests, only a murmur is heard. Manuel: "I'm not dealing with faggots." Rodrigo turns his back to him. *I don't want them to see me, maybe I'm crying, maybe it's sissy stuff.* "That's better, move it," Manuel shouts. And he himself goes to tighten the wires. He calls me and I help him. Rodrigo disappears into the woods. "Okay, hit the ground, on your backs," Manuel shouts. We place the tips of our rifles by our armpits and he presses the butts of our rifles against the ground. We serpents start to slither towards the barbed wire. "Don't get off course or you'll get tangled up, no shit!" Manuel angrily shouts. I try to have crab eyes so I can see behind me, and I figure I'm getting closer to the wires. The serpents start to make headway. I try not to lose my way towards the guitar strings, using a familiar tree to orient myself. I keep going. To one side the dirty boot of a compañero passes by. I stretch my hand backwards to feel the barbed wire. Nothing. I look at the blue leaves of the trees and here and there a patch of sky. The rifle is slipping.

I put it back in place, the strap should be tight on the shoulder. Finally my head runs into something sharp and pointy. I've arrived. I rest a few seconds, observing another little patch of sky through the foliage. I touch the barbed wire. How wonderful! I prefer this to running bent over. "If you're not careful you'll poke an eye out," Manuel warns us. The barbed wires sway, someone has started to go through, to possess the barbed-wire tunnel. I move my head closer, until it bumps into the wire spikes; I raise my hands to my forehead, I squeeze the rifle in my armpit and I lift the web of wires. The boisterous Manuel begins to howl again: "Don't act like you're touching a woman." That's the good thing about him, he has a sense of humor, especially if he's just watching us from his coffee tree trunk with a forty-five in his hand, like *juan charrasqueado,* the Mexican Cowboy in the songs. Covering my eyes with the same hand I use to raise the wires, little by little I'm able to get my head under the wire; with my other hand, I secure the rifle, because it shouldn't be left behind. "If I didn't have to carry this piece of shit it'd be a lot easier," I think, referring to the rifle. Manuel is so damn good he knows what I'm thinking: "Make sure you don't get the rifle entangled in the wires, it would be suicide." In this manner this *mazacuata* snake keeps moving, with one hand over his eyes and the other struggling with the rifle which, with its barrel pointing forward, caresses my check. My stomach is no problem, I think each time a barb scratches my abdomen. I keep penetrating the entanglement, my youth-league soccer-player's feet are still outside the web. An hour or a century after it started, I begin to raise my head. A normal delivery, just a few scratches on my hairy chest and belly which previously had been full of beer. "Quickly," shouts Manuel. "When you're up against the enemy they're not going to be waiting for flowers." *The enemy has never had a bouquet of flowers; nor did my compañeros when they voted so that I would go to prison as a heartbroken guest.* I scratched my belly, mostly when my boots got stuck in the wires and I had to twist like a "u" to reach my feet and untangle the strands, my struggle to free my boots from the wires and continue advancing. "Manuel is right," Rodrigo explains later, or I dream that he said that anytime, "Those scratches are nothing if you think that, from now on, this training could be what will save our lives."

— *ii* —

(I walked all night, with a backpack on my shoulders. "I should have stayed in Mexico, writing poems." Forty pounds on your back is a good reason to turn around, honestly, forty days and nights, taking care not to trip, in the darkness and in daylight. Rodrigo was the first to realize that they were pursuing us, just after we had left the road and entered the forest. First we saw a truck with armed civilian men. We hid on the side of the road and nothing happened. They were peasants. We had gone down to the town. "I'll wait for you guys here, don't forget the big *ceiba* tree." After doing the shopping we regrouped in the outskirts of town to take the truck; up ahead, Rodrigo was waiting for us behind a few bushes near the *ceiba* tree. A few miles ahead we went down, one by one, with five minute intervals between us. "Thirty electrical posts, more or less, between us," Rodrigo ordered. Then we regrouped on the crag on top of the bald hill. We picked up our weapons there and divided up the load of food to carry. "Now we should go to El Encanto." The whole group is depending on us. The three of us know it. When we see the blue hills, it looks difficult: the bluer the mountains, the farther away they are. "They're following us." Said as if one didn't care, in the same way one observes that it's raining, so what? They're probably not after us. It's just ridiculous, wishful thinking. The load is a hindrance, but we shouldn't leave anything behind. For now we can't leave behind a single kernel of corn, much less a grain of sugar. *When I got to your house, Genoveva, I was beat, in some way I had ceased to exist, before that I was dead, I had abandoned the other world, the one of my origin; I was born of a little green iguana, covered with vines, lying there beneath a river of stars with dew falling on us like a waterfall, the gushing waters flowing over a layer of brilliant plastic. It's true that I think about you, I'm in the undergrowth the same as any humble amphibious animal, looking over grasses as I wait for the contingent pursuing us that is coming with its teeth bared hunting the animal that has escaped from the cage with two sacks of food and some aspirins.* Jorge breaths at my side with his suffocated mania of making noises as if he were a tractor climbing a mountain. The lives of those at El Encanto depend on us. Rodrigo continues moving forward, we can no longer see him. Behind they come tracking, slowly, the hunters. There's no doubt they'll get us, you can sense them coming, breathing. *All these things were different, I would arrive from one place to another to see you and you thought I was different, sprung from a green iguana, son of the* jiota *iguana and of the Lempa river* garrobo *lizard.* When Jorge left with his bag of provisions, I started getting rid of mine, as I went farther and farther, throwing away cans of milk, chucking sardines, bags of sugar, hiding them so the pursuers wouldn't find any clues. *The important thing is to advance until sunset.* I had offered to stay behind. We realized they were hot on our trail, sniffing out their prey and our path. Jorge climbed up a mountain, to its peak, Rodrigo followed a little behind him, the two of them disappearing. A wave of lead went flying by like a flock of doves, above the tree leaves. They were bad shots, but the bullets were coming in our direction. I climbed a little more, propelled by the noise of the automatic rifles down below, the howling of the machine-gun dog. There I was, lying down, with my Garand rifle resting on a fallen tree trunk, until I saw them appear; moving from side to side, sniffing around, they look upwards, they run; and my eye is glued to the sight of my Garand. A new burst of gunfire and another flock of doves, this time they pass closer to my head. *The important thing is not to fire helter-skelter, wait until you're sure you won't waste a single bullet, don't ever forget that they are different, they've got bullets to throw away, that's why they fire their weapons, to overcome their fear and to cling to life.* I held my breath. Years passed from the time I started to squeeze the trigger and the moment the downward shot sounded. War was declared, the war of the ants, the lone ant. The group that had come into view disappeared. "Hit the ground." There they were, crouched down, waiting for more shots, trying to locate their source. And they don't get up. They have me surrounded, I think. And I am forever lying down, waiting for them to receive orders to get up. I arrived at your house in that condition and you didn't recognize me. I went up to my room, to the wooden room, and then to the terrace where you hang your clothes, your flowery dresses. I barely look out the door and you think you are dreaming and I tell you that you might possibly be dreaming, one never knows the truth about dreams. Wounding a man who falls headfirst, as far as I can tell when I see two men in a ravine carrying another. It's the first man I've wounded, I proclaim with melancholy. I imagine his life pouring from his chest, his blood like a church window lit up from outside. The holes of my eyes rest in the air, on the dry branch of a tree, and then swoop down upon the group of people down below, I observe the first one to get up. The idea was to procure enough food for a month, for the El Encanto group that is waiting for us. *Alfonso, Rodrigo, and Jorge must go down.* At noon we were approaching the houses. We hadn't seen roof tiles in weeks, the red rooftops,

the moist moss growing on the rough mud walls. We hid
our rifles by a bend in the river, in a space created inside
the branches of a weeping willow. We bathed for a while
before crossing the river. At nightfall we were at the town's
gate, sleeping in a field planted with rabbit grass, beneath
the shadows of some *tihuilote* trees. We spent another day
removing ticks that had attached themselves to our bodies,
I lit a cigarette—following instructions—in order to put it
near the little bags of blood stuck to my skin, the heat didn't
even make the ticks move—but you shouldn't fry them. I
decided to pull them out by force—against instructions—
which meant ripping out my own skin, but that way I would
keep them from sucking up my blood. My skin was covered
with ten tiny bags that were black with blood. One by one, I
ripped them off me, after having failed with the cigarette—
according to instructions—I smashed them on the bark of
the *tihuilote* tree that shaded me. It took half an hour for
Jorge and Rodrigo to get rid of all the bugs. The clarity of
the sky approached, spinning around like a cat. Jorge says
that we should march. I dig through my pockets. We divided
up the money equally. Then we headed towards the highway.
Rodrigo would wait for us on the outskirts of town.
Someone informed on us. I saw Jorge and Rodrigo for the
last time. The peasant man-hunters stayed down, waiting
for nightfall to surround us. You must be brave, my mamma
would tell me when she dug spines out of my foot with a
needle she had heated until it was red hot. It's goes beyond
bravery, of course. *Jorge leaves first and then you go, Rodrigo.*
Who knows where I got my courage. Especially because of
my fear of the dark, even worse in the woods, a fear that
climbs my back with its paws that give me the creeps. *One
man needs to decide to get up so that the others will follow
suit.* Perhaps they lack that man. They remain lying on the
ground. Better for us. The shot put them to sleep. It was
then that I aged a hundred years, face down, protected by a

tree trunk. Suddenly someone shouts: "Get up!" And I saw
their labored breathing among the trees. I held my breath
for several seconds and then I pulled the trigger, smoothly,
backwards, with the tip of my index finger—I could never
do it any other way, I mean with the second joint of my
finger, the way you're supposed to. The center of the sight
enclosed a moving shadow. I, following it, the cat after the
mouse. I felt my brain fly like a hat blown into the air by
the wind. A noise of nocturnal birds traced a golden line
across the growing darkness. The bullet hit a rock; three
more shots and I prepared to get up. Jorge must have been
far away by now, with Rodrigo behind him. If I reach the
summit they won't find me. Another burst of gunfire, and a
pack of dogs, illuminated by the shadows, advance. Dogs
that don't bark, but create poom poom sounds in the
foliage. Because they are campesinos, they have more faith
in their machetes, they must be surrounding me; I hope my
head separates easily from my shoulders, you suffer less if it
comes off with one stroke. Something like that happened.
By then, almost a week of constant pursuit had passed. And
fatigue and hunger set in.)

— *iii* —

Manuel's bad mood was understandable, run until you
vomit, play the barbed-wire serpent, race and race until you
leave pieces of your knee on the ground. Something
fortunate happened. Or these inexplicable things happened
from the start. They weren't after the three of us, but the
group. We found that out much later, once we were back
with Manuel. After we came out alive, the three of us, who
should have died much earlier, the pursued ones, lost in
caves and finding one another again after forty days of
playing a game of cat and mouse. They had the patience and

we had the ability to resist. That's why Manuel's bad mood was understandable, run until you vomit, play the barbed-wire serpent. *They were more than peasants, Manuel, that's why they tried to kill us, because it was better to follow us so we'd think about regrouping to stop them, falling right into their trap.* Manuel tried to take advantage of our defeatist attitude. The thing is, you guys are shit. And what could we say if we didn't have the nerve to respond? And then: You guys are required to be brave until the end. And we, agreeing with everything, letting Manuel threaten us even for sneezing wrong. With his forty-five in hand and his *cojones* philosophy. That was the deal: destroy our hides and knees, toss our cookies. Manuel knew it. Besides, he was the boss who knows everything. *My head was also blown to pieces, diced brains, because the bullet that touches a person touches me. That was my first man—I say as if it were from a cherished song—and perhaps my only one. Another burst of gunfire from the opposing band and the little lead balls turning around, playing the lottery in the green and yellow urn of trees. And the sunlight, the dying afternoon, scratching my back. The afternoon is clear enough so that the men don't dare get up. In another hour Rodrigo and Jorge will be far away, they'll be greeted with joy, they'll congratulate them for their prowess and they'll remember Alfonso, left behind, protected by a tree trunk, the sight of his rifle aimed downward, waiting for nightfall, to end up surrounded or to break through the circle.*

— *iv* —

Space trips, projectiles guided by television, counter-insurgency. Twelve years later, the panorama has changed, there are not eight, or ten of us facing the cataclysm. Everyone must be involved. That's the problem. And mine in particular. Manuel maintains that the revolution should be made with *cojones*, I say that we should use a little—to be modest, a few scraps of—grey matter, get with it. It's his problem too. Twelve years later that is the difference of opinion. It couldn't be any clearer. We argue about that. We lose track of time. Manuel loses the arguments and I think I'm winning them.

— *v* —

Madness, you shouldn't get drunk on your birthday because you don't want to stop; besides, you start making dangerous decisions. So what? Blood is just a little tinted water, if you swallow it down in one gulp it doesn't hurt you. It isn't important. That's it, you should take your first step and not waste time, going from your room to the University and from the University to your room. At night, go listen to nelson pinedo at the Margó cantina, ask the lame guy to play that faggy song that moves you so much, especially because it's your birthday. Yes, my poems must be authentic, I ought to live that life that appears in them, I should suffer them, suffer with them, because when I write I'm an illuminated hallucinating masochist. Or perhaps something else and I'm not aware of it. Any day now you're going to get involved in the organization, in the other world, and you're going to realize what life is and you're going to abandon your cry-baby poems, after all you're not the great Pablo Neruda, getting involved in fashionable writing, the poems that you like. One of these days you're going to know what's good, like in the Agustín Lara song "Raising Hell." The song comes back to you, when you were ten years old, a spoiled, rotten kid in shorts, son-of-a-bitch kid, pinocchio nose for behaving badly towards Mamma; mischievous behavior in the river, spying on your kissing cousin when you snuck up on her while she was bathing in the bathroom. Joining the organization fits perfectly well with poetry: First, be a grassroots militant, that is, put posters up on walls, hold meetings on buses, challenge the police, sitting in the front row, in the street so that the cars must stop, under the sun, as the policemen look at you with the eyes of strangled oxen and bloated toads. Son-of-a-bitch cops! Say it nicely, with your big fat mouth. Martian mask, gases that produce tears and crying, vomiting and shitting, our enemies, give us ours today and forgive our heavy burdens; scandalous masks that make them feel like important gentlemen; masks, made in the united states. Pig cops. Two hundred gas masks per hundred pounds of coffee. One hundred bombs to make piss and shit, for a thousand sacks of high-altitude coffee, "Very Smooth" quality. It happened when I was going to drink beer at the Margó cantina, a few yards from the Corner of Death. Before creating enmity with the policemen I was already shouting obscenities at them; toad-eyed, cat-nosed pigs. Define matters: Genoveva demands that I go visit her every day. Until I rebel. I'm sorry, but we won't be able to continue seeing each other. I'm leaving. Will you write me? Maybe. It's probably a way of getting rid of her. I don't tell her because the poor thing! But if I know everything, my love, her fat china woman's eyes tell me everything, her long lashes, her train headlights. Okay then! I'm going away with Jorge. Delighted to have the chance to do something for the fatherland. The important thing is being honest, Jorge says; and I: that life is beautiful like a sunset, contemplated from Playas Negras. We are wasting ours. I had already done something for the fatherland: my anti-crime poems and the ones about our rulers. The first meeting was on the third floor of the apartment building on November 5th Street, Building F, in the apartment of a railroad worker, where a mythical baker who had set the record for spending the most hours in the torture chamber appeared; and two students, Jorge and I. We place our hands on the red and white flag, it's time to take an oath. Red war, white peace. We place our right hands on the symbolic rag that the mythical baker has removed from a plastic *lintorrey* bag of *kraft* paper made in the Cartel—Common—Market. He has been pursuing Jorge and me since the sixth grade. The oath goes something like this: In order to keep living it is necessary to fight against those who do not want us to keep living. We're talking about those who pardon our lives only because if they didn't they wouldn't have anybody to pick coffee. Difficult battles to overthrow the master-owner, take from him his whip, rebel or die. It's sensibility, it's poetry. Until we're actually in the saddle, we don't realize the seriousness of our commitment. *It'll only be for a few months, Genoveva. You'll be faithful as long as I'm alive. You bet she will.* A knot forms in my throat. From boardinghouse to boardinghouse, from bus to bus; in the street they put a bullet in you and it's all over. Your photo appears in the newspaper, another dead person, goodbye dear poems, day-to-day life. The dead on the pages of newspapers, a typographic cemetery.

— *vi* —

Fifteen years later, it was my fault for thinking too much. No nation is worth a damn if it doesn't have a rifle in its hands, Manuel says; his facial features exhausted by so much leadership and heroism, so many compañeros and disciples killed or disappeared. His eyes are vacant. I refute him by demonstrating that his concepts are ridiculous, that he's stuck in the year 1965 or in the stone age. Think, you mother! I tell him, guns aren't everything. That he has to open his mind. Think, you piece of shit! In more poetic words, of course. And I finally end up telling him all at once that he is a phony hero. Things are getting hot, is it too late to rebel or too early? His only defense: that I am still a shitty poet. I laugh in his face. Poor Manuel. Poor little poet am I.

— *vii* —

Our beloved dead ones, join their ranks, find solitude like the verdict in a farcical trial. Valid poetry cannot exist if I don't remember my brothers beforehand, imitate them, not with my death but with my actions. To survive in order to continue until they catch up with us or until the years arrive. Recover lost time. Become a bandoleer of liberation. A pistol to your head and your blood are the salvation of others. Someone grabs hold of something, he climbs the mountain, breathing with difficulty, like a tractor, two packs on his back and a rifle as his third leg, sweating tears, a path in the night that is the umbilical cord through which oxygen penetrates. I see the blue-grey mountain ranges, when there is no trace of sunlight because night has fallen in defeat. It's raining cats and dogs. I know because the humid earth becomes more humid, filling itself with cold, a smell like when one walks through the countryside on the day of the cross, with bananas, mangos, *pepetos*, and *paternas*, and green, purple, yellow, and red *nances*. A way to introduce sadness into the streams of water that slowly turn my dwelling of four walls and one 25-watt light bulb into mud. I think that imprisonment is rebellion disguised as mourning and that there was no other alternative. He, they, denounced me for treason and revolt, for selling out to the enemy. Paradox of paradoxes.

— *viii* —

(...Well, the national guardsmen, unable to find bandits, take it out on us, they burn our planted fields, they throw us off our land and take us to another place and we leave behind everything that we can't carry with us; we go carrying our things on our backs, our children behind us, shoved along by rifle butts. They take us to land fenced with barbed wire, near the coast with blue-tailed mosquitoes, where there aren't any bandits. They say it's to protect us from evil. We don't want their protection, but if we don't let them protect us they kill our youngest children because they say that they are the seed of evil. That's why we accept their orders. What else can we do? No one protects us, no one gives us even a crumb of bread. We abandoned our cemeteries, our wells, our plots prepared for yucca and beans and corn. Yesterday there was an explosion at the military detachment that sounded like thunder, like an earthquake, our houses shook like hammocks from side to side. And it was deafening to our ears. That's when they arrived, we should leave, for the good of everyone, and they struck us with their rifle butts for dragging our feet. Let's go, move you lousy sons-of-bitches. Gathering our things in a hurry and then they burned our houses to ashes and we cried because of the smoke in our eyes and for the burning of our houses that had cost us so much work and they said that they would give us new ones on the coast where cotton is grown and hands are needed and you can make a lot of money and you can plant beans and corn in May; smoke makes eyes water, motherfuckers, they call us, even if you're going to be better off on the coast and they make us get into trucks, let's see if there's enough room for all of them, squeezed together on the platform of the National Guard truck; take only what you need because there's no time or room; wrap your junk up in your blankets.... We're moving. Let's get out of here now.")

— *ix* —

I don't know if it rains the same up there as down here, the drops of black water, a special sound, the most beautiful sound in the world. It's a little cold. My compañeros brought me a blanket. Here, shitty poet. Alfonso the crap. And they know how much I love them. Well, after all, this isn't a picnic in the country. For those of us who have been desperate, imprisonment is a goal of the rebellion. In cases like ours, no one has ever lost his or her freedom by being thrown in a cell. I also try to put up a good front. They left me a book that I can read with the help of the 25-watt light bulb. If it weren't so cold in this tomb for the living dead, it'd be different. How do you write a poem underground? I'm in an icebox. They take me out once a day so I can take care of my physiological necessities, because a dead man has these needs too. In the john, I stretch, I scratch my butt, but that's okay. The good thing about it is that it keeps me in shape. Corpses also need to work out. Two months spent in a cell that was originally intended for our enemies. Now I'm an enemy for breaking with the party line. At three they bring me bread and coffee. They let me keep my watch. I don't take my eyes off the steaming cup of coffee. Locked up in here, I look like an earthworm, after all, I am skinny. It was the only thing I hadn't experienced: Having a biscuit in my hand that I never finish and a resentment in my stomach. The black raindrops between the cracks in the concrete blocks, dripping mud. *Your theories about the grassroots social base are treason, the compañero in charge says, putting his forty-five down on the table. I know I'm in the way of those who believe in the "cojones" thesis; you can pull the trigger and that's the end of it; I'm a good recruit, like in the Mexican song, one who wrote poems and made life better.* "You on the other hand are a son-of-a-bitch." *I didn't have any other way out, given his threats and bogus heroic gestures.* I get sunlight once a week, I'm in a farm house that could be anywhere in the country. I have nothing to fear but death. I'm awake, watching the water flow, my eyes swollen. I like to exercise beneath the beautiful sun. My sun. Solitary sun. Sun, you that gets up in the morning. Sun, you that sleeps. The small, important things. Goodbye Manuel. You are different, Jorge, but you aren't an asshole either. To see my pine forest, my cabins by the river where we began to die. *When will we be together again, Genoveva?* I have to urinate. I better get used to doing it just once every twenty-four hours, because I don't have a choice. Or I could urinate on the wall, by the edge of my bed, but that would be bad manners. They take me to the john when the sun is barely up, too bad. I try to take my time, to give the sun a chance to come up. Then I return to the humid cell, to this shitty basement. Through any small crack that I invent I watch the last stars fade away, it's a good sign because it means that in some way you are coming—joyous day!—with your bright, clear eyes, day wrapped in cellophane paper. Instead, I'd better take a stroll through the coffee farms. *Mounted on a horse more beautiful than light, a mountain appeared pawing at my horse, a wave of blood. They are secret things, Genoveva, I can't tell you when I'll return, I myself do not know.* We remain in a cadaveric, incomprehensible muteness. Will they understand me when I talk to them? It didn't appear that this would end up bad for me. A way of not existing in this unusual life experience, one sees things and doesn't believe them: eyes, touch, an abyss that flows to the sea which is death. The great lords of destruction, that's what we are. *A way to be forgotten, in a family house, attics where there's room only for mice,* toi et moi, *mice ready to eat your eyes out; I breathe the fragrance of pine trees when I see Genoveva.* Was it worth ending up in this incomprehensible hole? I'd like to go out on the streets and live. I myself chose this path that leads underground. *You and me, Genoveva, we are the product of imagination. I have everything here and I don't even have to be thankful, it's the rule of any prison. Obligatory rule: Don't look like a beggar, eat your food out loud, with pride, like you did in the mountains. Moral: Food is more precious than freedom. (Can I come visit you?) It would be better if you didn't, Genoveva, you'd make me feel naked and I have nothing with which to cover myself except for my hands, my strangely filthy fingernails.* I'm below sea level, but my sentiments—that I express in some fashion—are celestial. I expect to remain locked up until the day of my death. An hour of confabulation is worth more than a day of freedom. My name is Alfonso, but you can keep calling me Al, Genoveva. *He thinks that I'm asleep when he opens the room / cell. His omnipresent forty-five. For his satisfaction, I keep my eyes shut. His eyes are closed too, in this darkness the eyes of all are extinguished. Only the eyes of the forty-five shine. And my brain is blown to bits.*

— *x* —

I hadn't written you in days. I was nervous, you know. Anyone will tell you I'm not sane. It was impossible to write to you when Jorge came, because I had to do some outside-of-class assignments (Nowadays they really keep us busy with work in the night classes I'm taking at the University). By the way, we have to go to Acajutla tomorrow, for a job in the country; even though we do so with fear because the Guard takes us out of buses and beats the crap out of us, because we are traveling in the university bus, and that's very dangerous, as you well know, especially on the highways. I suppose you know about the massacre that took place on the thirtieth. I thought about sending you clippings or something, newspaper articles about the things that are happening, but I changed my mind. In one of those photos you can see me holding a poster. I'm going to be honest, we were all afraid that day, because in the newspapers they had threatened to repress our protest march, and, as soon as we were organizing in the Sciences and Humanities Park, there were small planes circling overhead, dropping leaflets on us. Despite that, everything began well. At first, I was up in front with a compañero named Carlos Fonseca. When we were passing the Children's Hospital, my legs began to tremble, you know, with the motherfucking planes (excuse the metaphor) and the number of threats in the newspapers; I started to fall behind until I was in the middle of the group, there at least I felt protected, from whom or what, I don't know, because up until then I was just uneasy about the small planes strafing University Avenue. When we reached the Polyclinic, I saw Carlos Fonseca, who had also fallen behind, or rather he was moving with the people looking for me until we bumped into each other and he told me that I should get out of there, that the police were up ahead; then I lost sight of him, he went to the front of the demonstration, where the banners were carried; what I did was go off to one side, along the sidewalk, and I continued walking with a group of people. When we got to the Social Security Hospital, I saw hundreds of heads running, and farther back, on the overpass, the tanks advanced with their headlights on, you can imagine, at four in the afternoon, with the immense sun like an egg cooking in a frying pan; the tank lights were distant stars that were coming to crash into us. I remained standing for a while and then I went back; when I was passing the Polyclinic, a woman who had a *pupusa* stand pulled me and two other girls over by her stove, that's why I wasn't able to tell what was going on up ahead; after a while we decided to leave because we couldn't take the smoke from the stove and also because the woman had pushed us under the table, she almost pulled our hair out, and the sound of gunfire increased; we weren't going to stay there paralyzed with fear. I saw several compañeros captured and carried away right before my eyes. Some Guardsmen had infiltrated the demonstration, singing and shouting, mixing in among the students. We realized this when from our own group several men started pulling out pistols. They tied the thumbs of some of the students together and threw them into the back of military trucks that came from the rear or appeared at intersections. I saw this with my very own eyes. They killed the compañeros who were up in front carrying microphones and banners, they were the first to fall. They killed Carlos. To this date his remains have not been found, I mean, that those who fall into their hands are never returned, not even the bodies of the dead, they say that this is to prevent them from being turned into symbols. It's their new tactic: making them disappear. There are only two casualties at the Social Security Hospital, the nurses and doctors picked them up in middle of gunfire, they were the only ones spared from being taken away in the military trucks and later disappeared. They saw Carlos fall with his head badly wounded, some other compañeros were going to pick him up when a national guard patrol appeared on the corner firing their weapons, someone shouted "hit the ground!" and we did so. Fifteen students died, some of them were women. Perhaps I felt the same when I was twelve and my father died, I mean it, it's a different kind of pain, I know, but I'm talking about how it affected me. Maybe I'd started to love him; well, I hadn't told you that he used to come to our house, Aunt Gracia thought highly of him. And now, several weeks later, they kill Flavio, they've killed Flavio, Carlos' brother! They say it was a coincidence, but the only certain thing is that a military patrol killed him as he was leaving the Regis Cinema, he was barely fifteen years old. They didn't even wait a month to finish off an entire family. They say the patrol asked him for his documents and when he was showing them to them, they filled him with holes. They shouted son-of-a-bitch at him while a fat man, in civilian clothing with his hair hanging in his face, discharged his machine gun on him. What can we do? A demonstration of mourning has been the most impressive, a demonstration of women dressed in black: students, women from the markets, teachers from ANDES—the National Association of Educators—workers, slum dwellers. The demonstration ended up at the cathedral where a meeting was held; before that we had passed by the Social Security hospital, we sang as we went along. What else could we have done? We all wore red carnations and when we reached the gate of the Social Security Hospital we placed the carnations in holes in the decorative bricks. It was a red wall of carnations. While we were placing the carnations there, a nurse from the hospital comes out and shouts out that one of the wounded students has just died. Then we stop singing, because the words won't come out of our throats. A while later there was a storm, one of those terrible August rainstorms. We didn't even move. Because we didn't know what to do, do you understand? We got completely soaked by the rain. The protest march turned down Arce Street in the direction of the cathedral. At that moment, someone came out from the middle of the group of people: It was a priest, he climbed the railing and from there he began to say mass for the dead. And it kept raining. As there was no microphone, he had to shout out the things he said; we couldn't hear anything. Yesterday, there was another demonstration. Tell me, don't you think we're doing something for the dead? It started at Cuzcatlán Park. The small planes once again started flying about overhead. I, frankly, felt like crying, and I cried, we all cried, at least those of us compañeras who were together in a group, with crowns of flowers and songs. Perhaps they were frightened too, and they didn't dare stop the demonstration of mourning. Do you think those people know fear the way we do? For us, an attack was imminent, because it always happens that way: If there are planes over one's head it's because there's going to be a massacre. They are like birds of ill omen, the *spitfire* planes or whatever the hell they're called. We reached Liberty Park at around five in the afternoon; until it started to get dark and the lights on the distant hills of Planes de Redentores came on. Halfway through the rally, inexplicably, they turned the lights off and we remained in the dark as night came on. People just kept talking from the pedestal of the statue of liberty. We started to hear gunfire nearby, they were shooting from the towers of police headquarters. You tell me, what else can we do for the dead? I forgot to tell you that I'm so nervous that when I close my eyes and open them one of them stays shut, it refuses to wake up. The doctor at the University says that it's psychotic. I don't know what's wrong with it. I'll write you again with more details, because this is starting to turn into a novel. A kiss from your ex-Ant.

— *xi* —

With a courage that is unexplainable at first. They go around with their rags displayed. Cotton fabric, from one stick to another one, and at each end a hand and a girl and a compañero. I am the girl who's going along touching her forehead. Because you know, one will try everything. That's the explanation. It was three in the afternoon. Like a party beneath the purple sun that rolls from the volcano, turned into little balls of fire. With rags that have writing on them:

"Down with Tyranny;" you know that all the rags say that; or "Fuck the Government." And children reading the phrases that are prohibited for children. We left the Second of April Plaza and headed towards the Francisco Menéndez Institute to ask the high school students to join us. That's me, wearing a scarf, walking quickly. Can't you see that air that is about me, following me? Not you guys! We shout to some little kids up on top of the Polyclinic bridge, who are barely twelve years old. They say yes, that they've been waiting for more than an hour to join the demonstration and that no one will keep them from marching. This isn't a children's march! Eat shit, you old people! "Well, come along then, you little shits, but you can't say that we made you do it! You'd better stay here, there's no telling what could happen! They whistle three times at us, their form of morse code to tell us: "Your mother!" We've got a right to march. We're tired of trying to dissuade you. Finally: Let's go, those up front are getting ahead of us! Carlos Fonseca with a megaphone pressed against his neck like a good luck necklace. Shouting: "Run, keep going forward!" And everyone turning at the Bloom Hospital down University Avenue. I'm running. That one in the yellow dress with the miniskirt, that's me. Hair tied with a scarf-souvenir from you. Everyone is happy, singing the songs we know by heart because we've gone to the streets to fight the police so many times. They throw tear gas at us and we throw it back at them. They, with their television Martian faces, and we, covering our faces with handkerchiefs that we dampen in the Twisted Figure Fountain, in front of the embassy, and then we'd dip them in baking soda to neutralize the gas. The wind blows the fountain water on us. The American embassy watching us with electronic eyes. The wind is purple from so much three-in-the-afternoon sunlight. The drops of water becomes large and then tiny. "Line up in four columns," Carlos shouts; but no one pays attention to him, because we don't hear him and we're all very close together. All of sudden he pulls out his megaphone and we can now hear his instructions. Everybody in four columns, don't get too close together. And the snot-nosed kids from the Francisco Menéndez Institute formed one single block, in their heavy cotton uniforms. Carlos shouts, if they want to join in they must stay in four columns. The school kids are mixed in together with the university students in Chemistry and Humanities. "We've got to make sure nothing happens to the little shits," someone shouts. (Go to hell, you old fogies.) The front of the group is getting way ahead of us, the person in charge of leading and taking care of our group warns. We continue down the avenue, leaving the embassy and Pete's Cafeteria behind. No provocations, the megaphone shouts. Because, all of us were afraid to do anything—even cut a fart—near the embassy. The fountain keeps spouting water of every color upwards into the air, confetti water drops. Damp rags, wet banners to use against the gas. Then that damn plane showed up. The same one that had flown over the University campus in the morning. Dropping leaflets with threats and other cowardly things. And that is why we got mad as hell when we saw it pass overhead, with its stinking leaflets against the cancer at the university, against the worthless students. From below we could see their green uniforms, with green stripes like Malaysian tigers, their berets of brave soldiers killing Japanese warriors in the islands of the Pacific, murderous John Waynes. We, raising our fists and shouting. That one with her hand raised is me and those are the snot-nosed kids from the Chico Menéndez Institute. This time the small plane didn't drop any leaflets, we could see their Malaysian-tiger uniforms clearly in the plane as it performed rolls and then strafed University Avenue. They were keeping us under control, the sons-of-bitches, determining our location: "They are now passing the illuminated Twisted Figure fountain." I can see the front of the demonstration from the Bloom Hospital and the Boulevard of (hog-wash) Heroes. To the right, the volcano with many small luminous fountains rising through the residential neighborhoods. From behind, from my position, I could see the first armored cars by the Social Security Hospital, their headlights gave them away. They were going down the hill by Rosales Hospital. I mean they were on one side forcing the traffic to take a detour on the overpass. They were changing the direction of traffic so there wouldn't be any witnesses. At first we only saw some twenty guardsmen and five armored cars waiting to greet us in the area where the hospitals are located. Our megaphones telling us we should remain in four columns and that we should stay calm and not disperse for any reason nor should we get too close together; if it became necessary, the best thing to do—for those who could—would be to head to the right, towards the highway that goes to the Miramonte barrio. Those in the middle of the serpent had to retreat and those in the rear had to disperse in the area of the Tutunichapa riverbed. Do not run, remain calm everyone, obey the megaphones. Because it was the first time we were face to face with armored cars. It was no longer a question of police and guardsmen disguised as Martian gas throwers. Suddenly we realized that up ahead, near Cuzcatlán Park, several squadrons of guardsmen were approaching with their respective armored vehicles. And we, our posters raised, with "Down with Tyranny" written on them, "Murderous Government," etc. The squads of guardsmen behind their armored cars, their Malaysian-tiger uniforms from some John Wayne movie. I saw Carlos again with his megaphone, ordering us to disperse. The columns went down towards the highway, to the right, and those in the middle of the serpent headed to the left. In the middle, I started up the hill by the overpass. Most of the people didn't hear the order to take the side streets and they pushed onward towards the hill. All of a sudden we were packed together on the bridge. Then we had no way to go except forward, to take Third Street. Everyone was running across the overpass. That's when the first shots sounded. They fired on the group packed together with no way to go but forward. The Malaysian tigers were firing on us. I took off running towards the highway, but it was impossible for me to make any headway, those behind me were pushing like a block. I could barely see because of the gas, confusion, and shooting. The brats from the high school were the first to jump off the bridge, they dropped fifteen feet below, one on top of the other. It was a trap, because we were boxed in. I was about to jump off the bridge but stopped when I saw my compañeros below moaning. The one in the flowery dress with a wet scarf in her mouth is me. The minions of the law were getting closer and closer, the ones who were advancing through Cuzcatlán Park. The same armored cars that had turned on their headlights. They advanced beneath the afternoon sun with their yellow lights. Anti-cancer, anti-student tanks. I couldn't wait any longer so I jumped. With an intense pain in my stomach, I started to vomit, vomiting on my compañeros who had fallen on the pavement. I touched my legs because I felt wounds, pieces of skin scraped off. I kept vomiting on the brats in canvas uniforms who hadn't been able to get up. The youngsters from the Chico-Kid, go-take-a-hike Menéndez Institute. I still had my pita fiber handbag over my shoulder, who knows how I kept from losing it. I took out my bag of baking soda, I'd forgotten about it, the little bag that I had soaked in the fountain—where there was a gush of water that got larger and smaller—and I drew it to my nose. Once again, the fresh, July air and the purple wind of the Jabalí Volcano reached me. We were still out of range of the Malaysian tigers, because they were detained up there, on University

Avenue. I'm saying we should get up before they start shooting down on us. We go through Tutunichapa towards the marginal areas. I mean that we escaped from under the bridge; others ran too, limping, but alive and moving. The marginal settlers received us with buckets of water and then gave us some dirty rags so we could dry ourselves off; and the women were crying: not because of the gas, but because they couldn't think of anything else to do but cry—the poor things!—and they told us to come in. We said no, that we'd better reach the Boulevard of (hog-wash) Heroes. Over there we skirted the dry river bed. A group of settlers leads us along paths, behind the San José Day Academy. We: Wouldn't it be dangerous for them to see us together, I mean, for you guys. And they: What the fuck! Excuse me, miss. Before that they invited us in and served us coffee, there were eight of us students.

— *xii* —

One of us had a broken foot, an armored car had tried to run him down and almost crushed him against the gate of the Social Security Hospital. We told ourselves it would be better to leave. Told the people: that we should leave in pairs, the women first. I went in front, an old woman with grey hair told us she would lead us. Other people from the poor barrio cried, until we reached the Metro Center shopping mall. Our clothing—wet from the water they'd thrown on us to neutralize the gas and to fight the heat and our tears—was now dry. We were all thinking the same thing: "I was in the second block of the demonstration; we took off running to the east but were forced to stop by gunfire. I saw when the megaphone shouted: 'Hit the ground' and we all got down; of course we couldn't hear it, but we saw the signal 'Hit the ground.' Other compañeros didn't understand and they tried to climb the wall of the Social Security Hospital, some were able to pull it off, but when the men dressed as tigers discovered that escape valve they went over there. They drove their armored cars against the wall, smashing those who were trying to climb it, a few were able to jump to the other side. Several were crushed. I saw the compañero with the megaphone fall, his head destroyed by a bullet. I saw him fall into a gully, with the megaphone still strapped around his neck. He had told us to hit the ground, but he himself didn't. Streams of blood began to flow in the gutters, becoming heavier, a red ball coming apart, fleeing from something. When I raised my head I saw that the zebras painted like Malaysian tigers were petrified, they had just gotten out of their armored vehicles, and all of a sudden they were immobile. A compañero let out a shout saying pick up the wounded. As if we were on a picnic! The tigers were not moving. One of the zebras was trembling, bathed in sweat, with a look of dirty water in his eyes, that is, water and shit, and he shouted at us to leave, to get up, as if we had been taking a siesta! We realized that he too was dead but didn't know it. That's when an officer arrived who slapped him in the face; he threatened us with a machete, he told us he was going to cut our heads off; the Malaysian tiger, who moments before was paralyzed, came back to life and started to shout at us too. They went up to a compañera, who insulted them from the ground; one of the tigers hit her on the head with his rifle butt. That's when I started vomiting and I saw a red liquid coming out of my mouth and nose, and I saw that the painted zebra was coming towards me, his machine gun aimed at the bloody vomit and I was the one who told him to pick up the wounded." Somebody else: "They grabbed me in the back of the demonstration crowd. Everything was chaotic there, because, besides the gunfire and the tear gas, we watched as agents dressed as civilians came out of the groups of spectators in the street, pulling out their pistols, firing them. We were also attacked by a group of 'spies' who had come from behind the demonstration, hidden in trucks covered with canvas canopies. The gas hit me in the face and I felt myself fainting and although I tried to get up, I couldn't. Suddenly I felt two 'spies' take me by the arms and they struck me on the head, take that you asshole so that you'll learn to think better, and more blows to my head and I fainted and they threw us in the same covered trucks. They took us in the direction of Guard headquarters. In the truck, I started to come to. When we reached Guard headquarters, we were separated into groups of five and locked in cells. Then they interrogated us, along with tremendous beatings on our backs and heads until they got tired and we started to shout to the heavens; they wanted us to denounce our compañeros for having instigated the battle, as they put it. They would come to our cells to tell us: 'Tomorrow we're going to give you fried pork fat,' which meant they were going to kill us; we remained silent, because they appeared to be drunk and they were always trigger happy with their machine guns. We didn't sleep at all that night. A compañero who by some miracle hadn't lost his watch told us the time. At six they began to beat their drums, the time for the them to give us fried pork fat had arrived. We heard the noise of boots that produced sparks on the bright bricks. They opened the cell door and screamed that our final moment had arrived. They made us line up near the swimming pool behind a wall. One of the guards came over to blindfold us, amidst insults and shouts. 'With these shitty students, we're not going to have peace in this country until we kill every last one of them, but there are so many of them that we're not going to have enough bullets.' And he said other things like this. Someone gave the order to fire and shots rang out! They were using blanks or maybe they fired into the air, who-the-hell-knows what they were up to, because our eyes were blindfolded. They laughed heartily like well-fed kings. Some of the compañeros started to talk, especially the weaklings that couldn't take the torture and preferred to sign documents denouncing the leaders of the demonstration." Another person: "I'm a nurse and I work at the Social Security Hospital. This afternoon we found out the students were coming, but we never imagined what could happen. We realized what was going on when we saw the planes strafing the hospital. At around four thirty we heard a great uproar, many voices and the sound of running feet and gunfire, machine guns being fired, someone shouted: 'They are killing students.' Yes, because we were already used to hearing about them killing students, but until then I had never imagined that there were going to be so many dead and wounded. We left the hospital without thinking that we could be struck by a bullet, the spectacle was sickening, a cloud of smoke in the street and blood flowing in the gutters, bodies left abandoned on the pavement, the guards still shooting and some children and young people falling down wounded, shouting to stop shooting, but the gunfire was terrible. I saw several little boys' heads peeking over the wall as they climbed it and then jumped into the grass around the hospital; others were unable to climb over and they fell back onto the street. Someone shouted to us to pick up the wounded and we went out into the street amidst the smoke and gas, but then they came at us with their rifle butts and fired shots into the air. They beat us. We were able to rescue several kids, among them a little girl completely mangled, she was one of those who fell from the wall when the armored vehicle started to scrape it. We tried to give her strength, as we carried her in our arms, already inside the hospital, telling her that she would get well, maybe she couldn't hear us, but just in case we talked to her although we knew that she was going to die, she had lost a lot of blood and was in terrible condition. I say she listened to us because she opened her eyes and it was as if we had been looking at each other for a long time and that you shouldn't worry, if she wanted, we would sing for her, and as she was hardly more than a little girl, I wanted to sing a song to her, but everything would have seemed unreal in that smoke that was getting into the hospital rooms. Instead I whispered something in her ear: that Mommy was going to be right here and that soon she would be taken to the operating room, sleep my dear child. And she responded telling us not to worry that I'm going to be okay, who knows where her voice came from. And all of us around her started to cry. We couldn't help it. Besides, the damn gas hurt our eyes. Our tears were another matter, of course, they were pouring down, filling our throats with stones."

— *xiii* —

That day they took you to the bathroom with a rag covering your eyes. But, what's going on? They sat you down on the toilet. The water tank began to overflow, getting you all wet. Your hands were tied behind your back. You wanted to get up to search for the door and you realized that your feet were tied together. You fell on your face. The water drenched your body. Time passed and you remained asleep beneath the water, you remember the puddle you fell into. Maybe I'm going to drown. My compañero Manuel was an asshole right from the start, you thought.

— *xlv* —

Dear Al: Congratulations on your birthday and may you have many more, just like Aunt Gracia. We spend our time here consoling one another sometimes, at other times fighting over any small thing. We're fine, although my Aunt believes that the ground is calling for her; sometimes she thinks she's very ill and she fights with me because I point out that there is nothing wrong with her. "Stop being a pest, niece, you just want to be the one who's sick and not me." The latest illness that she says she has is that "my heart is fluttering, I've only got one year of life left." And who told you that. My doctor. Then tell your doctor that your niece says he's full of shit, it's deceitful to make people feel ill. Those are my conversations with my aunt, Al. On another subject: this year they got rid of the water problem in the streets (they put in a drainage system), because in winter you need a canoe to cross the courtyard, a large lagoon forms there and the next day it has dried up. My Aunt says: "Bullshit, I just hear a wooshing noise, the sound of water escaping to who-knows-where, these damn rooms are going to sink and come crashing down on my head." She's no longer afraid the walls are going to cave in, but she thinks the neighbor's mango tree is going fall on her, every time it rains she complains: "Listen to that shitty tree creak, one of these nights it's going to crush me." Or she is afraid that some night someone will come in and strangle her, because the other people who live in the house never close the gate. So, in order to avoid problems, next year she's going to make another courtyard to separate our house from theirs, and then we'll see whether or not they close the entrance. That's life. *Ciao.* Your ex-Ant.

V

BACK IN THE FOREST

— *i* —

I don't know why it is that every time we come into this house we are two invisible beings. So to speak. When I look at you—I'm spying through a small crack anywhere—there you are, in spite of your vague forms. When you look at me, you pass through my body and end up running into the shelves with photographs in the hallway. And when my body goes through yours, you act as if you're driving away the gusts of wind that are created when someone passes by your side running, leaving behind that feeling of stalking flies. Or you simply get angry. At any rate, that matter of meditating upon whether or not it's beneficial to be two invisible beings, trying to safeguard responsibilities, what it does is avoid problems. This is to die, understand it, Ant.

We pass through objects, we don't bump into any obstacle. We are like radar. We've never run into a chair, we don't make noise when we eat, we don't need doors opened for us. Let's spell it out, it's as if we didn't exist. Two invisible beings, indescribable, inaudible, incredible.

"You don't take care of yourself, you're not a little copper coin or a pathetic piece of antique furniture, like in the song '*Tango Bar.*'"

"I feel kind of dizzy, sometimes I wonder if it's sleeplessness, I've had a hard time sleeping of late, did you notice?"

"Don't talk to me about that, I hear you when you move around in bed, the creaking of your bed beneath my room."

"You're not going to tell me that from your room..."

"Of course I hear you, that noisy bed in the silence of the night."

"I thought so. That's when I hear you too. I suffer when I think they could be listening to you. I wouldn't like for them to see you come in."

— *ii* —

I thought about the most isolated part of the house, perhaps there's room in the empty, unhealthy attic; I never thought it would be on top of yours, I mean above your room. Those inconveniences, of course. Mutual sleeplessness and no one is to blame for anything.

"You're imagining things, Ant, I wouldn't let them think badly of you."

"It's not that."

"It would be a lack of respect for you, breaking this silence which unites us. This separation has its advantages precisely for that reason: it joins us when we least expect it. We're in hot water."

"You're dreaming, that's all."

"I'm dreaming?"

"That's right, you're dreaming that I'm thinking and saying that you're coming to knock on my door; actually nothing's happening, we're each on our own."

"Sometimes I get up when I start to feel dizzy and my head spins around and around. Everything falls apart. Like a Ferris wheel with tiny horses made of sand, it turns and turns until it finishes me off."

"You ought to see a doctor."

"Yeah, I should."

"I'm not kidding."

My head rattles like those enchanted carts pursued by the howls of dogs, perhaps because only they can see the bones writhing in the bed of the cart. With a black bell on its mast. Peeling at midnight. Making the pale *amate* flowers fly away. My thoughts clatter, throwing off sparks. Sometimes I say: The reason we think about these things is because we don't have enemies. Our enemies are buried and they leave us in that depressing tranquillity. We ourselves are those beasts with ghost faces, invisible beings, enchanted oxcarts, etcetera.

— *iii* —

"I've got to get up to breathe some fresh air, when I start suffocating from being in this small, dark room when the mice—that go about the roof and get under my bed—won't let me sleep. I'd advise you to tell Aunt *Desgracia*, I mean Aunt Gracia."

"You always call her that."

"Call her what?"

"Nothing."

("Grandmother, why don't we shut the window?"

"It'll be dark."

"So that the cats and mice don't come in.")

I'd like to see you when you get up to think, I'd get up and follow you to the courtyard on those hot nights, get a little night air, a small breeze. Or it'd be better if you'd climb the stairs to invite me to go with you to look at the sky, always with the same stars, the same sketches in the night. I'm sitting on the overhang of the breakwater, the lights on a sea full of boats. A sea different from ours. Through a small window I see the house lights. I see myself twenty years younger, seated on the peer of the breakwater. The dark waters of the gulf.

— *iv* —

I tell her that everybody has to be happy, out of necessity. She replies that that is fine. Well look, I try to order my thoughts and I just can't express myself clearly. Everything seems to sink, it's an intense trembling. I'm talking about happiness, silly. Happiness is silly? I'm talking about you. You're offending me. I call you silly the way I'd say little flower or butterfly, you know.

"When you came to our house you seemed a rude person to me, you spent Sundays shut up in your ugly room. Who knows what you saw in that attic, where the cats and mice won't let you sleep and let's not talk about the stench. They were poisoned and they went off to die in their caves in the roof."

"I'd go out sometimes, you didn't notice, I'd go to the library."

"You'd go off for long periods of time without saying where you were going." "When I'd come home from school, you were already in your room, doing who-knows-what, reading, I don't know and you didn't show your face except at mealtime."

"They are habits of discipline."

"Asleep in your dark room."

"Concentrating on the noise of the mice."

"The first time I used the Mousekill, you got mad."

"It was because of the stench from the dead mice."

"Then you cooperated with me."

"I had to poison mice to be with you."

"Do you know that they came looking for you?"

You're asking me that to change the conversation. You're asking me that with a voice that is hoarse and weak, on the verge of its sixty-fourth birthday.

"I don't know."

"I had the impression that they were people of few words, they ask a question and remain silent; they look around with curiosity."

("Do you want to wait around for him?"

"No."

"Have a seat.")

"They didn't say anything else?"

"They turned around and left."

"And you were thinking about me?"

"I wasn't thinking, I looked at the strangers and that's all."

And I start getting really scared. Someone comes looking for you and I don't know who it is. A problem, Ant. When a stranger comes to your house, it's something bad, something is happening in someone's life. All of a sudden I'm at an important age. That happens, one turns twenty-two and strangers show up looking for him.

("Well, if you don't want to wait for him, don't keep standing in the door.")

"It's just an expression, right?"

"Maybe they're your classmates?"

"I couldn't say."

"It seems strange to me that they would come wanting to know about you, they ask for you by name and want to know about your background, and you don't know anything about it."

"Let's not make a big deal out of it."

"Of course it's a big deal."

"Is Alfonso home?" they asked. I: Perhaps he's at the library.

("If you want, you can leave him a message."

"No, it's personal.")

"They gave the impression they'd come back soon."

("If you don't find him there, look for him in the park,

he was carrying a few books under his arm. Do you want to know anything else?"

"No, thanks a lot."

"He's my compañero," I laugh nervously.

"They're all a bunch of whores," they said softly, and then I was terrified, you know.")

"Did they insult you?"

"But what can we expect from those strangers, Al?"

"I ask because it sounds strange to me."

"I didn't say compañero, that's the truth. I said that you were my boyfriend, and they looked at me as if I were spitting in their faces, because suddenly, their initial courteous attitude, changed. Imagine, saying that we're all a bunch of whores. It happened a few days ago, but I didn't want to tell you."

"You're not making this up, are you?"

"Next time I won't let them leave so that you can see with your own eyes."

She kept looking at me as if everything were true. She had been to the laundry room to chat with Aunt Gracia.

"Ant didn't come home for lunch, she has final exams," Aunt Gracia says, "but she'll be here soon."

Ant is a liar, one of these days when she's by herself ironing, Saturday, I'll calmly interrogate her. It's a question of intuition.

"It's true, if you don't believe it, that's your problem." As I look at her hair disheveled by the wind of the street; she's just returned from her exams. It's true, I state with conviction, image of the Souls in Purgatory. Now you can see my feet, my dirty shoes, they've gone a month without being cleaned.

"Next Sunday I don't have much to do, if you want I could clean them for you," once again changing the subject.

For the first time I realize that everything Ant said is true. You should forget about me. Maybe it has to do with my friendship with Rodrigo. You're suspicious, the next time I'm not going to tell you anything so you won't be anxious.

"Did they look like police?"

"They looked like hatred."

— v —

Like the mouse, in a cat and mouse game, that's the way I feel these nights and every night I dream and let out shouts that slither down the attic steps towards the hallway. The rat crawls over my body and the cat digs her claws into my dirty head which serves her as support for her mortal leap into the shadows. I turn on a light and the feline appears with an animal in her mouth, an animal between her teeth, kicking; her legs tremble, her fur stands on end. "What's going on?" someone shouts from the room next door. It might be Aunt Gracia. "Nothing," I say from the hallway and from the other side of the dream without taking my eyes off the red eyes of the cat who takes off lickety-split through the same window she came in, the window that opens to the dark sky at night and the sun in the day. The window is an open hole in the wood, with bars to prevent access to the roof of the house, where Aunt Gracia's imaginary maids sleep cockroach style. Beneath the stairway and behind the door that opens into Ant's room, I sense the special panting of every night (the light was just turned off) and I can no longer get any sleep because of that damn cat. Ant continues to pant, moaning, breathing deeply, as if at the time the cat came in she had rescheduled her sleep, like me. And then, just like band musicians when their director's toothpick starts moving up and down, they become silent to lead into the second piece, that silence that means wait, something else is coming. That's what happens when I turn out the light. A moan comes from Ant's mouth, not of pain, but of self-destruction, the assailant's knife penetrates the wound, continues, accompanied by lamentations, a blade breaking membranes with its sharp point, a knife in a previous wound, and the only thing it does is penetrate, because the lesion has already been inflicted, below the abdomen, in the intimate parts of her being; stuck in her mouth, in her closed eyes, tonight and all her nights of insomnia; I have opened the door first, it makes a creak that puts my nerves on edge. My molars chatter with the musical rhythm of a *sacabuche;* then I go down the stairs, one by one, measuring the steps, the distance in leagues per hour, until I reach the middle of the staircase, that is, level with the ceiling of her room; between the ceiling and her door there is an open space. I straddle the door, my dreams vanish, I see that the lights are out (I see them with my eyes turned on); the door squeaks under the pressure of my body. Ant lets out a sigh, here I am completely asleep. *I'm a person whose heart jumps as he places a foot on the threshold of the door and scurries along like that very cat that wakes me at night.* She sighs again with her asthmatic panting. I'm alone, accompanied by her breathing of an awake woman, but she pretends to dream about men who, when two o'clock in the morning rolls around, come down the stairs and pass through the door that opens into the solitary Ant's room. A person hanging from the roof, like the nest of a *chiltota* bird that hangs to the ground, via the creaking wood that passes for a staircase and not by the invisible thread created by flight. And what if she lets out a scream?

— *vi* —

i sense your arrival as if you were coming to rest in my body, from the time the door creaks i sense your arrival, the rhythm of your breathing, your bare foot on the landing as if it were a musical flute, the accent of your body in the air, a bell

i sense your arrival, i sense you my love; you're standing in the darkness, in front of the bed where i sleep awake and naked, with my legs closed and my hair over my face

i walk slowly, measuring the beats of blood until i touch the bed and i proceed to sit down, my soul thunders and the bed, moving me upwards, flying, entering the nest, and then i lie down with ritualistic lethargy, first my buttocks, then i place my hands on the open area of the bed

i move myself to one side to give him the opportunity to lie down, my tenuous respiration, a slight movement, his hand is burning

i don't know whether to hug her or go directly to her panties and pull them down as if i could take it or leave it, and touch; she's probably naked and i touch her close to her bellybutton and she shudders sending a message through my erect nerves, upright just like the bell tower of Don Rúa's Church

i become a statue again, without moving my hand from her tummy, i sketch a rainbow with my arms, without touching her skin, my hand is a little animal, a spider with five legs, moving down until reaching fear, a caress incapable of waking anyone

who is it?

i've dropped my arms on her naked breasts and i don't say anything to her; who am i; you'd be ashamed and me too; finally, i work up courage and i tell her it's me

who's me? frightened

the one who comes down naked towards a naked woman or who remains asleep in his room without closing his eyes, while the cat goes by in pursuit of the rat over my body and exits through the window and Ant sleeps in the room downstairs, panting mysteriously, alone, calling someone who would get up and go towards her and lie with

her and in the morning they'd greet each other as if nothing
had happened the night before
    did you hear those nocturnal noises?
    yes, it was the cat going after a rat.

— *vii* —

The one who always goes around in a flowery dress and
stares at the geraniums in the garden—everybody likes
geraniums, especially if they're not stained with blood—as
if she were giving them away, her moist and brilliant eyes,
swimmers in a fish bowl covered by a veil that lets you see
no more than her glance. Please leave, Ant, if you don't want
a tragedy to impound our misery, or something like that,
get out of my room, you're not being very prudent; I'm
capable of throwing myself on her and suffocating her;
don't grit your play teeth at me any longer. Why were you
born with those lips disposed to opening up and revealing
a contrite attitude, an eternal smile? Don't you have
anything else to do? *And dimples appear in your smile, where
the pure water of your goodness is gathered.* I see the
photograph pinned to the wall in your room. I close my eyes
to see if you've gone and to imagine beyond imagination
and you are the same one who comes to serve the meal,
moving with nervous reactions, with your cat's feet, placing
them to the side so as not to make noise or perhaps to move
faster; you give the impression that you're going to go into
a death trance or that after each hour of life's activities
they're going to take you to the hospital. You're more
nervous than the last leaf of summer dangling from the
highest branch of a tree that doesn't know whether to fly or
to conquer immobility forever; if you please, perhaps I can
stay for a while, long enough so that you can keep
palpitating my heart, but not long enough to wound you

with real fevers, the result of having walked in the rain without carrying an umbrella and lacking a layer of natural plastic, what for, if all this has been like a solitary cadence, soft dream music.

— *viii* —

it was when i was sick

you've always been well behaved, the best boy in the world, the youngest of all

i take care of you because my aunt tells me to, if she didn't, i wouldn't come up to your room, anyway, i do so with the greatest of pleasure; it's because you are really different, besides, i take care of your illness, not you

don't think that i'm going to leave before i see you drink this little coffee, this small, hot tortilla made of tender corn, eat it slowly if you want to savor it most, i can wait

eat it up, you'll die of hunger, you haven't eaten all day and that's bad for your lungs, you don't want to see yourself coughing up blood, do you? don't tell me you want to die, no one would believe you, besides, who dies these days with so many medicines!

if all this is a paradise, what's lacking is imagination, you just have to want it and be happy every second of life; i don't know where i got the idea that we are imaginative people, do you know? we must have something in common for me to think that we are different from others, don't you think so?

— *ix* —

i watch you start falling apart from the heat of my fever; you are a play-dough figure, your fingers traverse my illness and you become softer all the time, i think that you have the texture of honey or of meltable objects. Or could it be that Ant is like images in the air, the sensation of nonexistence, of something vague; i know that the way i see you, that's the way i am; i see you the way i am; when you melt, when you speak to me with voices that come from inside a box of fruit, that's my voice; my way of seeing you is my way of being. The light that my eyes see for others is shadow, you're always in front of a mirror, on the other side of my conscience, seeing flashes

you're not alone, if you have me and Aunt Gracia who doesn't charge you anything for your medicines, so behave yourself and eat this *rigua*, a golden tortilla of tender corn, when i said dammit to you, it wasn't my intention to mistreat you, i was bored, that's all, from fighting with you so much, as if you were a little snot-nosed kid. Drink your coffee and stop bothering me, i don't want any food left on your plate, so if you can, lick them clean

you can't come downstairs until you've eaten everything; if you don't feel like eating, that doesn't hurt me; stop being so finicky or you'll starve to death; dying of hunger is a way of being, that's the key to our national identity. Shh! Behave yourself! Here's some sugar and a spoon

you're sitting on the edge of the bed, and you're not even a servant, and your dark eyes to top it off, if i could i'd tear them out of you and eat them up

you'd better go because i don't like you talking to me with the voice of a *zenzontle* bird

get down, pretty Ant, get going, before my hands touch you, go downstairs Madonna or i'll throw you down the stairs just to see you fly, get moving you white cream-filled cookie, dove, colored light bulb

and you take away the bread crumbs, no sentimental gestures; here lies Al with much sadness, he was never to blame for anything, dead in the attic of a house in the red light district of San Salvador, the pallid condition of his skin, an indication of the path of sleep eternal

then go to hell, Ant, if you don't want me to pinch you on your shameful parts; because it's my way of besieging you; we'd stay together until we got bored if you don't leave before I count to three, which means I'm saying goodbye to you, get going because that flowery apron makes me want you more, someday we'll say goodbye for good and the emotional debts will be paid off and we'll put on the greatest theatrical performance of our lives

think it's just a matter of a few days that you'll be healthier than a cat, making strange noises in the kitchen and telling those jokes about somebody's ass and a flute which is a way of looking for trouble; you should be obedient, you're too old to be going around telling distasteful jokes, you need a shave, look at your mustache, maybe you were a spoiled child, you were served your meals in bed and you always wore white britches until you were five

then why are you so silly and such an ingrate; i tell you not to touch me, it's just a joke; but be still if you don't want me to bind you by the hands; i'm not a ball of honey, i'm your companion, Ant, and i like you, that's all

watch out, don't let the coffee burn you; well, i'm everything you want me to be, but eat slowly, eat your rigua, eat your tortillas.

— *x* —

From the kitchen door, Ant: "Would you like a cup of coffee with cream?"

I go to the door and tell her to wait a moment, my intention is to turn it down, I feel lousy, it really is a sickness caused by this room, by these four walls that close in and move away from me singing, running, confining. Ant's steps on the stairs:

"I'm coming."

"Don't bother."

I remain there waiting to take the plate of bread and steaming cup of coffee from her. She gives me a look of disapproval and passes by me, pushing me to one side; she bumps into me as if she wanted to knock me down, to force me to lie down because I'm sick and I should be in bed, as she says five seconds later. "I'll get well, I've got to be patient," I respond without conviction. He that doesn't work shouldn't eat, but he that doesn't eat starves to death and I should accept Ant's way of offering me food. If it were up to me, I'd spend my whole life being thankful to her.

"It's a present for you," referring to the special banquet. "How can you stand to be in the dark?" she demands to know.

"It lets me think," I tell her. She acts like she doesn't understand, as if she were standing at the foot of a dead statue; but she watches with delight, scrutinizing, wanting to knock me off my pedestal. A jar of instant coffee rests on her tray; a small mug of coffee with cream would be good for you. She sets it on the combination shoe and night stand. I keep looking at her and I thank her for her courtesy. "Why have you taken bread from your mouth to give it someone like me to whom you owe nothing; I've never done anything for you, neither good nor bad, it'd be better for you to eat it, you look a little pale and there is sadness in your smile." The tray trembled when she set it beside the pitcher on the shoe and night stand. One movement and everything came crashing to the floor, Ant jumped up; as she picks up the bread, I help her pick up the dishes that have rolled under the bed.

"What a shame!"

She, confused, about to sink into the earth: "It was my fault." "Don't worry about it, what counts were your intentions, somebody else deserved that cup of coffee with cream and just offering it to me, from downstairs when you shouted at me, was enough for me. Leave me the bread," I tell her when I see her put it on the tray.

"I was frightened, you're going to think I'm a cripple."

"No, you're a person from another world; it was my fault."

"I can't replace the milk, the other things I can."

And she takes off running down the staircase. I watch her descend in the darkness. I look at the bread. I caress it and eat it up.

— *xi* —

it so happens you have a mother complex and I a son one. No one is going to like us this way, with that calloused way of being and expressing ourselves, a mixture of anxiety and desperation, like Mexican boleros

stop trying to sweet-talk me, and I'll give up my seductive poses. Give me my freedom, Ant, let me die of hunger, be my amorous euthanasia, I want to be famished, undernourished so that people will take me into consideration and say poor fellow, he just worries about everybody and has no hope of having his needs met. Poor guy, after all he is a being who barely hears about the things that are happening; am I perhaps the other nocturnal voice, inaudible, that no one sees whose mouth it is coming from, the word that expresses more than gratitude, surging from a place called the inside twice over, crannies of conscience, subterranean wing that is led by the sound of nocturnal murmurs

leave me, then, with my sicknesses, which is a way for

me to withdraw from mundane concerns, and i'm not saying this for you, but for those who think that there is another, better life than being a recluse. It'll be better this way. It's not as if you were the wolf and I Little Red Riding Hood; don't treat me like a weird person. That, far from helping me get better, makes me worse, understand it Ant, if you really hold me in any esteem, leave me now, don't bring me coffee, the best coffee in the world, because there are cockroach legs in it

you look like the word colloquy, especially when you stare at me wanting me to see you; you're like the strange voices, like the song that goes pih rih pah oh, knickknack, gloating, etcetera, metempsychosis; i'd drown you if i kept mentioning names; i won't climb another step, going up and down the stairs is not fun; i come up because i like you, dear compañero, the way you carry yourself, and nothing else; i could very well stop coming up; stop getting my dress dirty from these filthy walls, avoid the rats, but you don't appreciate what i do, you act as if i were here to get in your way; in this room you can't even think

now then, if you're staying here to get away from who-knows-what, that's a horse of a different color, but then I'm going to think that you're just acting ill

your long hands and equally long fingers, your fingernails of Castilian soap, crazy Ant, devourer of gardens, now you're here to bring me back to health, to remove my eyes, leave me blind, to whistle pretty songs to me while my ears hear only the sound of the storm. It'd be better if you don't come up, keep looking in the mirror down there, like other days, when I spotted you beyond that mirror, which was like a mirror to see you better, because I can see you without your knowing it, your rain-dimpled smile, your words that you say to yourself. So, it's preferable that you go downstairs now, it's better for both of us, and it'll be a way to die a little less.

In the afternoon, while I was taking a siesta, Ant came up to my room again. I heard her steps on the stairs. Here you come Ant, I tried to say to her, but it only occurred to me in my dream. I woke up with teary eyes because I was dreaming about my death, stretched out on a long pine table covered with flowers, my corpse too, yellow flowers, you could barely make out my face: a mask of bee honey; the only one crying around me was myself. Ant told me my eyes looked irritated. You're crying. You know that men don't cry, like it says in the military bible. Besides, I've slept since twelve-thirty. Ant looks at the clock: four o'clock in the afternoon. You're right, she tells me straight in my ear. I've come so you'll invite me to go somewhere, anywhere. I tell her that I can't, your aunt is angry, she's a fiend, I mean friend; if she finds out she'll kick me out of her attic. She tells me that she doesn't see anything funny about confusing fiend with friend, I tell her I don't either, but sometimes my tied gets tongued. I wouldn't have wanted Ant to come into my room. She always criticizes the chaos in which I live, the darkness, wretchedness, and mice. You chose this place, she says, she doesn't know why: she wanted to isolate me and have me above her room. You'd better go downstairs because Aunt Gracia could find out that you come up to my room, I tell her; because I don't want her to discover the wet dreams that force me to possess Ant every night. "I like to come up to your room, because we talk about all these crazy things," she tells me without specifying what she's talking about. And confronted with my question she replies: "The things that entertain us and make us live happily even though you are sick and I'm afraid something will happen to you." I don't tell her that I always want her to come to my room, and that when she is upstairs it's as if she were invisible and all my desires deflate. Maybe it's because of

Aunt Gracia who could throw me out of the house. "Are you good?" she asks me in a polite tone. She lifts her hands and places her open fingers over her eyes, looking from behind the bars, the cell that encloses her insane, dark eyes, within basins of jewelry, opening up excessively, trying to escape their prison. She lowers her hands and once again she's Ant with her eyes liberated. You're pretty, Ant. It has to do with nature and affection, that modesty of hers that never leads anywhere. Modesty is slavery. Then it does lead to something. Slavery is nothing. Those who enslave are another matter, they do exist. She asks again: "Are you good?" this time she takes my hands, she squeezes them as if she were getting rid of something. I don't know why we are libidinous and then I tell her to touch me here. She acts like she doesn't know what I'm talking about and for the first time I notice that she has a Leonardo Da Vinci smile on her face. She pretends she doesn't hear me so she won't have to slap me; she doesn't get upset, on the contrary, she has sat down on the bed, she is the queen, but I have to do something to dispute her throne. Caressing me, she moves from my hands to my arms. I wish you'd get over your sickness, she says as she slides her silky fingers up and down my arms. A wind on the surface of the sea, skin and wind whip my sheets. A bolt is about to fall killing both of us, I believe it. I lose my composure and I see little stars beyond her mercury eyes. "This bed squeaks," she says as she moves to a more comfortable position and I begin to wake up, because I've been dozing the whole time.

I think it'd be better for us to see each other tomorrow, she says, trying to get up. But now I take her by the arms and I never could have imagined that I would feel that softness that I can't feel on my own skin. I realize today that I need you, especially because of the red dress and blue flowers, I always see you different when you look like this and you wear a little red cap on top of your straight thin hair, unlike mine which is curly. A shadow passes across the ceiling and she uses the occasion to say that she's lost her fear of shadows, and she lies down beside me and lets my arms rest on her stomach and then I move them to her heart that is pounding on the verge of losing control. She pushes my hands aside. I explain to her that I only wanted to know whether she was about to die so that I could help her. The warmth beneath her dress is eternal. A few seconds later we aren't there, in the room, but in a distant place, where there is a river and a forest of young pines in the background. A heron crosses the sky and dives. "That's an airplane," she tells me. "A what?" I ask with surprise, because it had been years since I heard that word. "I can't explain," she says as we both watch the heron disappear behind the tree tops. "It committed suicide," I tell her softly. "You're crazy, herons don't commit suicide." Suddenly I know that I'm dreaming. I see a blue sky, the same small cloud hanging a few yards above the pines or my eyelashes. The heron climbs again and makes noises like those war planes and makes us think that they are planes that want to invade us. Poor heron. There ought to be a special sky for beautiful birds. The small cloud hangs on the end of a branch of the pine trees. "Did you know, did you know?" I tell her that I always have the same dream: I arrive sniffing around her place, a wooden two-story house, but I never work up the courage to go in to see her; then an enormous desperation overcomes me, because I can't see you, and because I can't rid myself of that dream it means that I'll never stop loving you. "You're always crazy," she says.

"It'd be better if we talked about other things," I tell her, fearing that Aunt Gracia could return from the market at any moment.

"Okay," she nods her head and withdraws her hands that have been close to mine, under the table. It's true, we have eaten together and we are at the dining-room table when Aunt Gracia appears and tells us that it's better if we don't sit down at the table at the same time, because neither of us eats anything, as if we were in a trance, hypnotized, get with it kids. I don't know if it's an accusation, but I take my hands from under the table and Ant does the same.

"The table is for eating," Aunt Gracia says.

"We digest our food conversing."

"If you don't eat you can't digest," and she repeats again that the table is for eating.

"And for dreaming too," I think I say.

— *xiii* —

And I tell her the fable of the cat and the mouse.

you are like the silky animal, the cat, your long television-antenna ears in the Jabalí Volcano your nose your eyes purple under mercury lighting your pampering all that that makes animals pretty you have frightening claws you are a domesticated animal beauty darkened by your teeth and claws you can see the blue eyes of the cats you're my kitty cat and I'm the mouse the one that appears at night up above my room my friend in the suffering his malignant illnesses propagator of incurable diseases assaulter of pantries cereal thief you do not respect respectable houses unbridled penchant for waiting around sharpening your nails honing your fangs a non-ferocious toothless cat is inconceivable and pursuer that generally makes it direct its attention on another animal the mouse

you inspire reservation damaging private property without submitting to the owners

of course the mouse is not an animal inclined towards piety or mercy modern science has relegated a place to it in the highly touted space of essays to discover the truth years more of life and cure for cancer on other planets the spirit of fear in rodents could be justified to a certain degree of course when they decide to hang a bell around the necks of cats the felines will become vulnerable and their beauty will be a silky mask mice will become the most courageous of the animals for the benefit of all

moral you've got to put a bell on the mouse.

— *xiv* —

One of these days is my birthday. Let me know. I'm going to give you a mirror, I've seen that you like mirrors, when you don't look at me it's because you're looking at yourself in the mirror. You keep your eye on me for sure. I can't tell you my secrets. I like to do what I like to do. I laugh, dance, assume poses, etcetera. I don't do anything bad, I'm sure of that. I don't tell you to do anything bad. You have to tell me what you do to see me, I can't be so trusting then; I don't like for you to do it, if you really do do it, tell me if you can spy on me. I hide behind the mirror. Impossible, because it's attached to the wall! There's the secret. I underst... I'm not crazy. Don't interrupt me, I tried to say that I understand. Once again the blue sky. That heron is an airplane, can you hear the noise it makes? A heron is a heron, silly. I'm not silly. You interrupt me too, I was going to say I'd get rid of it. What are you going to take back? I don't know. Were you crying? When? When I came in. I never cry, because since childhood they've told me that men are brave. Bored, then? Ant inquires. No, I reply.

177

Like a fourteen-year-old, Ant will show up with her choppy steps, flat turned-out feet, yellow or red dress, her canary or saint andrew or tree-of-fire complex. It's a nice thing to tell her, but she doesn't understand, she always feels like she's being talked about, especially when I call her crazy, silly garden ant. Ant rolls her caramel-colored eyes. Match-stick legs. Is that true? Mint stalks. She sits on the shoe and night stand. We talk as if we weren't there, but we understand each other well. Don't you love me? As a companion, yes. Do you think I'd be here in this room? We're lost in the mountains. What are you saying? Nothing. You illuminate the paths with the *ocote* pine torches of your fiery eyes. She throws herself from the shoe and night stand, she almost falls on the bed. Can I lie down? Lie down. What did you say? Nothing, sniff the deer's butt. Control yourself, I'm tired. Are you going to go help me in the kitchen? Do I have permission to sleep in your bed? I raise my head to look into her eyes. The Venetian windows of her eyes that speak. Did you sleep? Yes, said with a tenuous voice.

"Wake me up at a quarter till two."

"Did you think you were leaving like that?"

"What?"

"You're half asleep."

"Are you worried about it?"

"It doesn't matter, your Chinese peasant's eyes won't give you away."

Be quiet because you know that I'm about to besiege you. Everything is a product of the imagination. Having you tonight after the mice and the cat on the roof tiles. You get up from the table and my skin continues to sniff, pretty bitch, you gave yourself away for the last time. Follow me, she said. I went right behind her, I climbed the stairs. Two invisible beings. We always dream when we're seated at the table.

"Do you want to let me sleep?"

"I couldn't."

"I only have an hour to rest."

"Then why don't you leave?"

"I thought you liked me."

"Of course I like you."

"I came to your room to sleep for a little while."

"To place my arm on your tummy and sense you."

"Stop it."

"It's somebody's fault."

"What?"

"This."

"And what if Aunt Gracia comes?"

"She's not coming, that would be a *desgracia*."

"You're always adding an extra syllable."

"I've already told you that sometimes my tied gets tongued."

"Don't you like her?"

"I adore her, it's just that sometimes I stutter."

"What about your parents and brothers and sisters?"

Much of what is mine is mixed up with what is yours. Much later, I realize that something is happening in her tummy. I'm going to have a baby. You tell it to me in dreams. I'm an only child and an orphan, so I don't have any parents or brothers or sisters, I respond to her question.

"I'm inviting you to come with me."

"Where are you going?"

"To the Institute."

"What am I going to do at school? You've never invited me before."

"I'm inviting you now, it's a prize for letting me sleep."

She attends the Francisco (Kid, go-take-a-hike) Menéndez Institute.

"I can't."

"It's up to you."

"Letting you sleep is torture for me, I'd rather you talk with me. Asleep, you live in another world, where I can't follow you."

"Do you agree to go with me, yes or no?"

"Sometimes you get stranded between the states of sleep and alertness."

I am that son, I'm in my mother's arms, Mom sits on Grandmother's lap, this is the womb of my great-grandmother; in short, an interminable chain that binds all human animals in society. You say nothing. You keep eating atrociously. I haven't eaten in many years. Ant pretends she doesn't understand. She ignores any agreement between the two of us, she protests my lack of solidarity, my plans made behind her back. I act silly for a change. She insists. I tell her she's right, but that she has to understand. I watch the beans jump in the hot soup. I remember a woman who was my mother. I stop eating. My legs are asleep. Mamma in Grandmother's womb. Bring the midwife, but tell her not to smoke those stogies. Ashes could fall in the newborn's eyes. Did you know, Grandmother, that Mamma was a little girl? Yes. Grandmothers are wise.

You laugh with joy, then your eyes open like the headlights of a train in the night. Then I'll close my eyes, if they bother you, Ant says. And she continues:

"Your dreams make me laugh."

"Tell me why, if you're making fun of me," I say.

"You act as if you were full of pain, you remind me of the principal at the Kid, go-take-a-hike Institute. Don't you have a sense of humor?"

"What I don't like is not understanding you."

She's afraid she'll get pregnant. Her belly is swollen, on the verge of knocking the roof off the house if it keeps growing. Something is being born in my body. She's not talking to me about the baby or anything having to do with maternity. I kiss her enlarged bellybutton, the lower part of her tummy. I kiss, more than skin, what was the dream of a wanted child.

"I don't understand."

"You are my lungs, my laughter, my weariness and everything that has to do with breathing."

"You always have to say strange things."

"And your sense of humor?"

"It's not your gibberish, why don't you learn how to talk clearly?"

"Well, you laugh for me, I suffer for you, you speak I listen, you sleep with me I sleep in other heavens."

"You can't talk seriously, you're hopeless."

"Besides, the man wearing the bowler hat—I think his name is Don gibberish—I don't even know him."

Once again she is remembering any old thing. With her reflectors, she scrutinizes the most minute details of my expression, I can tell because she keeps looking at me and I have to cover my eyes with my hands. You dazzle me. You make me translucent.

She wakes up startled:

"Do you think it's two o'clock yet?"

"It's ten till, you're my alarm clock."

"It's my routine," she tells me. I give her a kiss.

Aunt Gracia shouts: Ant, where have you gone off to? I'm coming, I was hanging the clothes. She almost nabs us. Straighten your dress. The afternoon took us by surprise. See you later. Another kiss.

VI

BACK IN THE RED
LIGHT DISTRICT

You still have the old, faded newspaper clipping. You were a skinny guy then, now you've changed a lot; your cheeks are fat, you've eaten well since your scholarship to the San Juan Bosco school, with milk three times a day. When in your goddamn Catholic life had you gotten milk at each meal? Before, you were starving. Then other things happened: your desire to stay at the bakery, a loan to gain your independence. Then they tried to destroy the bakery that had cost you so much to start. Someone denounced you saying you had harbored a union member. Nothing happened because your buddies vouched for you. Nothing really happened until Noel showed up.

"Will you accept, yes or yes?" Noel asked.

"You know he's my brother."

"The poet?"

"No, he's not a poet, he hangs out with poets, which is another thing altogether. I'm the poet."

"I'm not saying you're an idiot, getting yourself involved in that monkey business. Work with me instead and things will go a lot better for you."

"You don't have to make decisions for me," and he stuck his gorilla-like hands in his pockets. Through oven-baked eyes, he could barely make out the blurred image of his friend Noel. Blind at twenty-five. What a tragedy. We the proletariat. And you remember Charrier—that's what you called your brother after seeing the French movie. He certainly has been lucky in life—you think about your

185

brother Charrier—he married a pretty, rich girl. Too bad he's mixed up in that foolishness, but he lives well, that's the important thing. He's always been lucky. Now he has disappeared. What will happen to Charrier?

"If it's poets you want to see, all you have to do is go to Pavos Carlotas' or Verniers' and tell us the things they tell you, even if all they talk about is poetry shit. We're not asking much—as you can see—and it's the only way you're going to get out of this day-to-day poverty, you can even study at the University, which has always been your dream, you can't deny it. Look how many lawyers we've been able to get to cooperate with us. Why, we even had a government minister work for us and we helped him out. You're smart too, think it over. Or are you satisfied with your bakery business? What little you earn you piss away in *guaro*, you have no goals in life. You gotta study, be somebody. Keep the photo as a souvenir. Remember how I helped you when they found that subversive union organizer in your house."

"I'm sorry, Noel, but I can't, he's my blood brother. You understand. And the others are poets, my brother's friends, how can you ask me to betray the things I love? And poetry as well. Who do you think I am, Cain?"

"Don't be stupid, telling us what they talk about is not a sin, it doesn't matter if they talk about poetry, tell me about it even if I don't like that crap. Besides, I won't do anything bad to them. But it's my job, and it'll be yours too."

Then he pulls his small simian hands from his pockets and begins to get animated. That way it'll be okay. You can study and compete with your brother and show him you aren't some kind of mental retard. You've seen what he reads, don't deny it, only books with red covers; red, just like their content. I'm not accusing him of being a commie, it's just an example of the kinds of things you can tell me. Get even now for all his put-downs, because you're a proletarian and he's an intellectual.

186

Several years earlier, I went to see him. I'm here to borrow a book of poems. He didn't invite you into his room, instead he criticized you, he said you were disorganized, that you didn't read, that you drank too much. You stayed there at the door until your brother was hoarse from letting you have it, come in then, and sit down. Shitty little bourgeoisie—you think. Read this and get some culture, it's poetry by Nazim Hikmet, and he handed me the book. If you understand poetry you can understand life, don't just stagnate. I'll return it in ten days, you told him. Put a cover on it so you don't get it dirty. My brother records the loan of the book in a small notebook. He thinks he's such hot shit. He doesn't trust me.

"And why do you want to know what they say in their poetry, if you think poetry is shit?"

"It's a matter of security, you know. One can never know too much, and besides, you shouldn't ask, I'll let you get away with it this time because you're my buddy, but I'm not going to tell you."

"I suppose you're going to want to know about the poetry my brother Charrier reads."

"Don't be silly, at first we won't ask you anything about your brother, let's begin with his friends, even if we were stupid we wouldn't expect you to be a Cain right off."

"Why don't you look for another informer?"

"Because I'm doing you a favor. It saddens me to see how your children are neglected and how your talent—your knack for reading and writing—is being wasted. You've already finished high school; that shows you have ambition. And I helped you, remember? Now it's up to you whether or not you get a university degree. Do you think I'd offer you this deal if I didn't think highly of you?"

And your wife and kids are suffering. Let me think it over.

"We'll see each other sometime, think it over."

187

Noel, you swine, son-of-a-bitch traitor. Do you take me for an asshole, do you think you're going to impress me with your cashmere suits and ties. Sure, go screw yourself.

— *ii* —

I picture her sitting at the table by the window, gazing with her eyes closed at the hazy curtains of the Grand Hotel of El Salvador across the street. You could wait for me in that hotel, but they charge in dollars. What! That's an outrage! Charging in a foreign currency, damn it all! That's inexcusable. Calm down people, I say with a hoarse asshole-president-of-the-republic voice. She lights her stars behind the Venetian eyelids. We are seated in the Latin Café.

One of these days I'm going to drink a beer in the Grand Hotel. You heard me, I say but she didn't hear me because she's not with me—I remember a song-poem of the profound life. Behind the curtains of the Grand Hotel one can sense the plush chairs with buttocks gently sinking into them; the silent steps on the Persian carpets—as in the advertisement—made in San Sebastián, in San Vicente; my eyes encounter immense mirrors that give depth to the main room—alias *hall*. One of these days I'm going to invite you to the Don Quixote Bar. All of a sudden we've turned Don Quixote into an alcoholic character; that was the man, it's true, only he didn't drink *pilsner* (Ayau family piss). The Don Quixote Bar will serve him a cold, executive smorgasbord. And I start to feel like passing through those curtains in front of me. That would be the last place I'd visit in the event my premature death were announced. And I'd cook up some scandals (and eat them up, because with that expression I can only think of a meat dish), and offer you goodbye kisses, rolling around like a cat on the Persian-cat rugs from San Sebastián. I would write the name Little Red

Riding Hood on the convex glass of the anti-thief mirror until I had converted the walls into a serious newspaper column. But you're at the Latino Café, with a window looking out onto the street. She won't come. I start thinking nonsense. Thinking is a physiological act, only there is no payoff, it's finding yourself by this window watching the funeral processions of students killed by the police pass by. And I realize that it is horrible (not burial) to think.

Requirements for living in this country:

1) Don't think.

2) Don't even think.

3) Think nothing.

Then, what do you want us to do with our gray matter? What do we do with that magic box we carry in our heads? It'd be great to sit on it, wouldn't it?

Five years ago I was sitting at this same window when I saw Rivas Salfuero's funeral procession go by; but I was also in the procession, with a combative attitude, that's me, I point at myself with my index finger like someone brushing a piece of lint from his shoulder. But how can that be if I'm sitting behind the window drinking a cup of coffee? Or maybe not even that, as all of a sudden I have landed in a cement cell sealed by a metal door with five small holes in it (that flow to the sea that is death) the size of my eyes so I don't suffocate. In Guatemala City it gets cold as a witch's tit; snuggling up in my own skin before I turn purple, that is, before I kick the bucket from the cold. I rub my hands together until they produce sparks. It's all nonsense, I tell myself: No students were ever killed by the police. It's a way of staying in the café and to go home and forget I was ever involved in activities that are anarchic and contrary to democracy and other crap. It'd be better for me to go to a two-bit whorehouse, I recall my favorite verses from Mayakovsky. A little more respect, Sir. So you call me Sir, eh, well, know that you are more Ma'am than I'm Sir, I answer her, as my twenty-five years of weight gain approach obesity. I realize something is happening, like returning from a trip to outer space, I've never taken an extra-terrestrial trip, but I imagine that it must be like this. One closes one's eyes and stops breathing, all of a sudden you turn into a tiny, crazy ant devouring a worm in the garden, one of those worms that stand up with legs on their backs and twitch around trying to free themselves from the merciless stings. After you close your eyes you turn into a shitty earthworm, an oly-hay it-shay, it-hay ells-smay ike-lay uh-hay art-fay, oo-hay eh-thay ell-hay ut-cay un-whay? The stuff that happens when you think deep thoughts. Guatemala, Land of Eternal Spring, and cadavers wrapped in cellophane or polyethylene pass by, made in USA. If they make me push soil I'm going to lose my manhood, I say like the big cynic I am. Push soil is being nude on your hands and knees and then they stick an eclectic prod in your ass. It's the best truth serum. The pain makes you push the soil, the Earth, to the point where you almost nudge it from its orbit—that's the way the Nicaraguan—your cell mate—describes it to you, when you think they are taking you to the "little hospital," at the Fourth Police Corps. If they take us to the little hospital, then we'll be saved, he had told me. Don't worry. But they took me to the so-called railroad car with steel doors, completely closed up with just five small holes so that five threads of sunlight can come through. I didn't see the Nicaraguan again. I wrote a poem about him.

Why is it that Nicaraguans are so old? Because the young people have died, you know. They've been getting rid of them. To fight the demographic explosion, they use thirty-caliber explosions.

This is a freezer, I think when I notice the cell's shiny cement, my eyes remain fixed on those holes which like dragonflies bring and take oxygen from the cell.

"Where are you from?" the Nicaraguan asks.

"I'm from Cuzcatlán, alias El Salvador," I respond.

"That's funny" the Nicaraguan says. "A Chocho and a Guanaco in a jail that is neither Nicaraguan nor Salvadoran. I protest because this is a foreign jail, an attack upon our nationalities! Just think, a Salvadoran and a Nicaraguan in a Guatemalan jail, it's like the regional integration of three divine personages and only one true God.

Why did I invite her to this café when there are other little cafés that are less expensive? I check my pockets and discover that I can barely pay for myself, maybe I'm entering social decline. That's when one decides it's better to have torn pockets, to give poverty a tragicomic tenor. Well yes, look, the coin fell through the hole in my pocket. A fifty-centavo piece and I didn't notice when it disappeared. It's too much, Little Red Riding Hood, I can't pay for you, instead I'll go with you to the Institute and return from there, it's nothing new. But goodness, what am I going to talk to you about if I only know a few verses by Neruda and nothing else?

"Whose great big little nose is this?"

"Yours, the better to smell you with."

"And these enormous ears?"

"The better to hear you with.

And you go along with your basket over your shoulder, among the lilies of the field (Let's look at them!). With your appetizing footsteps.

— *iii* —

"We've seen all this, we've verified it, we've felt it, in an interminable series of abuses and injustices, with the lamentable and discouraging complicity of a press pitifully silenced by economic threat and the pressure imposed by a front office that has made light of and has played around with journalistic ethics. Inexorable history will pick up the story of this horrible nightmare and relegate the perpetrators of this drama—that the fatherland is living—to the bench of the accused, convicting them for centuries to come.

"The Church cannot, it should not, it does not wish to be an accomplice and probably in these lines wants to let it be known that it wasn't fooled, much less was it a participant and that, in spite of the dirt that some wanted to heap upon it, it maintained its dignity—although shaken, it was not knocked down from its pedestal—because its foundation is divine and its policy is that of Our Father forgive us as we forgive.

"Beloved brothers of the priesthood. Dearly beloved children; these are heroic times for us. We are called upon to play the role of the Good Samaritan: To console the poor and afflicted, and to *chastise* those who abandoned their neighbor who was injured and alone by the side of the road; it's time for us to dispense love and charity.

"Let us continue to side with the poor, they are our sacred heritage. It matters not that they persecute us because of them, it matters not that they speak ill of us, it matters not that for this they call us New Wavers. The words of Christ have been in the gospels for twenty centuries, and for much longer the prophet Isaiah has clamored relentlessly against the eternally opulent, the pharisees and scribes. These passages from the Scriptures strike hard at the hardened consciences and that's why they avoid reading them, they are not meditated upon or preached. The gospels' teachings are misrepresented and emphasis is placed on a charity constructed after their fashion. It's true, very true that, as with the apostles there was a Judas, in all ages and latitudes there have been others like him, and they appear defending injustice and serving as vile instruments against even the evangelical and canonical principles and against the dispositions of the prelates, so as to earn a beggar's gift and the fatal thirty pieces of silver, in the end strangling their faith, their dignity, and their very ministry; but death exists, there is a judge and a calling to account. Beloved children let us pray for them, they are priests after all.

"Unfortunately we must lament that our *alma mater*, disregarding its mission of training researchers and scientists for the needs of the fatherland with respect to the preparation of professions with integrity and devoted to knowledge, to raising civic spirit, has committed itself to cheap, petty politics which bring it no esteem. Individuals who have left its classrooms make up all the power of the State; the nation's justice is in their hands, and with pain and sadness we verify that there are individuals from those groups, the ones already practicing their profession, who lend themselves as members of the judicial power, to illegal acts, injustices, abuses, and fateful military coups. Signed, Monseigneur Aparicio."

— *iv* —

I think instead of Little Red Riding Hood and her five-o'clock-in-the- afternoon eyes; ten minutes have passed and I am still sitting in a chair in the Latino Café, waiting for her. Doña Gracia was good to me, she didn't ask my name nor how I was going to pay her. "We only have a room in the attic." It was filthy, but they were going to have it cleaned. She knew I didn't have a cent to my name; I decided to stay. I am climbing the steps as the black woman, Eduviges, watches me sadly from the kitchen, it's the look of a mistreated dog, singing "Mamma I want, Mamma I want a lollipop." At that time I don't know her name, later I learned her name was Eduviges, beautiful, black like the night face down, covered with white *amate* flowers. Someone arranged a date for me with Little Red Riding Hood ahead of time and that's how I came to this house. I see Aunt Gracia. She is so good—the poor woman—and I must keep quiet so she won't see I'm afraid. Well, I had nowhere to go and they told me I could stay here; stuttering, y-you n-know, I-I'm not sure, but I-I like the house. My tongue is tied and then it's free. I'm not looking for luxury, I said to her quickly, without thinking so as not to stutter. Then I spoke to her serenely, as one says things when they come from the heart (that madness of speaking in poems).

In the street I observe the five-thirty sky, when the trees begin to blossom and fill with birds. Suddenly I'm illuminated by the eyes of the *esquinsuche* tree that blooms on the corner of Eighth Avenue, the one whose flower gives birth to bats. The sunlight begins to redden the leaves of the trees that get larger as I walk among them, along the sides of the street. It was my first different day in the city, newly arrived, remembering vaguely the time I was lost in the jungle and got shot in the head, it's a miracle I'm alive. Besides, I was my country's most important poet and poets never die. It was when my mother recited to us at the door of the shrine by the light of a kerosene lamp, as large tears of emotion poured from our eyes. I say goodbye to the trees, to the birds, I see them one last time, conscious that it will be the last time. I never liked the idea of hundreds of birds arriving to roost in front of the house to create an uproar, perched on the branches of the *esquinsuche* trees.

It's all right, I tell Little Red Riding Hood with a trembling voice. The day we run into each other again. I had just gotten off the Route 4 bus heading downtown, first I had to cut across Cuzcatlán Park. There she was, seated on a park bench, feeding the *clarinero* birds. The thought occurred to me that she was waiting for someone and that that someone was me. Hello! she says, as if we had seen each other just yesterday and that the encounter was of no major importance. The *clarineros* would come up almost to her feet, as she tossed out bread crumbs or something that looked like bread crumbs. I see the top story of the Military Hospital, it rises above the foliage of the park and the flowered branches of the *maquilishuat* tree, and I am afraid. I'm thrown onto a bed and a man searches for the piece of lead in my head. It's very painful, we have no anesthetic. The black steel scrapes the bone and I hear the drums inside my ears. And voices of desperate people crossing the river.

"You won't believe it but I knew you would show up in this part of the park."

"I've come from Guatemala," I tell her, although she doesn't ask.

She empties the contents of the bag, perhaps bread crumbs, and shakes them over the heads of the *clarineros*. The small birds gesture, raising their wings, and fling water as they shake their feathers. I see a rainbow form in the mist beneath the three-o'clock-in-the-afternoon sun. "There's no more bread, beat it, bluebirds."

An hour later we're on a bus. She is Little Red Riding Hood, but I can call her Ant. This is my city, the same golden *totopostes*, sweetbread sold in the street by women, the same yucca with fried hog fat, slabs of roasted meat in the eateries beneath the late afternoon of the sidewalks. The commercial billboards. "Can I help you feed the birds?" I had asked her a few minutes earlier. I stuck my hand into her bag at the same time she did, and I felt her characteristic heat of future years, I discern her aroma of sweetbread. Feeding the birds, who would think of it. I see the photograph, the two of us on the lawn in the park. When I drop my hand, after removing it from the bag, the *clarinero* flies towards me. Little Red Riding Hood is pretty, that's the way I see her profile through the frame of a bus window.

"My aunt has a large house, you can stay with us."

I: Thanks a lot, if it's not very expensive, tha-that perhaps it's not possible. I realize I'm stuttering. She: My aunt isn't going to charge you, she already knows you're here; don't forget that you're also a member of the family, besides, where seven people can eat, there's food for one more: the Samaritan's philosophy. In order to help the household she is working in a shirt factory and at night she attends the Kid, go-take-a-hike Menéndez Institute. She has nearly finished high school.

Two days later I invite her for coffee. We could drink it at home and it wouldn't cost us a thing. I: I'm embarrassed. Don't be silly. Besides, outside we can talk to each other. Okay. I rummage through my pockets with the tip of my memory and my fingernails. The horse-biting spider of my fingers touches the lonely cloth, not even a single coin. We look at each other in the Latino Café. I confess to her that I don't have a cent to my name. I shouldn't tell her anything. She has only allowed me to accompany her for a while when she whispers to me, we'll see each other after five, that afternoon she wouldn't go the Institute and I'm going to wait for her at the exit door of the factory, behind the San Esteban Church. I plead to her in silence, please don't put me in the terrible position of having to invite you, because I don't have a cent to my name and I feel like drinking coffee in my country of coffee growers. I'm still convalescent and I show her the scar on my head. Then I'll wait for you on the steps of San Esteban. Okay

"Aunt Gracia might find out that I went out to have fun, but I'm glad we can see each other."

"Me too, to smell once again the same smoke, the streets full of danger and death."

I'm very sorry about what happened to you, she tells me in complete confidence, knowing that I could have changed a lot. After being shot in the head one is never the same. I observe the climbing, green grass, it rises to the crest of the hill. When I'm stretched out on the ground, the Cypresses look taller to me. "He's got a head wound and he's losing a lot of blood," the paramedics in the mountains say, their troubled respiration, their hearts jumping out of their chests, kneeling over my wounded body.

Little Red Riding Hood got me out of the fix. Don't worry, I pay for the coffee. I realize I'm poor.

— v —

"All those belonging to the military class since 1932. We shall never allow ourselves to be recruited by those who want us to attack those who command, those who bring wealth to the country, those who have created a nation, I'm referring to the coffee growers, the cotton growers, and the owners of industry. Without them there can be no prosperity, nor can there be any without us, we who are here to defend what has been accomplished in several centuries of history. We are the peoples' armed forces, we also defend those men who produce wealth.

"And to those who accuse us of viciously allying ourselves with the rich, we say, remember before 1932, how we used to have to go to the river to wash our uniforms, every Saturday we soldiers would go single file, we bathed once a week, we'd get skin infections. The people, the riffraff that is, called us *chichuichosos*, the mangy ones, because most of us really had mange. It's true that in 1932 we killed thousands of people, but without those deaths the republic would have not been saved nor would we have saved

197

ourselves, we who have always been vigilant to keep the republic together. They treated us like dogs, just like animals and we barely earned enough to feed our families. And now they would like for us to give up those achievements, that progress. May he who was born poor remain poor, and he who was born rich remain rich, what else can we do, that's the universal law. We aren't here to change things, he who wants to live well, let him work. We protect private property because it's the only way to have order and prosperity. What would happen if the poor were given milk? No one would be able to wean them from their habit; then we'd see them stealing and taking from those who have, as in the Communist countries, where some work so that others may eat. Besides, as long as man has been around, there have been rich and poor.

"We were all raised eating salted tortillas, why then is there such an outcry for the poor? We are here so things don't get out of hand, to look after one another, because it's true what Hobbes, the great philosopher, said, yeah I think he was the one who said that man is a wolf to man. That's why no one should touch what belongs to another, peace is respect for the rights of others, as that great Mexican statesman said, even though he was an Indian. May no one misinterpret our benevolence, nor should our patience be an excuse for some two-bit leaders, just because they have attended the university, to go around inciting the poor. Leave them alone, just the way they are, there's no alternative, otherwise, more blood would have to be spilled than in '32. On the other hand, I don't believe in the university students, who, once they have earned their degrees, are going to increase the ranks of the rich. Would they like it if what they earned by the sweat of their brow—after burning the midnight oil as students—was taken from them? No, right? Do you think, perhaps, that being in the military is a piece of cake? We're the guardians of the nation's wealth and if you think we're going to take that role lightly, you're wrong. They accuse us of killing thousands of peasants. That's not true, but let's suppose that it is: The peasants wanted to steal from the rich that which had cost them years and years of hard work to accumulate.

"To those who preach exotic ideas I'm going to say, with all the dignity becoming a career military man: There can be no workers if there is no capital to give them work. Let the poor go to work and they'll see how their money chests are filled; let them save, not get drunk and spend their centavos on alcoholic beverages. A centavo saved is a centavo earned. On the other hand, we protect the country from attack from any other continent and those who wish to distance us from the great people of the United States are very mistaken, they buy our coffee at good prices, our cotton too; they're helping us become great, they lend us money to build railroad lines and highways. Do you think there could be so many factories without that country's valuable involvement? Just to give one example, before we had no instant coffee, now we have the best instant coffee produced in Central America; we have bicycle assembly plants, match factories, Coca-Cola bottling plants; we make medicines—although they slander us saying all we contribute is water and air—but, we make them, that's the important thing. Soon we'll have a refrigerator factory and we're going to export refrigerators (although we'll only export them; it pains me to admit it but our people aren't used to using these modern things). We have factories for foreign brands, we already make Arrow and Manhattan shirts; we produce American brands of cigarettes, which is saying a lot. In all, I could never name all the advances we've made in industry. Then, what's all this bullshit talk against the rich and the Americans about?

"And as for you measly little nouveau priests, I'm going to give another warning, your mission isn't in this kingdom, Christ already said it, give unto Caesar that which is Caesar's and unto God that which is God's; this earthly hell is not the domain of your ministry, you are here to satisfy spiritual needs, to provide guidance about eternal life. Well, I, who have been a Catholic and would give my life for Christian principles, tell you to stop whipping up discontent among the poor, you aren't here to instill in them vulgar materialism, telling them that only with material things are they going to satisfy their needs, leave that to us; leave the poor alone, they are content as they are, why be more Catholic than the Pope? We have been very patient putting up with speeches by the priests in their churches; besides, don't forget that in accordance with the Constitution, using the pulpit for political purposes is prohibited.

"Talking about the rich is getting involved in politics, to tell the poor to struggle for their demands is also politics; I say to you nouveau priests, don't break the law on me, much less the bounds of the magna charta. And if, for the good of the fatherland, we have to be forceful and intractable, we won't hesitate an instant—in spite of our religious beliefs—because duty comes first and we know how to do our duty.

"Don't provoke us, don't ask for blood, because if it's blood you want we're willing to spill it as well for the good of the fatherland and the free world." (*Announcer's voice: You have heard His Excellency the President speaking before the diplomatic corps, civil, ecclesiastic and military authorities, on this day of national independence. The President exits followed by his ministers, the supreme court justices, legislators of the National Assembly and, finally, the presidential bodyguards. You are hearing the sounds of the twenty-one farts, excuse me, the twenty-one guns that commemorate the day on which the chains of Spanish subjugation were broken. A big apology for the unintentional, tremendous, conceptual mistake I've just made. Good night.")*

— *vi* —

"Thirty-one," Margó shouts hysterically, picking up the twenty-five centavo coin. She has the most money on her side. "I'm not playing anymore, it's bad to win too much, I already have two *colones*. We've got to get up early. "Don't go, let's play one more time," Pichón demanded. "All right, I'll stay for one last game."

"It's good for you, Charrier, because Margó's winnings go into your coffers," Al says.

"We are on our own here," Charrier defends himself. "Twenty-two in hand," Al announces. "Thirty-one," Margó counters. "I'd better go, you're having a lucky streak," Al says. "If you leave I'll keep playing with Charrier." There are knocks at the door. "It's Old Man returning from the movies." I rise to my feet to leave. I open the door for Old Man, "Don't get up. Goodbye." "I'll join the game," Old Man says.

With a book in your hand as sleep overtakes you; a few minutes later you realize that tonight you'll have difficulty sleeping. The book over your face because you don't want to turn the light off. "Let Old Man turn it off when he comes," you think.

(And through that gate, on the side of the fire station, you enter the black palace of the security guards, with your thumbs tied together with string, your arms behind you, the men inside the car push you so you'll get out of the car quickly. With good manners, they barely give you a gentle push, so you won't fall down. "Now you can see for yourselves, you people say we are murderers, but it's just the opposite: We're here to give you anything you want, that's what the students can't stand, they just want to fuck everything up: We're for a revolution with freedom, that's the only difference, we agree on everything else, then what's the problem?" The chief invites you to a cup of coffee, right this way to the officers' club. A *sui generis* invitation, as my high school anatomy professor who reeked of semen used to say: "Communism is in the country, but it doesn't matter, they're not going to do anything; look, I'm in the government and nonetheless they let me do anything I want and they even let me disagree with them, I can work, that is one of the advantages of democracy, you guys think that when I attack the oligarchy I'm joking, but I'm not. I'm against the oligarchy, and I'm also against extremists, whether they are on the left or the right. I've always fought in the ranks of anti-Communism, but I'm against illegal acts by the government; for example, they were going to buy twenty-five airplanes at twenty-five thousand dollars apiece—a symbolic price offered by the United States—to get aircraft to thwart extra-continental aggression, and I was greatly surprised when, from the same company selling them, I learned that the invoices being prepared by the government were for two hundred and fifty thousand dollars, *per capita*, in other words they were just adding a zero, do you understand? That's right, that was the original price, but the United States was selling them for a symbolic price. What happened to the two hundred thousand dollars for each plane? There can be no doubt but that it was a million dollar operation. I went immediately to the Defense Ministry and demanded an explanation, at first I thought it was an error or that some outsider was swindling us; then the defense minister told me: 'Look Chele, keep your nose out of this matter, we know what we're doing, it's a military secret, you worry about your national police, you have enough power there, what more do you want?' I raised hell and slapped the defense minister's face. Do you think you could do that in a Communist country? They'd shoot me in a second or they'd send me to Siberia, where the Siberian ice cream comes from; but the only thing I lost was that they didn't nominate me as a candidate for the presidency of the republic, those mistakes that one makes; but they keep me as nothing less than chief of public security, I'm not doing bad, so I can't complain. I defend democracy and I earn my livelihood honorably. I once was young too, and I fought against General Martínez's tyranny, I know what it's like to be dishonorably discharged, they take away your uniform and your insignias and your comrades look at you as if you were shit, for us, wearing the uniform is what reading is for you, it's like what oxygen is for plants. I'm not going to take a chance just for the hell of it and lose the privilege of defending our country against outside intervention and internal subversion, that's where I draw the line. So, you can see, I'm even letting you talk with me, if you were in a Communist country you'd be doing forced labor. From now on this shall be my policy, send all detained students to me and it's not to torture them as you people proclaim in the park or in the newspaper you publish at the University. That's democracy. I exercise it everyday, and I believe in it more and more. Of course there are always details like that business about the planes, but these are the risks of the free world. Some people are always looking for ways to cheat, like stealing, but they are unforeseeable things, human mistakes. That's why I slapped the defense minister. You people have to understand one thing: When you attack the military, you are attacking democracy; when you consider us enemies, you are attacking patriotic unity." The general extends his hand and you feel it in yours; as if you shouldn't wash it for a year. Audrey Hepburn's hand must feel like this—you think to yourself—not for its delicateness but for its transcendence. "It's a new tactic," you think. At first you were confused. If things keep going like this they'll offer me a scholarship to the military school or they'll give me a ministerial job in public security.)

Sound asleep.

Margó says: How did he let himself get caught? Who knows? He felt like going to the University when he shouldn't have gone out. At first we thought someone had detained him, but we were mistaken. After a month in the Forest. And the general didn't even ask you where you lived? Imagine that! We really lucked out this time.

Old Man comes to turn the light off. That's why we have such a big electric bill, he says. You don't hear him because you are out like a light; or rather, dead asleep.

— *vii* —

She fell asleep with a piece of bread in her hand and an orange at her side. I didn't eat lunch that day simply because you forgot about me. For half an hour they've been passing plates around me. Poor little girl, they demand so much from you; she carries two bowls of hot soup; helping Eduviges; beef stew with ripe plantain. The bowls tilt and she trips. The absent little piece of bread, she is asleep, hypnotized. My hunger goes away if you don't stare at me. I'm famished, look at me. And finally you see me, that's when the houselights went on.

Well, I'm going to tell you, I'm a senior in high school and in the afternoon I go to a shirt factory. At noon I help Aunt Gracia serve lunch. You're something else, mysterious man; I'm a normal person, do you want to accompany this ordinary girl to the shirt factory? And I tell her yes. We have always understood each other, even before we knew each other or when I thought that you'd never come back.

"I'm going to the factory."

"You're going too early."

And then she asked me:

"What about you, are you ready to leave?"

"I have to go the University, maybe I'll go study some more."

Lies. What was really happening was that I had that date with you. We would meet at the Latino Café.

— *viii* —

I took the seven p.m. train. I know that traveling by train is somewhat dreadful, to go along up there in those old, dilapidated cars that the English left us after a hundred years of exploiting their steam engines, chugging along over the rails on the dust with the dry trees running in the opposite direction, the burnt stones, stone lakes of the Chaparrastique Volcano, always venting smoke from its largest crater. The green lake farther away, the Jocotal lake with its green lizards. Mamma and Papa traveling with me; smoking a Copán cigar, my grandfather, and he's telling the same joke he always tells: *Hey you, chubby cheeks with the cigar, get your head back in the window!* At that time the passenger cars didn't have bathrooms, and grandfather had to stick his butt out the window when he felt like going poo poo. *Hey you, chubby cheeks with the cigar, get your head back in!* But it was my grandfather's butt, breaking the hot summer wind, the train going twenty-five miles an hour, a magic carpet. Towards the Usulután Fair and farther, on other occasions, Cojutepeque, Zacatecoluca, San Vicente. My eyes glued to the tips of the volcanoes. For long stretches the path was a dust cloud. My dusty country like a book abandoned on a dirty table; my country of mushrooms and malignant parasites. Cuzcatlán of flowers and moribund people bitten by malaria-carrying mosquitoes; village bellflowers, yellow bellflowers, red, purple, white, orange, possessed by the bite of hummingbirds. Most of the time the telephone posts are assaulted by birds, the fields planted in corn, the wild daisies growing in the deserted grazing lands with several tuberculin cows eating up the valley of flowers.

— *ix* —

Reye. We must use the border troops one by one, internal, over.

Guirre. Correct, you're saying that we have use them for the internal problem, if we need them.

Reye. That's right, because we have all... if it's necessary... we should be sure there is no movement by the green troops.

Guirre. You're saying that we can use the border troops because there won't be... of green troops.

Reye. Correct, General, Sir... if it's necessary to use them, we can do it, over.

Guirre. Okay, Reye, and I think it's necessary today with the operation we're going to mount this afternoon, I don't think we're going to move the troops from the border. Anyway, if it were necessary we would deploy them during the night or maybe in the morning.

Reye. General, Sir, the enemy is surrounding the air force, but they're going to get their teeth knocked out... enemy is surrounding today in the afternoon, at nightfall, the air force, but they're going to get their teeth knocked out... excuse my expression, over.

Guirre. ...

Reye. Enemy has troops around the air force, our troops will try to control the situation, over.

Guirre. ...

Reye. I can barely understand you General, we'd better cut, wait, the Minister, or rather, General Torre is going to speak to you... go ahead...

Torre. Hello, Guirre, what can we do to control Doctor Downhill... go ahead.

Guirre. It'll be difficult, General Sir, because I think that... I'm going to talk by phone... I think that Doctor Downhill is in the bathroom.

Torre. I want Doctor Downhill to report to military headquarters because I consider it to be easier, less dangerous, we have to pass a constitutional resolution, get the doctor out of the bathroom.

Guirre. Okay General, Sir, understood, we're going to control the doctor, because we don't know which bathroom he's in... I wanted to tell you another thing, General... decree martial law, decree martial law... decree martial law... over.

Torre. Okay, we have to do it, decree an eight o'clock curfew, no one can be on the streets after that hour, shoot to kill; now we need radio stations to instruct the people.

Guirre. Yes, General, we're going to Radio P.U.P.U., we're going to take over the tower, outside the studio, in addition we're going to... the immediate transmissions in the departments... martial law... that is, no one can be out on the streets after twenty hours.

Torre. From twenty until six hours, but it's very important that we control the vice president, the doctor, I want to see him, besides, now we want a civilian, let them be useful for something.

Guirre. Okay, General, Sir, I'll confirm Dr. Downhill's arrival...

Torre. If you can bring him in bound... I mean, if it's necessary, so that the constitutional emergency can be controlled... over.

Guirre. Yes Sir, General. Over and out.

— *x* —

"Who would think of taking a train at this time!" I say as if listening to the rain fall, with no intention of mounting resistance.

"We have to save every last centavo," Rodrigo says.

"It's not that bad," I rebut with my ambiguous gestures. In other words, gestures of a patient Job or of a militant pacifist. It's true that I only behave this way outwardly. On the inside, I'm a beast.

"You decided to travel by train."

"Agreed..." I just wanted to argue to calm my nerves which are giving me goose bumps.

When the train negotiates curves I love to watch the nineteenth-century smokestack and the blue flames emerging from under the engine. Antique machinery, the wild-west kind, that run on gasoline or wood. A museum with a white, painted sign that is burned into one's memory from childhood on: *Salvador Railway Company.*

"We're going to have a child," Little Red Riding Hood tells me. "That's a good joke," I respond trembling, remembering Caridad Bravo's most recent novel, *Chiclet Adams.* "We really are." "Sometimes you really blow my mind." "I wanted it this way, don't worry about it." "That's enough, I'm not worried about having a child." I think she's kidding.

Traveling by train sweetens my temperament, that's why I didn't wait to tell Rodrigo that we would make the trip in the antique passenger cars. Then I thought about how much we would save on the tickets and about security, it's cheaper and you aren't subject to the routine searches that take place at the bus stations. Well, I don't feel guilty about anything, but we should take precautions. Traveling by train is a real feat. I think: "Maybe this is the last time I'll see you, my little country." I'm sad, but I'm always sad, I'm forever reciting poems by Pablo Neruda.

Five minutes ago I was reading and the dust started blowing in, reading *Children's Stories* by Salarrué. My butt hurt from riding on the yellow boards of the old train seats. I feel like going poo poo, pinching a loaf, first. I pull out my stick and start to urinate in the Water Closet, which has no water, just a bowl with a hole in it that opens to the tracks and our nation's soil. Just knowing that I would be doing it on my country takes away my desire to defecate. I feel like vomiting, my conscience bothers me. "You haven't gotten to the scary part yet and you've already shit in your pants." I vomit in the bowl, the rails and dust pass by below me. That's what I get for reading "The Story of the Tragic Tale, The Fruitful Vigilance, and The Cancerous Surprise that Wasn't any *Mareña* Nun, but Sudden Death Herself." Since I was fifteen I've learned by heart some of Salarrué's children's stories. This time, they were a gift from Little Red Riding Hood. Besides, in her goodbye letter she wrote: "Take this book to read on the train," with her eyes filled with crocodile tears. "There's a note inside, you can read it later," she ends her letter written with pens with different colors of ink. Of course, one should try to be brave in situations like this, we preferred not to say goodbye to each other. "You shouldn't have bought me this book, Little Red Riding Hood," I tell her when she hands me the *Selected Works of Salarrué*. "I stole it from the library," she tells me with her eternal childish smile. Her eyes filled with tears. How could one's heart and whole body not be moved!

— *xi* —

Could you give me your opinion about the political situation? No, not much, you should know about politics, but I don't know what it is. Let's say you're asking my opinion, well, then, politics is, what they tell us to do, I mean, to train us to be soldiers, to trick us, let's say. It seems that way to me, but it isn't that way, is it? Because if they offer us something, let's say that, and even if we fight, right, we get ambitious, they always offer us something.

And you, who do you think runs things in this country: the military, the rich, the priests, the people, the political parties? Well, imposition rules here, they always want to rule, but it shouldn't be that way. *What do you mean by imposition?* Imposition, it's those who impose, let's say the rulers, let's say those who use machine guns, and that way one can't say what he's thinking, right?

Do you think you aren't free to say what you think? No, there's no freedom, because, look, if one talks about those people, saying they are oppressing him, he's a communist, man, right? That makes him a communist. It seems to me that it's crazy what they're doing for us, because we're poor, they say they are going to take care of the peasants and everyone, let's say that now with the high cost of corn, they don't follow through.

Is corn expensive, do you think that the current president, the colonel, is going to increasingly make things worse? Man, things are bad, because since he's been in power corn has been scarce, because we were buying corn, because we are poor, at first it was thirteen and a half pesos for a fourth of a..., and last month it was fourteen pesos, and today it's at twenty pesos a sack.

And do you think the government is to blame for that? Look here, yes I do, because let's say it should keep an eye out, with so many authorities, monitor, pay attention to what's being said, but how's a poor man going to let them know, they don't look out for the other guy.

Why do you think the government is always talking about communism? It's in their interest, maybe because they are soldiers, well, for the poor the more poverty there is, the better it is for the rich.

According to the rich, is it better for there to be poverty? I think so, because there wouldn't be so much poverty if it weren't, and besides, they run everything.

What do you think about communism? Look, I know that people, I mean, communism is misinterpreted. If one seeks the well being of another, that is communism, at least that's what we have to put up with when they call us communists.

What kind of communism do you believe in? Well, I guess communism is a community, no, wait, no, I can explain it to you better, as they have given communism a different direction, which is this communism here, that communism over there, when Ché Guevara was around, they made him out to be the devil, a lion, something you should fear. Because he we searching for the good of the community, of the people that is, according to what they tell me, because I didn't know him. If we had a man here that would fight, if they triumphed, but we're really backwards here, the time hasn't arrived yet.

Is a civilian the same as a soldier? Well now, it depends on their conscience, there are some who have a black conscience and others who don't; let's say you find a soldier who really has a good conscience, I don't know, he could be good; it's the same with a civilian; there are people who think poorly of soldiers; sure, because they do a lot of killing. I think that if changes are made it's good.

Do you think it's a good thing for the president to make changes? Let's say a free nation, where there would be opportunities to be had, just to avoid that, that people steal, that they provide work. But, if there is work and theft goes on, that's a calamity, because one doesn't want to work. Let them work. For example, there's Fidel Castro, what's that place called? Cuba, where they say he ordered all the prostitutes rounded up, so that they could learn a trade.

211

They say they all learned, went to school, got degrees. The person who told us that was a pilot for Lasca, of a plane that was hijacked; he told us that it's really nice in Cuba, there weren't any bums, I don't know if it's true or not. *Then, do you think that communism, real communism, would be good or bad?* I don't know, with all they said about Fidel Castro, what the Lasca pilot said. What about right here? How many women are there who can't find work, they can't find anything to do, then they could pick them up, the poor young women, they're just girls. They wander around in the streets, looking for a way to survive.

Has there been an persecution in this area? Well, a few days ago they carried off a boy against his will, there were a lot of people detained, he saw them, he climbed up a wall and when the guards saw him, bang-bang, they shot at him, fortunately he didn't die, but he's in jail.

Well, we're done, thank you very much. No, thank you.

— *xii* —

I don't know how much time I spent throwing up, I went to sit by a window when I saw that the dust had settled. I slammed the W.C. door. Only then did I examine the aisle and the seats occupied by the needy class, that is, those who are neither workers, nor peasants, nor rich people, nor poor. Something very special. People who travel with their baskets and their shoulder bags with ripe fruit to sell at the train's next stop; people with mesh bags filled with iguanas and garrobos, who travel to the nearest town market. The— *Guanacos*—Salvadorans— my brothers.

It wasn't my idea, but I didn't hesitate before accepting, well, we had gotten it into our head that we were traveling for the last time and we had to see the country by train. With sore rear ends. I've set Salarrué's beautiful volume to one side. Once again I'm alone in the aisle, now I don't even have the urge to look through the windowpane. I'm sleepy; I've never been able to sleep in a moving vehicle; an excuse to think, instead, and not feel the train's emptiness. I start remembering Little Red Riding Hood: You think you're tough, always challenging me and trying to keep me here to avoid this trip, although she is a girl capable of any sacrifice. I do my thing, for example. A way not to die of tedium or hunger. You'd understand me better if you lived in my country of lakes, volcanoes, and mountains, all those beautiful tourist things. She understands it perfectly well. Me too. She likes to bite my ears. We've known each other since we were kids, in fact we were raised in the same house. You should have seen her little colored-pencil legs, shivering from the cold. The first time that she comes up to the attic, I hear her *Incateca* brand shoes, she comes flying. That is very pretty, she tells me, after I read her my first poem. "You hadn't told me you write such beautiful poems." Her words made me inflate like a balloon until I bumped into the ceiling. I: "Dedicated to you, dear little she-wolf. Well, and all those beautiful things about being alone together."

"Be very careful," one of my friends tells me.

"Careful about what?" I say dryly.

"Little Red Riding Hood, you're going to leave and you shouldn't leave her," he told me this three months ago, when my trip was looming, Jorge said it to me.

"We think highly of Little Red Riding Hood," he says, speaking also for Rodrigo.

— *xiii* —

Don't believe it, Old Man is a nice guy, he may be the best poet of all of us, because poetry is a problem of sensibility; he enjoys life more than we do, he doesn't harm us in any

213

way; all in all, if you were to tell me that you are going to pardon someone, it's Old Man. *And are you sure he's not a Communistoid?* That I couldn't tell you, although if we really analyze it, whoever hangs around with assholes is going to get shat on, and whoever hangs out with wolves learns how to howl; in other words, his problem is the bad company he keeps. *How long have you known Old Man?* He's not really old, that's just what they call him, I've known him as long as the others; I can't give you information on the others, they're the ones who stir up anger against the institutions. *Are you saying that Old Man doesn't do anything with the group?* That's not what I'm saying, besides, I'm not sure, what I'm saying is that he's not a person with bad intentions. *Then, do you believe that if someone has good intentions, he is acting right?* Maybe. *And if that shitty Old Man is a Communist, but he has good intentions, then he can keep on causing trouble, is that your logic?* I want you to understand what I'm trying to say; I'm saying that there are good people and bad people in all segments of society, people who can take the right path, who can work with us. *Do you consider yourself one of us?* Of course I do, if I didn't I wouldn't be here with you. *Are you threatening us?* I'd be an idiot to threaten you, I respect you, what I want you to understand is who your friends are and who your enemies are. *Are you trying to lecture me on what we should think?* I've said nothing of the sort. *Give us the facts, we're not interested in your opinions.* For example, Old Man says that no blood should be shed when the revolution triumphs, that means we'll have to use nooses for so many fucking criminals. *Are those his words, or are you insulting us indirectly?* I'd be a blubbering idiot to insult you guys. *You're not going to tell us you're afraid of us?* I'm not afraid, because I consider myself your colleague. *That's the way you should talk, do you know where they live?* I know that they always head for the Forest, but I don't know exactly where they live. *Then, you'll have to show us you are good by finding out as soon as possible exactly where they live. Is that clear?* Clear as a bell. *If you have nothing else to say, you can go, be careful on the way out, you know the commies won't forgive anything, and if something happens to you, we're not responsible, that's not part of our deal, is that clear?* I know how to take care of myself. *Leave through the firemen's door and don't turn around.*

And you leave thinking about your hard life, if it weren't for the wife and kids you wouldn't be involved in these things, but how you adore them and they've endured so much hunger and suffering since you've been out of work that you have to take on work as an informer, you've been in bad shape since they threw you out of the bread union because you proposed a salary increase of one hundred percent for the bakers and that was taken as a provocation by your own buddies, you got angry and told them they were a bunch of cowards. And they: Show more respect compañero. And he: My balls are my compañeros. And they tried to beat you up. You didn't come around for a month, when they came looking for you, you told your wife: Tell them I'm not home. They took you back again, but then you double-crossed them by buying some paint and wood to build some benches. That was when Noel showed up and said to you: "Remember that false witness job?" "What," you ask, because you don't want to remember. Six years ago I paid you by getting you a scholarship to attend the San Juan Bosco School, you didn't graduate because you're stupid and then I got you money so you could set up your own bakery, that's what I call a good friend. And then you were crazy enough to harbor the union leader. An informer recognized him and tipped off the police. "And they went and ransacked my business, I'll bet you were involved in that." Don't insult me, how can you think that. "And they broke all the furniture in the bakery, they threw the palates into the oven fire, they destroyed everything. And then they kicked the shit out of me just because when they told me 'come with us' I said 'and where's the guitar?'" That's what's wrong with you, you know you shouldn't fool around with cops. And the people: Leave the boy alone, you fucking pigs. And the police: Shut up old whores if you don't want us to beat the crap out of you. They threw me into their jeep. You always blame me for squealing on you, since then you seemed to be angry at me. "That's not exactly right, Noel, I know that you didn't do it," although he knows he did. Of course, I consider you my bosom buddy and I'd never do anything like that to you.

"I don't know where you're going with all this, Noel."

"You like poetry, imagine, if you had the means you could devote yourself completely to writing."

I don't know what he's getting at and I say:

"Don't beat around the bush with me, tell me what you came here for."

Noel: Don't get angry, it's nothing.

"I'm not getting angry, I just want to know."

"You can get a lot from poetry, you know a lot of poems by heart, besides, you have a brother who is college student and there's no reason you have to be less than he, the one they call Charrier."

— *xiv* —

Little Red Riding Hood starts biting my wolf ears and I start biting hers. That's how we stuck our foot in it up to our knees. Three days ago she laid the bombshell on me. As if playing the leading role in a radio soap opera. She told it to me all at once, in *toccata* and *fugue*:

"I'm going to have a baby."

Or I imagine she tells me that. But that day I'm not

suited for fatherhood and the news doesn't turn me on in the slightest. Besides, what a time to tell me. I've never thought about having a child as long as I live in this sublimation of a man *disappeared*, open to anything, except sitting around a table and eating three meals a day and hearing in the morning her greeting with a bouquet of perennial flowers in each of her gestures.

"I said I'm going to have a baby," protesting my lack of attention. My eyes fixed on the flashing rays of the sun from the foliage of the *mamey* trees in the neighbor's yard. We've spent the whole afternoon playing the same game as always in bed. She was biting my wolf ears. "Life is a motorcycle race." Little Red doesn't understand: My wise-old-man parables, having established myself at the University while she has just started classes.

Losing Little Red Riding Hood is the least of the risks; I'd prefer not to tell her about my trip so as not to sadden her. Besides, her tears have devastated me. From before, when we said goodbye. I mean, I don't tell her the reason for my trip. Out of discipline.

"I'm fine," she tells me.

I: "Because you're having a baby?"

"Because I believe your trip is for a good cause."

I feel like hugging her. At last I hear words of support. You're going to kill me, unwittingly. It was what I wanted to hear from her since the time three months earlier when I had broached the subject of my trip.

You're not in a Roman circus, she tells me, and I feel like the most important person in the house. I have been in a Roman circus since the last time: Señor González told me that if I kept screwing around they were going to shoot me. He said it to me in a fatherly manner, of course, with a Good-Samaritan face. Your time would be better spent writing poetry. He hasn't realized that poetry isn't going to break through this black palace of policemen, where Señor

González is a kind of jailer. I got a distressed look on my face when the cops came to remove me at gunpoint from the cell where they had confined me. My worries disappeared when I saw that Señor González, in his priest's cossack, was going to break and hand out the Host of communion. I had the bad manners to smile. He offered me a cigarette. No thanks, I don't smoke. Father González ought to be in a toy store, with his jovial temperament like an effeminate Santa Claus. I am in a Roman Circus. "The next time I won't be condescending and I myself will see to it that the 38 is emptied," he tells me with his pistol still out. "You guys would do the same with me if you triumphed." I don't answer him anything. I become melodramatic, or cowardly, which are the same thing. Roman Circus Central-American-style, the order on the menu.

I'm going away, Little Red Riding Hood, I decided several weeks ago, I had told her at that time.

She asked me to explain, I had to keep my heart from coming up my throat. I'm going to go. Everyone has a heart, I don't deny it. At first she saw it as a project in the distant future, a desperate phrase: "We're going with Jorge and Rodrigo. Don't ask where we're going; I can't tell you that."

— *xv* —

I introduced myself to them, they were talking about poetry. "I know Nazim Hikmet's poems by heart," they had their mouths agape. And what do you do? I'm a baker, a humble worker who had the luck of studying with the Salesian brothers, I learned a little something. What you see here is a high-school graduate, maybe in a year or so I'll attend the University, but more than anything else I see myself as a proletarian; I've got my little business, but I work with my workers, as an equal, I don't think I'm an exploiter.

— *xvi* —

In four years I've turned into the most dangerous man of the pre-university generation. Sometimes it makes me laugh because I take it so seriously, at heart I'm not as serious as I seem to those who know me. I became famous since winning second place with several poems devoted to poor little Central America; a short time later I fell into the clutches of Father González, giving me political advice, as he threatened me. I was scared to death, unable to utter a sound. That's when I was apprehended with other university compañeros in front of the Central Electoral Council, for painting slogans in favor of political prisoners. Father González gave a fire-and-brimstone speech about the youth they wanted, respectful of the University, and the bad young people, that we should devote ourselves to our studies, because the young were hoodwinked by the professional politicians, and another string of stupidities that he was telling us. Being a charitable soul, he wanted to scare me so that I would devote myself to my studies, writing poems, he had read one of them in the newspaper and it wasn't bad. He almost whimpers with sadness; it made me want to call him Cry-Baby González. "I don't want to catch you again because then it will be serious."

— *xvii* —

You can go to the Avenue, go up to one of them, if you want I'll get you a photo, don't forget about your kids, about your little-deer, about little-grapefruit; he called them that, the first because of the way he skipped when he walked, and the grapefruit because her cheeks were puffy and because she was so chubby and reddish. I told Noel that I was capable of any sacrifice for them, and it's been a while since I've seen them. And why don't you see them? You, telling him: "I'm separated from my wife, she won't let me see them because she says that I'm a bum, that the vice of *guaro* is to blame for everything," I admit that. You drink because of your financial worries, Noel adds, with a concerned look, it's like I tell you, you're in bad shape for no reason. You have to decide between your brother Manuel and your kids, because you're not going to deny that you're worried because you're afraid of your brother. You just have to tell us about the poetry, the intellectual stuff they talk about. We're not asking you to squeal on anyone.

"With no other obligations?" you ask him.

"Of course not, I don't know why you're so afraid, look how well you made out when you were my alibi witness in the kidnapping case. If later they burned down your bakery it wasn't my fault but because you stupidly harbored that union leader just because you admired him, just because you're a baker. Who made you hide him?"

"Let's not even talk about that."

Then came the walloper: that they were going to give me two hundred *colones* a month and books to study at the University.

"We want to know other things," says Noel, "or did you think that we were going to help you study and give you dough just for the nonsense you tell us?"

"That was the deal," I protested.

You ended up at the police station, the captain wanted to talk with you.

"Nothing doing! You're always causing problems for me," Noel complains.

And you get angry and tell him that two hundred *colones* ain't nothin and that he'd better not show his face around your house anymore.

"That's not up to you, little friend," said the captain smoothly. "Do you think we're going to pay you two hundred *colones* a month for the poetry bullshit you're trying to sell us, this month we're not paying you anything: As you well know, he who doesn't work doesn't eat, just like the commies themselves put it."

That's how the assholes were messing with you.

The Captain: "You have to find their house and if possible visit them." And you: "How do you expect me to do that If I don't have the opportunity to do so?" And you start getting scared.

The Captain: "Look friend, what we say goes, you're at our service, these are orders, we consider any refusal desertion and you know what that means, don't you? Do you remember when they destroyed your bakery and your ribs? Well then, you don't want to go through that experience again."

"Look," says Noel, "I don't understand your scruples, you're going to earn money that you badly need, get a little house, continue your studies. Think it over; besides, and this is not part of my plan, you're earning a good ass-kicking, for desertion, just like the Captain said."

One day, I was talking with them when a girl arrived, there in Verniers', they called her Margó or something like that; she's dark-skinned, wears her hair long and throws it over her shoulders; to tell the truth, she's not too ugly, you'll see. She's about 5'8", yeah, she's a little tall; she was wearing pants and a pair of boots, the first thing to attract your attention is her shapely figure. *Is she the one you're talking about? Because I don't think you only look at the body.* No, none of those photos. *And this guy, do you know him?* That's Pichón, he's twenty-two, light-skinned, straight dark brown hair, sometimes it gets in his face, regular mouth, he's well built, the son-of-a-bitch, he's short, that's why they call him Pichón; his eyebrows are thin, as if he were Chinese; he almost always goes around in a jacket and blue jeans. *Good, now you're getting sharp, and Margó, how old do you think she is?* Twenty, perhaps, she's young and somewhat authoritarian, I noticed that when she approached them. *Did she go into Verniers'?* For just a few minutes, she handed a paper to Al, who knows what it was; I remember they said we're almost there now. *Then did they go to the house, I mean Margó's place?* Maybe. *You're an idiot, you don't know shit, you're always hesitating.* You guys want to know everything; yes, I know that's what you're paying me for, but you've even got their photograph, I don't know what the hell you need me for.

"Don't get nervous."

"I'm just scratching myself, I'm not nervous."

I ask them if I can go take a leak. They let me; I'm going to see my golden urine, the color of bee honey. All this I do for my gillyflower buds, my children. And just think, one's children don't appreciate the sacrifices. Today is payday, I'd like to drink some beers with Old Man and Pichón, tell them everything and end this Christ-like suffering.

"Damn!" someone shouts, "You took a crap," reprimanding me because I'm piddling around too long in the filthy W.C.

"I have trouble urinating."

Those assholes are getting more aggressive. Son-of-a-bitch Noel. A little later: *And this photo, do you know her? She looks like Margó, but I'm not sure, how did you take the picture? That's none of your business and don't ever say you're not sure again because we'll kill you.* You know too much, I think. I don't know why you pay me if you say I don't tell you anything new. And that doubt stays with me.

— *xviii* —

Then that matter with the bus happened. I didn't learn my lesson. You had to get on right where they're building the

Bloom Hospital and get off at the third stop, the second one is for the gringo embassy. You couldn't get off sooner, because it could be dangerous to walk four hundred yards in the open; it wasn't convenient that way either, because we would run into other groups waiting for the bus in order to do the same thing I was doing. The "short meeting" would last longer than it should have, in other words it wouldn't be so short. However, we already had too much experience to think about chickening out. Talk about the political prisoners being detained at the penitentiary, get off at the Polyclinic and get in the car behind the bus. We hadn't foreseen that the driver of the bus was from the Poly; when I pulled the line to get off the bus, after having chatted with the passengers, he refused to stop the vehicle and he took me several blocks farther, until the people themselves forced him to stop. They almost lynched him. I was out of luck: When my two compañeros involved in the activity had leaped out, the bus took off and I got caught in the automatic door. The son-of-a-bitch almost killed me; the car had disappeared; I was left on the pavement, looking at the red, flashing eyes of the patrol car. Father González changed into Stepfather González. "I warned you the last time we had you at the police station," that if they didn't shoot me it was because it was a shame to lose a poet, "but now you're going to learn your lesson, throw him into the cell with the thieves." And that was it. Cry-Baby González lost his patience and took off his charitable nun's mask. Nothing serious happened to me with the thieves. After a half hour, we were friends and I taught them the civil war song from Spain. From nowhere, an apple appeared in the cell. We pigged out on apple; of course, we split it into twelve slices and showed it no clemency, we even ate the seeds.

"The cops told us we could grab you," they say as they let out their pains and their penises.

"You'd better not touch my schoolboy," Death Warmed-Over, the boss of the cell yelled, when he saw that they had knocked me to the ground with two surprise punches, a shove, and a *garrobo* fall. Death Warmed-Over, with his face of visible and invisible scars, was the one who had the last word. He surmised that I was a university student and for him that was enough to consider me as being on the same side. That's how I was spared a possible rape.

"If you don't mind, High-School graduate, let out some screams so that the cops think we are screwing you, because if we don't, they won't feed us tomorrow."

Seeing my hesitation, someone offered to scream for me; but Death Warmed-Over said that they would recognize the scream of a thief, a university student's screams are different. I screamed. I don't know if they heard me or not.

It was a story from A Thousand and One Nights; splitting the apple with fingernails, close to the wall, next to Death Warmed-Over, turned into my defender against future rape, his skeletal body defending me, tall like a rocket that hits the roof of the cell. "They brought me in because I touched a cop's behind, I couldn't resist the temptation," Death says, "his butt was hanging out into the entryway, where he was mounting a girlfriend, and I was passing by, I reached out my hand, like a tongue and I didn't even realize it when he was pointing his gun at me; to tell the truth, Schoolboy, I thought he was just any old neighborhood gigolo dressed in blue; the cop's whistle broke my eardrums and a short time later he had other cops surrounding me. He hit me five times with his nightstick as he tied me up. And so you see, I haven't seen the sun in six months, or a decent meal, just locked up, I'm in bad shape but happy, even though some people think that I have tuberculosis."

He asked me if I knew that when they threw me into the cell it was with the idea that they abuse you. That's what he said, "abuse," to give himself the air of the one in charge of the cell. I answer him with a "hah hah," acting innocent, sucking my piece of apple, which was a way of hiding my anxiety. "We don't eat much here," he stated, "but that's not important, these days those who eat die, from their heart, of cancer, they go to the doctor once a week, because they have too much." He looks at us, all of us with our mouths open, his dry eyes, mummified prunes. "Just imagine," he insists, " they almost kill me for touching a cop on the ass, and maybe I'll die in this cell without a trial, because there's no law against touching a policeman's butt."

— *xix* —

You've got to work with this photograph, buddy. It's easy, circulate it so they can see the kind of leader they have; but first come by so you can see that it's not a doctored photo. On the other side of the glass was Chele, the famous colonel, drinking coffee with a student, it was the same student in the photo he was giving me. Do you know him? Of course, he's the poet. Well, we'd already taken this photo in that same place; you're not going to tell me it's fake, because you have your doubts, that's characteristic of shitty little students that sell out for a few of Judas' pieces of silver.

Noel is responsible for this whole mess, for getting you in a fix and who knows how it's going to turn out; you're looking through a transparent window on one side and a mirror on the other, towards the national-guard officers' club, where you recognize Alfonso chatting with the chief of security, Chele. You smell a rat, but there's little you can do. What do I want with the photograph! So you can carefully show it to Alfonso's compañeros. Or if you don't want to do it, keep it as proof of what students really are.

For example, you don't want to cooperate with us, or you do so with great reluctance, I think that after this you're going to give it more thought. You want to be faithful to your profession as a baker and it turns out your leaders drink coffee in the officers' club, let's see if you still have those shitty scruples, let's see if you decide to volunteer service to the fatherland. Do you understand the game? Or you could show it to Alfonso instead so that he could autograph it for you, he says with scorn, it will be a nice souvenir. You guys are tricking me, you think. See for yourself, the captain says, as if he had guessed what the baker was thinking, that's why we brought you here, because we like you and so that you can become conscious of your work with us, being a policeman is nothing to be ashamed of, although I think that you'll never be one, but at least we have you as a friend, believe it and forget about those ideas the intellectuals have put into your head.

You put the photo in your shirt pocket. I have to go along with these assholes so they don't beat me up or kill me. You remember your brother Charrier—involved in that nonsense; that's why you never liked him, and you think he looks down upon you, that he despises you because he was able to study at the university and that he doesn't trust you, your little brother from the same mother and father shuns you just because you are a proletarian.

— *xx* —

While I am taking my siesta, she comes to lie down with me. We take advantage of that opportunity because Aunt Gracia has gone out for a walk after lunch to help her digestion. When I tell Little Red Riding Hood about Death Warmed-Over, she doesn't want to believe me, she says I'm making it up, the poet's bold imagination; and I reply that if she wants to believe me fine and if not that's fine too; demonstrating my conciliatory philosophy. Nonetheless, I know she likes to listen to me, I can see it in her tender face of an angel, or the face of a dedicated football fan listening to his radio on Sunday. We spend hours and minutes lying in bed, two of life's innocent living beings. When I start at the University I hope we'll see each other more often. I have my leg on the fresh cloth of her little panties, a half hour of suffering because we love each other so much and we shouldn't go any farther. Genoveva with her tourist calendar face and I reading poems and telling my risque stories. You're my best listener, I tell her. "Everything you tell me is so nice," she repeats every so often; but I know that she is brown-nosing me underhandedly. She gives me a kiss on my cheek every time she repeats the word nice. That may be why I feel I can't leave her, her praise lifts me up, it raises me higher than Death Warmed-Over.

"I won't let you leave me like this, so unloved," she says.

"I'm not going to leave you."

"If you really do leave me, I'm going to start mistreating you."

I tell her again, with a kiss on the cheek like the ones she gives me, that I'll never leave her, even if I go far away. She laughs with her slanted eyes, incredulous, trying to discern my feelings. It happens when we are lying down, I fold the cotton pillow, I prop it against the wall and I don't pay any attention to her, reading, enjoying the *Selected Works* of Salarrué, a publication of the University. She, snuggled up by my side, without interrupting my reading; besides, when she interrupts me I just answer with uh hums, which in this situation means don't bother me, pay attention so that you can enjoy the humor of these stories written in the Salvadoran idiom. After several interruptions I tell her to let me finish. She gets up, resentful, and takes her dress from the hook that holds up the portrait of

Neruda. I speak to her with a wide, large-toothed horse's smile. She puts on her skirt as if she were being chased by dogs from a wealthy plantation. She slams the door behind her.

— *xxi* —

"Why are you so sad?" you went to the kitchen to ask with that sentence as long as a freight train.

"I'm not sad," she was thinking.

She seemed worried to you, as if an ugly presentiment had dampened her eternal good humor; a jungle full of torrential rain, her hair, her eyes, her whole face; her hands on her chin, reading the newspaper, with Pepino the Brief on her lap, holding his little hands, teaching him the alphabet, reading the old-fashioned way, spelling out the words. Pointing out the letters with a long stick; to one side, Pichón slices vegetables.

"Hello, Al."

"Hi, Margó."

"What's up, Unpublished Poet," Pichón, who sometimes helps Margó or stays with her in the kitchen, greets him.

"Hey Pichónidas," Al responds.

Pichón with a blindfold on his face, covering part of his nose. The frame of his eyeglasses had opened a raw wound in the spot where it rested on his nose.

"I went to see the doctor," he explains.

"Did he tell you anything?"

"The beginnings of cancer."

"I don't believe it," Al gestures with surprise.

"From now on I'll devote myself to celebrate my death."

"Don't be ridiculous."

"We'd better not talk about these things in the kitchen, Unpublished Poet."

Pepino the Brief pops into the kitchen. "Pichón brought me this teddy bear," he says to Al.

"Where are the others?" Al asks.

"We're alone," Pichón answers.

Meme-Charrier went to see his family, he said he wanted to talk to his brother. Suddenly, some guy, who he said was his brother, showed up knocking at the door. Meme asked him what he was up to, and who had told him that he lived in this house. And then he saw us, guess who it was? None other than the baker who invited us to drink beer. It can't be. Yes, that's who it was, and he's Manuel's brother.

"Well, there's no need for such mystery, although he shouldn't visit us, Manuel knows that."

The doorbell rings and we were frightened by the bad timing of the interruption; Manuel showed up looking exhausted.

"We have to change houses."

"I don't think so," Pichón butted in, "he's your brother."

"Well I do, my brother is an alcoholic and it's not good for him to know I live here, no sooner do I get him off my back than he meets up with you guys."

"You know best about your own blood," Al says.

"Better still," Manuel says, still distressed, "You'd better leave this house today, Al. My brother told me that he heard something about you from a friend that visits him at the bakery. I didn't believe him, but he showed me a photo of you talking with Chele, when you were detained. I don't get it, how could someone have that photograph and have the luxury of divulging it through my brother? He said he must have shown it to him and perhaps forgot to keep it and forgot about it, that was his explanation to me."

"A strange story," Al says.

"We're going to take you to our friends' house, the ones who live there near Centenary Park."

"You have to put us in this tight spot when we were already sad about Pichón's bad news."

"Don't pay any attention to Manuel, we don't have to worry about it tonight, I even bought a bottle of *Cane Spirit* brand poison."

"It's not the time to think about vices," Manuel, who hadn't even greeted Pepino or Margó, protests.

"I'm going to celebrate my death," Pichón says.

"What nonsense is this guy saying," Manuel asks.

"Seriously, they found a cancer on my nose and from now on my life is going to change, I'm going to always be happy. But you bring up that matter of your brother! It's more of your poetic imagination."

"That's right, there's no reason to move Al this very night," Margó interjects. "Were you aware that these guys knew your brother?"

Negrita yelled from her bedroom calling for her daddy. No, he's not going to sleep in the house tonight, telling a half truth, because he doesn't want Negrita to get up, and they have already decided that Manuel and Al are going to leave, but it depended upon Guapote coming to take them.

"Yes," Pichón told me, "but I don't want to know anything about him."

"You had never told us about your brother."

"You don't have to mix family in these matters," Manuel says impatiently.

All of sudden Margó's eyes fill with tears, Margó alone and with others at the same time, with the responsibility of a underground press, the presence of Negrita and Pepino the Brief. I don't know how she copes with these things. And fear. Someday they could find the house surrounded by uniformed men, armed with machine guns, traversing the streets like ghosts, shooting at the first shadow that moves. Someday those men will not walk the streets with impunity, because you, Margó, will also have a weapon in your hands, or perhaps it will be Pepino or Negrita, let's hope not.

"Are you going to teach us sometime, Al, how to use these shitty things, since Manuel is so dense that he'd never show us?" Margó demands.

"Let's have a drink to my death," Pichón says, tilting the bottle. "Cheers Al, those who are going to live salute you."

"You and your dark humor, Pichónidas."

"My coldness surprises even me, you'd better believe it, I'm a kind of walking death, what can we do?"

"Here they come," Margó mutters fearfully.

"Who's coming," Alfonso asks.

"Who do you think?" Pichón asks, "Death comes looking for me."

Margó goes to open the door with Pepino in her arms.

That's why they had been sad that day, as if they had a presentiment that something bad was going to happen. But it was Guapote who arrived and he would take Al and Manuel in a car.

— *xxii* —

Remaining still as I place my arms around her shoulders and you drag her to you-know-where. "I have a secret." She says it in a natural voice; having a secret is the easiest thing in the world. But a child, and to say it like that, like one who removes a butterfly from her hair. That's another story. It was a day later, the news almost made me ill.

"You're leaving tomorrow?"

"It's almost set," then, impatiently, "is what you told me true?"

"Yes, I'm going to have a baby."

With a bunch of flowers in her hands and a smile from

the time of the principality of Cuzcatlán. A children's party in the ball court plaza. Fragrance of jasmine. Yellow dress. She is radiant.

"Are you sure?" And I move on the bed and bump my head against the wall. What does one say in these situations? I'm very happy. Congratulations. And she answers congratulate yourself, be happy, because both of us are pregnant. I'm not that happy, because a child before it's born is a burden for only one.

"Are you sure that you're not happy?"

She knows that I'm not in any condition to be happy, my trip is one day away. I look at her impassively and the right words just won't come out of me. "Do you know that I'm leaving tomorrow?

"What do you want me to say if you've announced it to me several times?"

"And you get even with me by announcing your maternity one day before my trip."

She's obligating me to play a part in the weekly soap opera. And she maintains her serenity as if she were watching ducks fly by.

"You don't have any obligation," her heavenly face with stars and diamonds.

"Take the two volumes of Salarrué's works as a souvenir, there is a message for you in one of the 'Children's Stories,' but I don't want you to read it until you come to the page where I put it. Do you promise?" Of course I do, because it could be the last promise I make to you. Do you have your toothbrush? Your underwear, socks? It's the future mother that is speaking.

At the other end of the tunnel a steam engine's whistle sounds. And I start feeling like waking up. I take out the Salarrué volume. "These books are going to be a bother on my trip, but if they're from her, I ought to keep them." I explain to my fellow passenger, an indigent man across from me: "It's a present from my girlfriend Little Red Riding Hood," I tell him pointing to the two volumes of Salarrué's writings. If you met her you'd really like Little Red Riding Hood, he tells the indigent man, who doesn't pay him any attention because his eyes are lost in the distance of the dusty railroad tracks. "Besides, I'm carrying a goodbye letter which I must resist reading." He speaks to the indigent, even though he knows he's not listening to him. I leaf through the book, looking for the note. And forgetting that I had promised not to look at it until I had read to the page where it was placed, I open the note and read: "I can't even keep you with those life tricks that supposedly never fail." I watch the engine as it negotiates a turn in the tracks. My marvelous country behind the mountain ranges.

Little Red Riding Hood appears baring her mouse teeth. You were only pretending to cry. Listen, you're becoming invisible. Love-e-e, my tied gets tongued. Dear wolf. Your moist tongue on my skin. Mint candy. Food is shit backwards. Forget it. There you go with your two-bit philosophy. Wolf of each day. Wolf of each night. The soul, well, that timeless fine dust. I keep reading the note: "I didn't want you to leave and I tried to stop you."

The indigent awakes from his sleep by the window, he says to me: "Watch out for the guards on the platform." And I wonder what he's trying to say to me if he doesn't even know me. He replies that he can see everything in my eyes. I act like I don't understand, I want to explain to him but the train has already reached the station and the old man gets his shoulder bags ready. He gets up: "Go with God." I can barely utter: "Thank you." The train's whistle blows and it speeds away.

"You must hide."

"Why? Don't give me your bullshit again, Noel."

"They say you told Manuel everything, that's why they weren't in the house when we arrived, neither he nor Alfonso. No one important was in the house, except Pichón, Feliciano, the children and Manuel's wife. You betrayed us, you forgot about your children for a brother who never loved you."

"You're making that up, you always come up with something to harm me."

"If I had made it up I wouldn't come to tell you to hide, I wouldn't even have looked for you, because I realized you were a shithead, well, you've made both of us look bad; for the people who hired us, the price of betrayal is death."

"You got me into this, you're a son-of-a-bitch, excuse me for saying so, but I don't want to offend you."

"Get it out of your system, you have a right to."

"What more do they want? I did everything they asked of me, I went against my brother, I showed you the photo of Al with the colonel; besides, you should know that that photograph exists, but it was Chele who invited Al to the officers' club at police headquarters."

"You saw it with your very own eyes."

"The poet was beaten up, and that doesn't show up in the photo."

"I won't get involved with details, I just came to warn you that they're looking for you and if you don't get out of here as soon as possible, don't say that I didn't warn you, although I think if they do grab you, you're not going to tell them the story."

"Why don't you eat a cartload of shit?"

"If you'll join me, I will."

"You guys want to screw Alfonso by using my brother

and from what I see you got yourselves into some deep shit; now you want to wipe it off on me."

"What makes you say that?"

"Because my brother never believed the photo, nor did he give it any importance, you guys think people are fools."

"We never make mistakes, but I didn't come to argue with you. If I can help you, let me know, I'm not bragging, I came to warn you, I defended you, I told them you were a straight arrow, incapable of betraying us. They didn't believe me and you pay me back with insults, as if it were my fault. Forget you."

"You're responsible for everything."

"I can't get it out of their heads that you didn't say anything to your brother and Al, that it was pure coincidence that they left the house that night, they don't even believe you had the courage to give that photo of Alfonso to your brother."

"You do that to your friend and your children?"

"If you knew the ins and outs of these matters you wouldn't be blaming me for anything."

Outside, the red lights of the police glared.

"It's too late, you never wanted to believe me," looking out the window. "It looks like Chele himself—in person—is getting out of the car to look for you. You can't even go out through the courtyard because they've got you surrounded."

The colonel gets out of his special jeep. Manuel's brother goes out the door facing the courtyard.

— *xxiv* —

One of the three of you has to stay: I'll stay, go ahead you guys. They left me three rifles, forty rounds, enough to keep the squad of pursuers in check. "I plan to use all of them." "Good luck," Jorge answers, saying goodbye, and he keeps seven rounds, just in case, well, you are going to need them, Al. I'm not leaving this spot until you guys are far away. I'm lying down on a mat of pine needles, with my eyes on the rifle's sight. As Jorge is reaching the crest of the hill, the same rhythm is heard, a burst of two shots. That's how I'll know it's my compañeros. When I hear the two shots I know it's my compañeros facing bursts of ten rounds that mean to bite them. I think Rodrigo must be ahead and that Jorge has stopped to fire. I hold my breath and the first part of my index finger does its thing. My lungs are pathetic. I'm panting like an old lion from the San Salvador Zoo; in this foreign land where I find myself, I can't help but remember my country. The park and the zoo's emaciated animals, the keepers throwing live dogs into the pit, dogs just as emaciated. Workers approach the cage, they raise the iron bars, while the audience applauds their bravery; I am also observing the spectacle, I think that some day the lion is going to lose and the skinny dog will come flying out of the cage. At least if he can't do it with his body may he do it with his eyes. The hungry lion and lioness approach the dog. After a few seconds, the dog is trembling from cold or death, he curls into a ball. The people have stopped applauding. The silence lasts a few minutes between the glance of the lion and the final pounce. Every Monday I go to the zoo to see the wild animals eat, but with the hope that the dog will someday win, that he'll take to the air. But it never turns out that way, it's just my dream, next to my mother who holds me by the hand as if she were afraid that I'd jump into the cage. I'm awakened by the noise of my own breathing as I climb until I reach the top and see the black sun of the afternoon behind the hill. The first mission, to gather weapons, had almost been a success, so I came back for this second one, because of my experience. Months later I learned to throw pipe bombs with their fuses lit, as far as

236

possible, to get them to go through the window of the barracks of this foreign country. I listen to the noise as the bombs break windows. "The fuse shouldn't be so thick that you don't have time to throw it," Manuel had told me. "Just barely the size of your index finger, at the most." "That's crazy," I commented. "Mathematically there's no problem," Manuel asserts. "But the bomb doesn't know math," I reply. "There you go again with your jokes at the most serious times," he chastises me. This second mission, which would lead to another and another, remembering everyone, my compañeros, my brothers.

CURBSTONE PRESS, INC.

is a non-profit publishing house dedicated to literature that reflects a commitment to social change, with an emphasis on contemporary writing from Latin America and Latino communities in the United States. Curbstone presents writers who give voice to the unheard in a language that goes beyond denunciation to celebrate, honor and teach. Curbstone builds bridges between its writers and the public – from inner-city to rural areas, colleges to community centers, children to adults. Curbstone seeks out the highest aesthetic expression of the dedication to human rights and intercultural understanding: poetry, testimonials, novels, stories, photography.

This mission requires more than just producing books. It requires ensuring that as many people as possible know about these books and read them. To achieve this, a large portion of Curbstone's schedule is dedicated to arranging tours and programs for its authors, working with public school and university teachers to enrich curricula, reaching out to underserved audiences by donating books and conducting readings and community programs, and promoting discussion in the media. It is only through these combined efforts that literature can truly make a difference.

Curbstone Press, like all non-profit presses, depends on the support of individuals, foundations, and government agencies to bring you, the reader, works of literary merit and social significance which might not find a place in profit-driven publishing channels, and to bring these writers into schools and communities across the country. Our sincere thanks to the many individuals and to the following organizations, foundations and government agencies who support this endeavor: Josef & Anni Albers Foundation, Connecticut Commission on the Arts, Connecticut Arts Endowment Fund, Connecticut Humanities Council, Lannan Foundation, Lawson Valentine Foundation, Lila Wallace-Reader's Digest Fund, the Soros Foundation's Open Society Institute, Andrew W. Mellon Foundation, National Endowment for the Arts, Puffin Foundation and the Samuel Rubin Foundation.

Please support Curbstone's efforts to present the diverse voices and views that make our culture richer. Tax-deductible donations can be made by check or credit card to Curbstone Press, 321 Jackson St., Willimantic, CT 06226 Tel: (860) 423-5110.